D1055160

Inspector Abberline and the Just King

By the same author

Midnight Bizarre – A Secret Arcade of Strange and Eerie Tales
This Rage of Echoes
Ghost Monster
The Gravedigger's Tale: Fables of Fear
Inspector Abberline and the Gods of Rome

Inspector Abberline and the Just King

SIMON CLARK

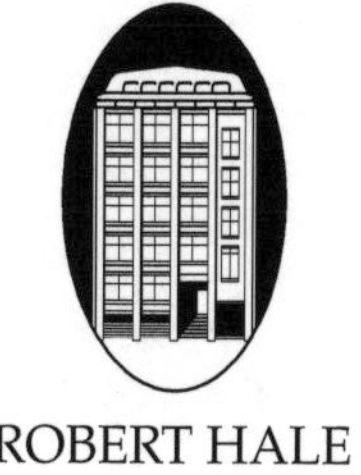

ROBERT HALE

First published in 2015 by Robert Hale, an imprint of
The Crowood Press Ltd, Ramsbury, Marlborough Wiltshire SN8 2HR

www. crowood.com

www.halebooks.com

This impression 2016

British Library Cataloguing-in-Publication Data
A catalogue record for this book is available from the British Library.

ISBN 978 0 7198 1656 7

Printed and bound in Great Britain by TJ International, Padstow

Who is Inspector Abberline?

IF A MAN could ever be described as a rival to the legendary Sherlock Holmes then the real-life Inspector Frederick Abberline is that man.

Frederick George Abberline (1843-1929) rose to fame in his search for the serial killer Jack the Ripper in 1888. He was widely featured in newspapers, which portrayed him as a heroic figure tirelessly fighting crime. Although Abberline never did catch the notorious Whitechapel Ripper, he was an enormously successful policeman, receiving eighty-four commendations and awards, as well as earning the loyalty and respect of his colleagues. Abberline retired from Scotland Yard at the age of forty-nine in order to work as a private detective. His legendary stature continued to grow and, without doubt, he became the most famous detective in the world.

Chapter 1

Isle of Faxfleet, Yorkshire, 1890

Benedict Feasby of Camelot House climbed the tree with all the gusto of a saint climbing a ladder towards heaven. Pixie-like, bright eyed, he moved with the vigour and energy of a man of twenty. Benedict was eighty-one years of age.

He whispered eagerly, 'Halfway from the bottom, halfway to the top. Up, up, up, Benedict, sir. Seek and, verily, you shall find.'

The sun rose from a flat horizon. Smoke from thousands of chimneys formed a hazy cloud over the city of Hull in the distance, while the mighty River Humber, which surrounded this island, glinted with flashes of silver. Sailing boats and steamers rode the ebbing tide towards the North Sea, which would carry them to mainland Europe and beyond.

Benedict paused to check nests in the branches. 'And the contents thereof,' he sang under his breath. Using a pencil, he noted down species of bird, number of eggs, or chicks as necessary. He took the utmost care not to disturb the nests or their chirping tenants.

Benedict continued his ascent of the oak tree. By now, he was fifty feet above the ground. Leaves rustled as if the tree whispered to him. A squirrel darted along a branch above his head.

'Good morning, squirrel, sir,' he said with a cheerful smile. 'A lovely day, don't you think? Though thunderstorms by dusk, I'm sure.'

Benedict pictured his twin brother's expression of delight when he returned home, armed with a list of birds' nests he'd visited and animals he'd seen. All creatures were objects of wonder and delight to the Feasby brothers.

Benedict's hands and feet darted to branches and footholds in the trunk with the speed of a monkey as he climbed with absolute confidence. For a moment, he was enveloped in greenery. His view of the landscape was non-existent. In fact, being in the heart of the oak was like being in a green room, entirely shut off from the world.

'Behold – a jade realm,' he murmured. The air was warmer here, rich with the aroma of leaves and bark. Seconds later, he broke through into the open where an astonishing sight met his eyes. 'Goodness gracious.'

Benedict Feasby stared at the creature on the branch in front of him. Swiftly his eyes took in the wolf with the outstretched wings of an eagle, the legs of a crocodile and the oversized teeth of a leopard.

'No ... no. That's not possible.' He froze in shock, staring at the bizarre monstrosity. 'You shouldn't be up here. Not you, Sir Terror ... you should be on your perch in the parlour back home.'

Benedict moved further along the branch, away from the mass of greenery, and into the open air. Fifty feet below him he saw rabbits scampering across the grass. He continued to walk along the branch, while holding onto a higher branch above his head.

'You are Sir Terror, aren't you?' He leaned closer to the wolf with the eagle's wings. Its eyes of blue glass seemed to stare back into his. 'Yes, I recognize my stitches on your neck.' He reached out to pat the furry head of the stuffed beast. 'Don't worry, boy, I'll soon have you back home. But who should be so naughty to put you up here?'

The wolf hissed sharply – No! Not the wolf. An object hissed as it flashed through the air.

'Oh?' Benedict sang out in surprise.

An arrow had whistled out of nowhere. Its point embedded itself in the man's chest. Pain seemed to flash through the very marrow of his bones.

Benedict released his grip on the branch above his head in order to clasp the arrow's shaft with both hands. That's when he toppled from the branch on which he stood, and began the swift, and decidedly lethal, journey to earth below.

Chapter 2

London, 1890

'THERE HE GOES! Catch him!'

The warehouse boss waved his arms as the thief erupted from a stack of empty boxes. Two constables in uniform pounced on the man. All three crashed to the floor. Arms blurred as punches were thrown.

Inspector Abberline rushed towards the two constables as they fought the wild man.

'Hold him down!' Abberline shouted. 'Watch out! He has a knife.'

Before the thief could stab the policemen, Abberline kicked the knife from the man's hand. He pulled manacles from his coat pocket and handed them to one of the constables.

'Chain him,' Abberline ordered. 'Careful! This devil has put men in hospital before.'

The thief roared with fury. Thomas Lloyd didn't hesitate and joined the fray. He knelt on the raving man's back while an officer locked the steel cuffs around their captive's wrists. Thomas Lloyd was a journalist. He'd been assigned to accompany the legendary Inspector Abberline and write reports for the newspaper about the man and his work. Thomas had shadowed the inspector on several cases now, and hoped this assignment would never end. He respected Inspector Abberline and considered him a friend. In addition, police work fascinated Thomas. There had been many occasions when he had been drawn into the heat and fury of the action – just like now, in fact, as the thief tried to squirm from beneath Thomas as he knelt on the man's spine.

'I'll cut you!' thundered the man. 'I'll chop your faces so bad your own mothers won't recognize you!'

He tried to bite Thomas's hand. Thomas shifted his weight to the back of the man's thick neck. Their captive's face turned crimson, his eyes bulged, and veins stood out from his temples.

Abberline patted Thomas on the shoulder. 'Good work. Just try and refrain from choking the fellow to death. I'd like to question him later.'

'Oi!' The warehouse boss waved his fists again. 'There's another of the devils. O'er yonder. By them doors.'

Thomas leapt to his feet as a thin man with a shock of black hair disappeared through a doorway. Thomas raced after him. Abberline shouted what seemed to be a warning. The excitement of the chase had caught hold of Thomas now and he dashed out of the warehouse. He found himself in a paved yard next to a canal where barges waited for their cargos of tea to be loaded on board.

The thin man bounded along the canal's edge. Thomas had the hunter's fever on him now. Catching his prey was all that mattered. The journalist saw that this second thief certainly lacked the physical power of the first. What's more, the man had a distinct limp. Running appeared painful to him.

This will be a short chase, Thomas told himself, exhilarated. *I'll soon catch him.* Thomas easily gained on the limping man.

Then the man did something unexpected. He quickly stooped, pulled a rope from an iron post, before leaping into a small boat that lay out of sight beneath the wharf. The thief immediately used an oar to push the boat clear.

Thomas judged the distance in a flash. He leapt hard. Cool air blew into his face. A split second later he realized he had, in fact, badly misjudged. Thomas fell short of the boat. Instantly, he was beneath that cold, black water. Bubbles rushed by his face.

It's all right, he told himself. *I can swim. I'll make for the boat. I can still catch him.*

The moment he surfaced the oar came crashing down onto this head. After that: stillness, silence. He realized he was floating face down in the foul water, unable to raise his head.

I'm drowning, he thought. *I am actually drowning.*

The water closed over him. He knew he was sinking to the bottom of the canal. Sinking down into death everlasting.

*

The constable saw Inspector Abberline jump into the canal after the young reporter. The middle-aged man disappeared into those black, greasy waters and the surface became still again. The constable crouched at the edge of the wharf trying to see through the murk.

'Inspector?' he called, even though he was sure his superior wouldn't hear him. 'Inspector, have you found him?'

The warehouse boss lumbered up, puffing, red-faced.

'Both will drown, mark my words,' panted the man. 'I've seen it before. One falls in, another goes into rescue 'em, and both drown. That canal's the work of the devil – it's made many a wife a widow, I can tell ya.'

The constable took off his helmet. 'I'm going in.'

'Then you'll make it three dead. That's hell water, that is.'

Before the constable could jump in, however, the black surface flared into dazzling white. An arm appeared, thrashing hard. Then two heads broke through into the God-given light.

The constable found himself in the midst of the fury and drama of the moment as Abberline swam, pulling the still figure of Thomas Lloyd. The second constable appeared. Soon the two men had successfully hauled Thomas from the water and laid him face down on the ground. The warehouse boss helped Abberline climb from the canal. He gulped for breath. Water poured from the heavy coat he wore. His side-whiskers were matted to his face.

Abberline shouted, 'How is he? Does he breathe?'

The constable rested his hand on Thomas's chest. The newspaperman lay absolutely still. His face had turned completely white, even the lips. Almost immediately the constable noticed a faint bluish hue creeping into that uncannily pale face – this blue colouring was a clear sign of death.

'Constable? Does he breathe?'

'No, sir. I'm sorry.'

The warehouse boss gave a knowing grunt. 'His belly's all swollen big, too. He's swallowed a gallon or more. He's beyond our help. His soul's gone from its mortal shell.'

The constable and Abberline rubbed Thomas's hands, patted his face, and repeatedly checked for signs of a pulse in his wrist and neck. The man lay in a pool of water. He hadn't moved so much as an eyelid. The flesh took on the aspect of cold marble.

Abberline knelt beside the man. 'Thomas. Oh, my poor Thomas.'

The constable wasn't an imaginative fellow, yet at that moment it seemed as if the Angel of Death had alighted in that place beside the canal. The waters became still, silence prevailed, nobody moved.

'The body should be covered,' Abberline said at last. 'Find a blanket.'

An elderly man, carrying a broom, stepped out of an outbuilding. He had a white beard that reached down as far as his chest.

The old man asked, 'How long was he in canal?'

'What does it matter?' Abberline sighed with such regret.

The warehouse boss spoke up. 'This is our sweeper.' He glared at the man. 'Get back to your work, Smith. This is no business of yours.'

To the boss's surprise the elderly man tossed the broom aside. What he did next was absolutely shocking. He knelt beside the body of Thomas Lloyd and ferociously punched the corpse in the back.

The constable wrenched the sweeper away from the corpse. 'What the devil do you think you're doing?'

The sweeper said, 'I worked on a fishing boat with a Russian. He told me that you mustn't give up on the drowned. If luck's on your side you can beat death out of 'em.'

The constable snarled, 'You should be in the madhouse!'

The sweeper shook his head. 'Death can be driven out. How long was he under?'

Abberline looked up. 'Four minutes. No less than four.'

'Let me try the Russian ways on the gent. Let me try and beat death out.'

The warehouse boss shook his fist at the sweeper. 'I'll beat the foolishness out of you! Clear out or I'll break your filthy old bones, you—'

'Let him try,' Abberline said. 'If there's a chance ...'

The boss started to protest.

Abberline silenced him with a glance of pure ice. 'Let the gentleman try.'

The constable released his grip on the sweeper and he lowered himself, with some discomfort, down onto his knees. Clasping both hands, as if in prayer, he brought them down hard onto Thomas's back. Once, twice, three times. The blows sounded hollow. Like a fist beating upon the lid of a sealed coffin. The sweeper rolled Thomas over onto his back. He repeated the action, delivering hard blows to Thomas's chest.

The constable cried out, ‘Inspector, don’t let him do this! Thomas was your friend!’

The sweeper delivered another resounding blow to the cadaver’s chest.

‘Enough!’ Abberline cried. ‘Enough! Leave him!’

His words still echoed from the surrounding buildings when Thomas Lloyd coughed and opened his eyes.

Chapter 3

THOMAS LLOYD WOKE up in his bed. Sunlight flooded the room. The sounds of London reached him: the clip-clop of horses' hooves, the rattle of cart wheels, shopkeepers bellowing prices of everything from potatoes to boiled eels, a train whistle cutting through the sunlit day.

Despite the brilliance of the sunlight he felt distinctly foggy inside his head. *Yes, foggy,* he thought, wondering why he couldn't more precisely describe the sensation of blurred thoughts. *After all, I am a journalist. Words are my business. Now I have gone all foggy inside ...*

A hand touched his arm that lay outside the bed sheet. 'Good afternoon, Thomas.'

Thomas rolled his head on the pillow in order to gaze in the direction of the kindly voice. He saw a middle-aged man with brown eyes. He could have been a clerk, who worked quietly in the back office of a government building. *However, that face ... the small scars around one eye. Something familiar ... ah ...*

Thomas coughed. His lips tasted strangely bitter. 'I've seen you before ...'

'Yes, you have.'

'You are a ... yes, I recall. You're a policeman.'

'I am that.'

'You are here to arrest me?'

'Good heavens, no.'

'Why have you broken into my rooms?'

The man's expression became worried. 'I've done no such thing, Thomas. Mrs Cherryhome invited me.'

'That I did, Mr Lloyd.' This came from a shadowy figure beyond the doorway.

'Then why is a policeman visiting me? Here. Today.' Thomas spoke with difficulty. 'I've committed no crime. Am I not a free man?'

'Don't you remember me, Thomas? I am Abberline. Inspector Abberline of Scotland Yard.'

'Abberline? You never did find Jack the Ripper, did you? When was that? Two years ago? Yes, the summer of 1888. I wrote articles for my newspaper. Those poor women. They say the streets of Whitechapel turned crimson … I must sharpen my pencils. I have so many of them. They're blunt. I must sharpen them all!'

'There, there, old chap. Don't agitate yourself.'

'Is Jack the Ripper in this house, Inspector? Is that why you're here?'

'You must remember me, surely, Thomas? We investigated the Denby case together earlier this year. Do you remember the Gods of Rome?'

'Yes … Sir Alfred Denby died when gunpowder exploded in his workshop.' Thomas sat up in bed, tingling from head to toe as the fog evaporated. 'It's all coming back to me.'

'Good, but don't get over-excited. The doctor insists you rest.'

'I remember! Today we lay in wait for thieves at a warehouse. We arrested one scoundrel. I chased the other and … and … oh, it all goes to fog in here.' He touched the side of his head.

'You fell into the canal as you tried to catch a thief. I feared for your life, Thomas. Fortunately, there was a gentleman on hand who knew the art of … well … bringing the drowned back from …' He ran a hand over his eyes as if remembering a sight that distressed him.

'I was brought back from the dead? Resurrected?'

'Ha, no witchcraft was used. The fellow knew a medical technique of some sort or other. What's important is that I'm visiting you today: a living man.' He patted Thomas's arm.

'Then I must have been unconscious for more than an hour?'

'Not an hour, Thomas. You've not been properly awake for these past three days.'

Thomas Lloyd's face burned with anger. 'And today is the first day you visit me? You wait three days before coming to see if I am still in the land of living? Blast you, sir! I thought you were my friend.' Thomas flung out his hand. 'Get out of my room! Get out of this blasted house!'

Mrs Cherryhome stood in the doorway. 'Don't say such angry

words, Mr Lloyd.'

'I might have been lying here on my deathbed for all he knew, or cared!'

'Mr Lloyd,' said the woman. 'Mr Abberline has been here every day since your unfortunate occurrence. He has sat quietly beside your bed for many a long hour. He has shown you the utmost devotion.'

Thomas stared at Abberline. 'I'm sorry. How can I ask you to forgive me? My God ... why did I get so angry?'

'You aren't quite yourself, Thomas.' Abberline smiled. 'It's perfectly understandable that your temper might run away with itself.'

'But I don't remember you being here. I must have been delirious.'

'Put your head down. Rest will be good for you.'

'And Mrs Cherryhome?'

'Yes, dear?'

'Thank you for nursing me.'

'Oh, I did no such thing, Mr Lloyd. Oh, just imagine! Me alone with one of my lodgers in his most intimate of rooms.'

'I am wearing a clean nightshirt, so who ...'

'Mr Magglyn nursed you. Why, he sat here night after night, playing his accordion to soothe your nerves.'

'Magglyn's accordion sounds like a knacker trying to strangle a mule.' Thomas took a deep breath. 'I do beg your pardon. My nerves ... I become so angry, and I can't say why. I should be grateful to Magglyn.'

Mrs Cherryhome said rather primly, 'You are not yourself, sir. Otherwise you wouldn't have used such language – those bad words that sailors use – when Mr Magglyn tried to comb your hair this morning.'

'I'm sorry, Mrs Cherryhome, I truly am. I have no recollection of using unseemly language.'

Her rounded, apple-red cheeks shone as her cheerful smile returned. 'I'm sure you will be well again soon. Now, gentlemen, I'll make a refreshing pot of tea and bring you some of my elderflower cake.' With that, she pattered away downstairs.

'Hmm? Elderflower cake?' Abberline smiled. 'Rather unusual sounding.'

'And unusual tasting as well.'

They continued to talk. Thomas still felt weak. The fog came and went inside his head, yet he began to perk up a little more. Mrs Cherryhome arrived with the tea and cake, which she handed through the doorway to Abberline. The confection had a powerful, flowery sweetness. Not to Thomas's taste as a rule. Yet its striking flavour drove the last of the fog away, which had clouded his mind. In fact, the disappearance of that fog revealed a thought. One that burned so brightly. He was surprised by the decision he now made. It was the right one, however. He knew he must break some news to Inspector Abberline.

Abberline, meanwhile, continued chatting as he sat on the chair beside the bed. 'The thief we caught in the warehouse is now in jail awaiting trial. The second man, the one who tried to escape in the boat and who struck you on the head with the oar, wasn't so lucky. When he tried hitting you a second time he tipped the boat over. He couldn't swim. As the saying goes, he's now gone to his final reward. Are you all right, Thomas?'

'I have something important to tell you.'

'Oh?'

'I don't wish to say this too bluntly, because I have enjoyed my time being your shadow, as it were, and writing about our adventures for my newspaper.'

'Thomas, is this bad news?'

'Inspector, I am a journalist, not a policeman. Recently, I have allowed the excitement of our work to carry me away. I've become reckless. Foolhardy. I should never have attempted to catch the thief single-handed.'

He smiled in a friendly way. 'Then curb your appetite for such actions.'

'I'm sorry, Inspector. I've made up my mind. Some miracle brought me back from the dead. I truly believe I died in that canal. Now I've been given a second chance to live my life differently.'

'Are you saying this is the end of our association, Thomas?'

'What happened to me three days ago was a sign. I am leaving. "Quitting" as the Americans say. I will resume my normal duties as a journalist.'

'You don't know how sad this makes me.'

'I won't rescind my decision. Another newspaperman will take my place by your side.'

Abberline must have said his farewells, and he must also have tried to persuade Thomas to continue his work alongside the detective, yet Thomas had no clear recollection of the conversation. The mental fog had returned and he had to close his eyes once again. Presently, he heard the kind of cough that people make in order to attract someone's attention. Thomas opened his eyes to see Magglyn standing in the doorway with the accordion on his chest. The blond man smiled as he fingered the keys, and Thomas Lloyd smiled back. He thought: *I entered the realm of the dead, and I returned safely. Surely I can endure an hour or so of the man's accordion music.*

Magglyn began to play and Thomas Lloyd was grateful that he'd lain there unconscious during the previous recitals. Nevertheless, Thomas smiled and nodded to the rhythm of the music. Within moments, despite the rousing crescendos emanating from the accordion, his eyes grew heavy and he found sleep stealing over him once more.

Chapter 4

'I SHOULD STAY at home and write books,' Thomas murmured to himself as he lay, gazing up at the ceiling. 'A man sitting at a desk, pen in hand, is hardly likely to fall into water.'

A knock sounded on the door.

'Come in.'

Magglyn's blond head appeared round the door. The man's smile was as bright and as innocent as a baby's. 'Sleep well, Thomas?'

'Yes, thank you.'

'Mrs Cherryhome is setting out tea in the parlour. Ham sandwiches, pickles, and sponge cake smothered in delicious raspberry jam.'

'Tea in the parlour?' Puzzled, Thomas sat up in bed. 'We only have tea on Sunday afternoons. Today's Saturday.'

'You slept right through again, dear soul. It's just twenty minutes before five o'clock on a very cloudy Sunday afternoon.'

'I've slept twenty-four hours? Goodness gracious.'

'Do you feel well enough to come downstairs, or shall I bring you a tray?'

'Thank you, Magglyn. I'll come down. I'm feeling much like my old self again.'

'That is good news. Let me shake you by the hand. I'm so glad.'

Beaming widely, Magglyn left the room to lightly patter downstairs.

Thomas did feel much better. His head was clear. His limbs felt strong again. It seemed as if he hadn't suffered any permanent ill effects from his brutally close shave with death. He quickly donned a clean white shirt and his best grey suit. Soon he took his place in the parlour by a formidable aspidistra, whose leaves touched the ceiling.

He was joined by his landlady and fellow lodger in a feast of fluffy, white sandwiches, followed by cake lathered in crimson preserve. Mrs Cherryhome thanked heaven that Thomas had recovered, then launched into one of her favourite stories about a previous tenant of hers who had sailed through ferocious storms to New Zealand, only to drown after falling head first down a well in an undertaker's garden.

'I do declare it was meant to be with poor Mr Scroop. He always said to me, "Mrs Cherryhome, I can't begin to tell you the dreams I've had of not being able to breathe – and did you know, Mrs Cherryhome, that a grown man can drown in just one cup of water." More tea, gentlemen?'

After the meal Thomas felt too energetic to return to his room. He put on his hat and coat before leaving the house for an evening stroll. Hansom cabs moved smartly along, drawn by horses at a brisk trot. Most of the people out walking were in their Sunday-best clothes. Ladies in white muslin dresses with parasols. Men in shiny top hats with ebony canes. This street housed many of the borough's middle class who were, as the saying goes, 'on the way up'. The neighbourhood's residents weren't heading anywhere in particular. They were outdoors to be seen, their clothing admired, and to politely nod and smile at neighbours who were similarly attired. This was an evening of quiet grace. A slow-moving respite from the hustle and bustle of the working week.

Thomas doffed his hat to couples he knew, exchanging pleasantries about the warm spring weather. He decided to continue his stroll down to the River Thames. He enjoyed watching the boats there. Often he pictured himself on a sailing ship floating downstream towards the sea, where it would set a course for far-away Ceylon: the exotic land where Emma lived with her father. He imagined her delight as he appeared at the door. *'Emma. I'm here to marry you.'* He'd say the words calmly – as calmly as asking her to take a stroll in the garden. He smiled, lost in the romantic play that his imagination had created (and which cheerfully ignored the fact that he couldn't afford the price of a ticket to Ceylon). He pictured her throwing her arms around him and crying out—

'Mr Lloyd? A gentleman wishes to converse with you.'

'Pardon?'

Thomas found himself looking up with a degree of bemusement

at the stranger who'd spoken to him. It was the driver of a coach; the man was dressed in a long brown coat and matching hat.

'You are Mr Thomas Lloyd.'

'Yes, who wants to—'

'Please step into the carriage, sir. My master wishes to speak with you.'

The blinds were pulled down in the four-wheeler carriage. He couldn't see its passenger. Was this an elaborate attempt to rob him? If so, why would thieves go to the trouble of finding out his name? Would they risk attacking him in daylight with people nearby?

The coach door swung open. Most men would make some excuse and leave. Yet Thomas's journalistic nerve tingled. Curiosity burned brightly inside his head, and he knew he would not walk away. Removing his hat, he climbed inside, ready to face the mysterious occupant of this elegant vehicle.

Thomas sat on the upholstered bench seat opposite a gentleman of about seventy. He didn't have a single hair on his head. His face was so thin that Thomas found himself considering that it was as sharp as a knife blade. The grey eyes held the same kind of sharpness too, signalling a formidable intelligence. Thomas pictured this striking man, dressed in black, hunched over a chessboard, outsmarting and outplaying even the cleverest opponent. The man wore a gold lapel pin on his long black coat. The pin terminated in a small, milky-white pearl.

Thomas said in a direct way, 'You wanted to speak with me. Why?'

'Don't you wish to know who I am?' He rapped his knuckles on the carriage roof. A sign for the driver to continue to a prearranged destination? The carriage moved off along the street. 'After all, Mr Lloyd, I might be kidnapping you.'

'I doubt that very much, sir. And as to learning your identity, it is entirely your prerogative whether you give me your name or not.'

'Mr Lloyd, I see you are a man who prefers to get straight to the heart of the matter.'

'You have information for me, and do not wish to reveal its source?'

'I have information, yes; vitally important information. As for learning my name ...' That thin face tightened into a smile, hinting that the man in black wasn't as severe as he first seemed. 'Knowing my name isn't particularly important. Like an expensive bottle of vintage port, it's the contents that are important, not the vessel it arrives in.'

'As you wish.' Thomas found himself intrigued by his travelling companion. 'Of course, you know who I am.'

'Mr Thomas Lloyd. The son of schoolteachers from Yorkshire. Now one of the finest writers of newspaper articles in Britain.'

Thomas blushed at this praise; even so, the words made him suspicious. 'Thank you for holding my work in such esteem.'

'Not just I believe you to be the very best of writers; my friends do too.'

'I'm flattered.'

'Oh, we don't flatter, Mr Lloyd. We have examined your work in detail.'

'I see. Would you like to engage me for some writing assignment?'

'Firstly, I'd like to tell you about our work.'

'Very well.'

'Raise the blind. Tell me what you see through the window.'

Thomas did so. 'Ah, we're in the poor district of Pimlico. Squalid houses. These are rat-infested places; twenty or more people share the same privy in a yard. Scarlet fever, cholera, dysentery are rife here, together with malnutrition. See the little girl carrying the bag of coal? She has no shoes, so walks in horse dung and all kinds of dirt with her bare feet – those dirty feet of hers will carry harmful germs into her home, which will, likely as not, spread disease amongst her brothers and sisters.'

'And such a scene is repeated many thousands of times throughout London, let alone Great Britain as a whole.'

'Indeed it is, sir.'

The man nodded. 'You no doubt understand that the lack of education is the evil generator of disease?'

'Absolutely. If the girl knew that it was important to wash her feet before entering the house then the spread of harmful germs would be restricted. Lives would be saved.'

The man placed his fingertips together as he studied Thomas. 'My colleagues do what they can to develop civilization here in Britain.'

Thomas laughed. 'Surely you're joking? We have civilization. Look around you. Paved roads, railways, telegraph communication. Homes and factories lit by gas.'

'We do not have civilization yet, Mr Lloyd. Otherwise, would that little girl be carrying a heavy sack of coal that must certainly hurt her back? Why does she not understand that to tread dung into her home is to deliver illness to her siblings? Believe me, sir, not just dirt but death adheres to each one of those little toes of hers.'

'I agree wholeheartedly. If there was one girl without footwear in London I would give her parents enough money to buy the shoes myself. Yet there must be fifty thousand girls in London who do not own a single pair of shoes. That is horribly wrong, but I can do nothing about it.'

The carriage rumbled beside a railway track as a locomotive surged along in clouds of smoke and steam.

'Mr Thomas,' said the man, 'I spoke of building civilization here. My colleagues and I lobby parliament to introduce laws that will make the education of children compulsory.'

'That's entirely laudable, although I don't understand why you're telling me about your plans.'

'Because you are a vital part of those plans.'

'I am?'

'One of the essential components of civilization is an effective and professional police force that the public respect and trust. You accompanied a detective as he investigated cases. You wrote about his work for your newspaper in such a clear and interesting way that it fascinated readers by the million.'

'I simply wrote about what I saw.'

'And you portrayed, most accurately, that Inspector Frederick Abberline is a man who gives himself body and soul to fight crime.'

'You are well informed about my work, sir, but I have decided that that I will no longer accompany Inspector Abberline.'

'We do know that, Mr Lloyd. We know, also, that you recently had an unfortunate brush with death.'

'Then you must understand that I am done with that aspect of my career. I'm returning to work tomorrow as an ordinary journalist.'

'That would be very regrettable.'

'My mind is made up, sir.'

'Mr Lloyd, a great number of people still believe that our police force is little more than a legion of thugs who are corrupt – that they only patrol the streets with the express purpose of bullying innocent men and women, while filling their own pockets with money from bribes. You, sir, are changing those perceptions. Your articles about Inspector Abberline are transforming attitudes towards the police. In the public's eyes, Inspector Abberline has become a knight in armour that shines with honesty as he smites lawbreakers with his sword of justice.'

'Not words I would choose, sir.'

'I agree. *You, Mr Lloyd, chose exactly the right words.* You have the talent to transform the image of our police force. The public will see the police as guardians of law and order. As protectors of ordinary people. Abberline is the perfect example of such a policeman. You, Mr Lloyd, are part of a greater scheme to build a safe, prosperous society where slums and disease carried on the bare feet of a little girl are things of the past.'

'Those are stirring words. Yet I have made up my mind.'

'You will not continue to pen those marvellous reports of Inspector Abberline's work?'

'No, I will not.'

'Very well.'

'Is that all?'

'Yes, Mr Lloyd.'

'Then I should like to return to my stroll.'

The thin-faced gentleman rapped the coach's ceiling with his knuckles. The vehicle came to a stop.

'Oh, before you go, Mr Lloyd.'

'I will not change my mind, sir. I am done with danger. You do understand?'

'I understand. However, I should like to present you with a small gift.'

'A gift? What on earth for?'

'Nothing of great monetary value. The value is in what it symbolizes.'

'I still don't understand.'

'I believe you will understand perfectly when circumstances demand it.'

The man handed Thomas a slim box covered in red leather. The case, about four inches long, could, perhaps, have housed a single cigar. Thomas opened the lid. Inside, resting on a velvet pad, was a gold lapel pin, tipped with a very small white pearl. The gold pin was exactly the same as the one worn in the gentleman's lapel.

'This must be a joke,' Thomas protested. 'Why are you giving me this?'

'It is essential that you have it. Imagine I have given you a pistol before we enter a hostile land. The gold pin could be as useful as a loaded gun when surrounded by dangerous enemies. Keep the pin out of sight. Do not show it to anyone, nor should you breathe a word about its existence.'

'I am truly baffled.'

'Accept it, please. I beg you.'

'Very well. Thank you. I shan't tell a soul.'

'I am so glad.'

'Good evening, sir.'

'There's just one more item that I am required to hand to you.'

'I can't accept any more gifts.'

'This isn't a gift. It's a letter.' He opened a small cabinet affixed to the inner wall of the carriage and drew out a white envelope. 'By all means read it later.'

Thomas raised an eyebrow.

'Please take the letter, sir. It is written by the Prime Minister.'

Thomas Lloyd stood watching the carriage vanish amongst the horses and hansom cabs that filled the street.

'A letter from the Prime Minister?' He gazed at his own name upon the white envelope.

Thomas had been so astonished by this turn of events that he'd not even been able to gather his wits to say goodbye to the thin-faced gentleman. *Why does a lowly newspaperman such as I warrant a personal letter from the Prime Minister?* Thomas forgot all about his walk to the river. Instead, he quickly returned home, intending to read the letter in the privacy of his sitting room.

Chapter 5

Inspector Abberline stood in the hallway of Mrs Cherryhome's house as Thomas Lloyd hurried downstairs. The message conveyed to him by Mrs Cherryhome was that Abberline wanted to see Thomas urgently.

Thomas said, 'You've received my telegram, then. You know?'

'I've not had your telegram yet, Thomas. I'm here about the letter.'

Thomas surmised that Abberline had been told about the Prime Minister's letter, handed to him by the stranger yesterday. However, he couldn't be more wrong.

Abberline pulled a grimy envelope from his pocket and thrust it at Thomas. Thomas saw what appeared to be reddish-brown finger-prints close to the postage stamp.

'This letter?' Thomas said with surprise. 'I thought ...' His voice trailed away as he saw who the envelope was addressed to: *Inspector Abberline, Scotland Yard.*

'Read it.'

Thomas pulled out a scrap of paper and began to read: '"*Dear boss. Forgive me for being so lazy, and for dragging these idle bones when I should have been at work on the street. Ha! Ha! Cutting, slicing, raising cheery mayhem. Be it hereby known, Inspector Abberline, I will soon be back at my butchery, sending more harlots to bloody Hades – and you can do nothing to stop me, so help me Christ ... Yours from the warming pit of hell.*" My God, it's signed Jack the Ripper.'

After Abberline left, Thomas Lloyd returned to his comfortable armchair near the window. Magglyn, in the next room, chose that moment to practise his accordion. Perhaps he'd become more adept with that windbag of an instrument, because the lilting melody he played sounded quite pleasant to Thomas's ears.

What weighed so heavily on Thomas's mind were two letters. One apparently sent to Abberline by the murderer known as Jack the Ripper. The other, bearing the address of 10 Downing Street, had come from the very pen of Great Britain's Prime Minister, the Marquess of Salisbury. Thomas didn't doubt the provenance of the Prime Minister's letter, so Thomas brought his thoughts to bear on the Ripper message. Thomas recalled his days as a junior newspaper reporter in Whitechapel two years ago, when a spate of murders throughout that summer of 1888 were attributed to one perpetrator – a mysterious figure that had never been caught, and had never been identified. All that was known for sure was that several women had been murdered. Some of them savagely mutilated. A letter had arrived at the offices of the Central News Agency, claiming to be written by the killer, and promising to cut off the ears of his next victim and send them to the police. The taunting letter writer signed off with the words: *Yours truly, Jack the Ripper.* Until then, police had referred to the unknown killer as simply 'the Whitechapel murderer'. The press and the public seized on the name 'Jack the Ripper' – a vivid name that perfectly suited the grisly killings. Thus, a legend was born. People still talked about Jack the Ripper with shudders of fear and excitement. Thomas also knew that when newspapers reprinted the 'Jack the Ripper' letter, hundreds of hoax letters immediately inundated press offices and police stations.

As far as Thomas was aware, Inspector Abberline had never personally received a letter claiming to be from Jack the Ripper – until now, that is. The detective must be asking himself if the letter had been sent by the killer of those women two years ago, or if it had been sent to him in jest. Although Thomas couldn't think of a crueller joke. Clearly, Abberline couldn't dismiss the letter out of hand. He must be asking himself if the infamous murderer intended to attack new victims.

Thomas gazed out at doves settling onto the rooftops. He could picture headlines screaming from the newspapers' front pages: JACK THE RIPPER IS BACK! SHOCKING LETTER SENT TO INSPECTOR ABBERLINE – THE MAN WHO FAILED TO FIND THE WHITECHAPEL MONSTER. However, Abberline had told him that the letter would not be made public just yet, so those potentially disturbing newspaper headlines wouldn't be making an appearance for a while.

The 'Ripper' note would remain hidden, just as the letter he received from the thin-faced stranger must stay a secret. Last night, he'd read the Prime Minister's message to him many times. In truth, the great man had praised Thomas's newspaper articles about Inspector Abberline. Salisbury asked Thomas to keep the letter confidential, although it revealed no secrets. Moreover, it was the kind of congratulatory note that a senior politician could have written to many a sportsman, artist or businessman who'd been successful in their career. The last line of the letter encouraged Thomas to continue his work with Abberline. It read: *Your reports that feature this magnificent detective, solving crimes, and protecting the public, are of great value and I do beseech you to write many more.*

Thomas imagined asking his fiancée, Emma, what he should do in the light of such an entreaty. He pictured her smile as she explained that if the Prime Minister himself had taken the time to pen such an appeal, then Thomas's work was deeply important, and he should continue to portray Abberline as the warrior that battled evil. Thomas had then sent the telegram, informing Abberline that he'd had a change of heart and would continue to shadow the detective. At least for now, anyway. Abberline clearly hadn't received that telegram when he'd hurried here to inform Thomas about the Jack the Ripper letter.

Thomas took the gold pin from the box, the pin with the tiny pearl set in the end. He studied it for a while, pondering its significance. The gentleman in the coach had insisted that the pin would become extremely useful to Thomas at some point. *How would it be useful?* Thomas wondered. *Does the pin symbolize a certain course of events? Are there others with a pin like this? Do they recognize each other as colleagues in some clandestine organization when they see it?*

Thomas Lloyd listened to the haunting Irish melody played by Mr Magglyn in the next room. Tingles of excitement began their distinctive dance upon his spine and instinct told him that a new adventure wasn't far away.

Chapter 6

PROFESSOR CHARLES GIDDINGS woke late on that Monday morning. He'd stayed up the previous night to work on his new book, *The Future Philosopher.*

'Goodness gracious,' he declared with mild surprise as he drew back the curtains. 'Maude, have you seen what someone's done to the windows panes?'

Maude bustled in from the kitchen where she'd been writing a list of groceries. She joined her husband, who stood in front of one of the windows.

'Someone, I do declare,' he began ponderously, 'has an impish, albeit impenetrable sense of humour.'

'Some devil's scrawled on our glass,' snapped his wife in a much more forthright way. 'I'll have their guts for garters.'

'That's a vivid threat, Maude. Though if you execute such a punishment it will indubitably lead to you being brought before a magistrate on a charge of assault.'

'See, Charlie! They've painted letters!'

'Indeed so, Maude, indeed so.'

The professor raised a monocle to his eye in order to study the marks that so outraged his wife. Being a man of mild emotions, he didn't wish Maude to become so angry. Invariably, once ensconced in such a fury her rage would burn for days, which he would have to stoically endure.

'What do those symbols mean?' she asked sharply.

'Well, my dear, two panes bear the letter O, three bear the letter V, while this one in the centre has the letter X. One vowel, four consonants; they do not spell a word I know of.'

'Foreigners.'

'More likely rascal children, my dear.'

That's when he heard a loud popping sound.

'Goodness gracious.'

'What was that?' asked Maude, startled.

'I venture it was a hard projectile striking the brickwork on the outside of the house.' Another blast of sound filled the room. This time one of the glass panes shattered. 'Good grief!' he shouted. 'Bullets! We're being fired upon.'

He fell upon his wife and both tumbled to the floor. More bullets smashed through the panes on which were painted the letters O, V and X. A tall vase on the mantelpiece shattered. Then ... silence. The firing had stopped. The professor warily climbed to his feet. He surveyed the broken glass before helping his wife up. What she said next dispelled any concerns he had that she might have been hurt.

'Look at the state of my room! The mess! I'll scratch their blasted eyes out!'

Professor Giddings was relieved to see that Maude was unhurt. Though his heart sank when he realized that she'd be angrily telling him, for many an hour to come, what was wrong with this blessed island they lived upon.

When there were no more shots he ventured to the mantelpiece and picked up an envelope. It was addressed to Scotland Yard, London. A bullet had nicked off the corner of the envelope.

'I rather think,' he declared, 'I should, in the circumstances, send this letter as soon as I possibly can.'

Chapter 7

MONDAY AFTERNOON SAW Thomas Lloyd climb the stairs to the editor's office. The editor was Thomas's boss. They'd never been on friendly terms, and Thomas suspected that the permanently grumpy man wished he could dismiss Thomas from his post. However, the articles he'd written about Abberline's cases had been so popular, boosting the *Pictorial*'s circulation by many thousands, that the editor's own superior would never agree to Thomas being sacked.

Thomas knocked.

'In you come, then,' came the grumpy command.

The editor sat at his desk, a cigar clamped between his teeth. The bushy moustache was in danger of igniting as the glowing tip of the cigar crept closer.

'Good morning, sir.'

'Sit your backside down, Lloyd.'

'Thank you.'

'Hmm!' That was the editor's far from eloquent way of asking *What would you like to talk to me about?*

Thomas spoke politely. 'Sir. I sent you a letter last week saying that I would no longer accompany Inspector Abberline, and that I wished to work on more general news stories.'

'Hmm. Got that letter, I did. It drove the newspaper's owners into a panic. Those adventures of yours with Abberline have got the public hooked. The owners are terrified that their profits are going to drop like a damn stone.'

'I'm here to tell you, sir, that I've had a change of heart. I'll continue to write first-hand accounts of Abberline's investigations.'

'Thank the Almighty for that.' The editor plucked the cigar from his teeth and exhaled a huge cloud of smoke. 'The owners'd have kicked my bones out into the street if you'd gone back to being a blasted hack. What changed your mind, Lloyd?'

Thomas Lloyd couldn't reveal the contents of the Prime Minister's letter. Shrugging, he said, 'I wasn't myself after what happened in the canal.'

'I'm not surprised. You nearly went to your grave.'

'I realize I was too hasty in telling you that I'd stop shadowing Inspector Abberline.'

'Yes, remember you are his shadow, not his puppet. Stick close to him, Lloyd. Always write what the public want to read. Just don't let that Scotland Yard chap influence you.'

'I always write what I see as accurately and as truthfully as I can.'

'Glad to hear it. Here ... this'll interest you.' The editor wiped tobacco ash from a handwritten letter. 'It's from the paper's owners. What do you think? Bet it's come as a surprise, huh?'

Beneath an elaborate crest was a directive ordering the editor to gather up Thomas Lloyd's Abberline reports he'd written for the *Pictorial Evening News* and publish them in a book.

'So, Lloyd. You are going to be the author of a book, which will be sold throughout the empire. What do you say to that?'

'That's amazing, sir. Marvellous news.' Thomas felt a surge of excitement. 'I'll send copies to my parents, to my fiancée, and to Inspector Abberline, of course.'

'You will be provided with ten free copies, so you can do just that.' He stubbed the cigar out on a plate that held a sandwich. 'You won't get any royalties, though, or any additional fees.'

Thomas flinched with shock. 'I wrote the articles. They are from my pen alone.'

'You wrote 'em as part of your employment here. That means the copyright belongs to the newspaper, not you.'

'I've earned the owners thousands of pounds. The Abberline reports are so popular that circulation of the *Pictorial* has doubled.'

'The owners are grateful, I'm sure. No doubt they've nailed a photograph of you to their living-room wall and salute it every morning.' The editor laughed loudly at his own sarcastic quip.

'Dash it all.' Thomas grew angry now. Earnings from the book would enable him to visit Emma in Ceylon – after all, he couldn't afford a steamer ticket on his newspaperman wages. 'It's only right and proper that I receive a fair share from the sales of the book.'

'You signed a contract when you started work for the *Pictorial*, my lad. Everything you write is owned by the paper.' He then added reluctantly, 'There will be a small token in recognition of your work; the owners have stipulated a payment of twenty-five pounds.'

Thomas Lloyd left the newspaper office seething with the injustice of what had just happened. His book, featuring Abberline's criminal investigations, might sell a million copies. Yet he'd only be paid a few pounds – a nominal payment, nothing more.

Even though he walked at a furious rate, his instincts didn't let him down. He abruptly turned around. A middle-aged man in a bowler hat had stopped dead behind him. Pedestrians flowed by the two men on the busy London street.

Thomas spoke sharply. 'You're following me. Why?'

'I admire your writing, Mr Lloyd.'

'Very well. But why are you stalking me?'

'I have information for you.'

'Oh?'

'It is important.'

'Do you wish to make an appointment to discuss it with me?'

'Here is sufficient.'

'In the street?'

'It won't take long.'

'Very well.'

A boy carrying a basketful of oranges hurried by.

'Mr Lloyd,' said the stranger, looking him in the eye. 'Inspector Abberline has enemies. They plot against him. You should be aware of that.'

'What makes you think I will believe what you say?'

The man's expression remained serious as he gripped the lapel of his own jacket and turned it over. 'This is all the evidence you need.'

Thomas saw that the man wore a gold pin on the underside of his lapel. At one end of the pin was a small white pearl.

'Good day, Mr Lloyd.' The man politely lifted his hat before vanishing into the crowds.

Today had been an unusual one. Thomas Lloyd had visited his editor and learnt that his Abberline case reports would be made into a book, and then he had been followed by a stranger who had warned him that Abberline had enemies who plotted against him. The stranger had revealed that he wore a gold pin on the underside of his lapel. The gold pin, terminating with a small pearl, was identical to the one worn by the thin-faced gentleman in the carriage, and the pin that had been given to Thomas.

The business about the book annoyed Thomas, while the business of the gold pin perplexed him. *Am I to believe that I've been conscripted into a secret society?* He turned this question over in his mind as he walked toward the post office, carrying a small parcel, wrapped in brown paper. *What is the name of the organization? Order of the Golden Pin? The Pearl and Pin Society? No ... now I'm being flippant. Clearly, this is serious. Even the Prime Minister suggests that my work is important. The letter was genuine, wasn't it? I'm not being duped, am I? What if the thin-faced man and the stranger I met today are the real enemies of Inspector Abberline? Am I being exploited because I'm his friend? Will they get to him through me? Should I confide in Abberline? Tell him everything? Show him the gold pin and the Prime Minister's letter? However, I've been asked to keep all this secret. Even from Abberline. What should I do?*

'Wait and see,' he murmured to himself as he entered the post office. 'All this about plots and grand schemes to transform Britain may come to nothing. I might never hear from my gold pin friends again.'

A woman in spectacles and a long black dress gave him a very hard stare. He realized he'd been thinking aloud. She clearly suspected him of lunacy. He smiled and raised his hat.

'I'm rehearsing lines for a play. It opens tonight.'

She frowned and turned away.

That's so unlike me, he thought. *Why did I lie to her, or even try to explain why I was talking to myself?* Perhaps these mysterious encounters with strangers had left him feeling that he'd been plunged into a melodrama full of spies and intrigue.

'Ah, Mr Lloyd. Parcel for the lady, is it?'

Thomas knew the post office clerk from frequent visits to his counter. The young man always had a cheerful smile. Thomas liked him.

'Yes, a little gift,' Thomas said. 'Some Scottish lace.'

'Scottish lace will look fine indeed in her home out there. Surrounded by a jungle full of monkeys, I don't doubt, sir?'

'Monkeys, snakes, and all manner of creatures.'

The clerk weighed the package. It bore the address of Emma Bright, and in large clear print: CEYLON.

The clerk gave Thomas a sideways glance. 'I should warn you, sir. There have been some changes.'

Thomas felt his backbone tingle. Another warning? He watched as the clerk's hand moved up to his lapel. Thomas thought: *He'll be wearing a gold pin, too. He belongs to the secret society, and now he has a message for me.* Thomas's heart pounded. This situation became stranger by the moment.

'What message do you have?' His chest felt tight as he wondered what the clerk would reveal to him.

'Postal charges, sir.' The clerk's fingers did brush the lapel as he reached into his breast pocket to pull out a pencil. 'It will cost more to send your parcel to Ceylon.' He wrote the cost of postage on the parcel. 'I quite forgot to warn you that the charges were increasing the last time you were here.'

'Oh ... I see, thank you.' Even though Thomas had misunderstood, and now he realized there was no gold pin hiding beneath the lapel, he still found himself asking, 'There is nothing else you need to tell me?'

'Nothing, sir.' The man smiled. 'Other than have a pleasant evening, sir.'

Thomas stepped out into the busy street. Every man who passed by seemed to shoot a knowing glance in his direction. So, how many people in this great city wore a concealed gold pin? Goodness knows. Thomas suspected that there was much more to this than met the eye. Fascinating times lay ahead; he was sure of it.

The next day a telegram arrived at Thomas Lloyd's home. The message, from Inspector Abberline, requested his presence at Scotland Yard. The telegram closed with the word URGENT – a word guaranteed to make Thomas's flesh tingle with excitement.

Abberline had, of course, now seen the letter from Thomas, saying that he'd had a change of heart and would be joining him on future investigations. Abberline, a generally undemonstrative man, had been visibly pleased. He'd warmly shaken Thomas by the hand and thanked him. After that, nothing more had been said. Perhaps Abberline considered Thomas's original decision to return to general newspaper work had been something of an aberration brought on by the shock of almost drowning in the canal. Thomas couldn't reveal the real reason, of course. The conversation with the aristocratic stranger in the carriage, the gift of the gold pin, and the Prime Minister's letter would have to remain secret. For now.

Thomas arrived at the police headquarters at nine o'clock. A constable took Thomas to a room bleakly furnished with a single chair and a table. Abberline stood at one end of the room. He glared at a large man of around forty with a high, glistening forehead. The stranger's cold eyes clearly signalled he resented being here, and would have gladly thrown a punch at Abberline if it wasn't for the fact his wrists were held together by manacles.

'Ah, Thomas, good morning,' Abberline said. 'You are just in time to hear Mr Turton confess to murder.'

'I shall do no such blasted thing, Abberline,' the man snarled. 'And you best wish with all your damned heart that our paths never cross at night. Cos you'll regret putting me in irons, you devil.'

Inspector Abberline's eyes were rarely harsh. Today, however, those brown eyes of his were as sharp as knife-blades. His furious glare even made this brute flinch.

Abberline spoke firmly. 'You stabbed the gentleman. You took his watch, his wallet and gold signet ring, which is engraved with his initials, RWF.'

'Have you found them in my house? No, sir, you have not!'

'I know you, Turton. I've had dealings with you before. You attack men and women, and you take their possessions when they're lying helpless on the ground.'

'You've arrested me three times before, Abberline. But you aren't a good enough copper to get me convicted. I always walk free from court.'

'Not this time.'

'I'll be out of this building by tonight. You, yourself, have no evidence, Mr Policeman.' He grinned, exposing black teeth. 'You've got nothing to fix that killing on me.'

'You had blood on your hands.'

'I helped a poor little doggy with a cut leg. Got blood all over these two paws of mine.' He held up the chained hands. 'Doggy blood, not some gent's red stuff. Ha.'

'It is Mr Foster's blood.'

'You know that there's no way of telling if it was Foster's blood or the little pup's. All blood's red. Even fish blood.'

'I know you stabbed him to death.' Abberline pulled an envelope from his pocket. 'Because here is the proof. Photographic evidence, Mr Turton. Incontrovertible proof.'

The thug blinked when he saw the envelope. His aggressive manner abruptly changed to one of nervousness.

'What's this, Abberline?'

'I'm going to show you. But first there is something important you should know. Something that will shock you.'

'Like what?' Turton had become defensive. 'What you got there, you stinking dog?'

Thomas realized that Turton no longer tried to dominate the room with his loud bluster.

Abberline placed the envelope down on the table. 'Do you read the scientific journals?'

'Ha, I'd use them to wipe that smile off your damn face.'

'Recently, there have been reports in scientific publications that describe how it's possible to photograph the eyes of a murder victim.'

'What's the point of that?'

'Photographs of the cadaver's pupil reveal the last thing they saw. The image is captured in the eye and remains there for days afterwards. Of course, the last thing a murder victim sees is the person who killed them.'

'I don't believe it.'

'Mr Turton, I will show you a photograph of Mr Foster's eye. When I do, tell me whose image is captured within the pupil of the eye.'

'No, Abberline. No ...' Turton's chest expanded and shrank in quite an extraordinary way as he began to pant with alarm. 'This is more witchery than science. How can a picture of a face be fixed in a dead man's eye?'

'Images are captured by a camera, aren't they?'

Abberline opened the envelope and removed a small square of card, which he held out so the man could see it. Turton's eyes bulged as he stared at the photograph. Thomas saw that the picture was of an eye. In the black pupil of that eye was the image of a face.

'How did you do that?' Turton spluttered.

'You see the photograph of an eye?' Abberline asked calmly. 'Whose face do you see in the eye of the dead man?'

'That's my face! I see myself!'

'So, you admit that you recognize yourself in the pupil of the late Mr Foster's eye?'

'Witchcraft, blast you! That ain't science.'

'Do you now confess that you stabbed Mr Foster and stole his possessions?'

The thug raised his manacled hands and pressed his fingers to his lips. He appeared to be trying to stop the words he felt compelled to say from spilling out.

'Admit you killed him, Turton. I have witnesses that say you stood next to Mr Foster in the Black Horse tavern. One will testify he saw you stare at Foster's signet ring: a large gold ring, extremely valuable, worth a year's wages to an honest working man.' Abberline touched the picture. 'And here is the photograph I had taken of the dead man's eye. It shows your face embedded there in the pupil. Do you confess?'

Turton had filled up with so much emotional pressure that it seemed he would explode violently at any second. Nevertheless, he kept his fingers pressed hard to his lips, stopping any confession from coming out.

Abberline nodded. 'Very well. We move to the next stage of the investigation. Mr Foster's body lies on a slab in the next room. You will be taken in there. A doctor will then attach cables to the corpse. After that, electricity will be fired into the body.'

Turton's eyes had become bloodshot from sheer terror. Veins throbbed in his temples. His eyes began to dart in panic – the beast caught in a trap.

Abberline continued, 'Scientists have proved that a corpse can be brought back to life when a charge of electricity is delivered to the flesh. We have done this many times before with murder victims. The corpse returns to life just long enough to point at the person who killed them and say, "That is the man who murdered me. He is the one." What image does that put into your mind, Turton? Can you visualize the naked corpse as it convulses before sitting upright, and fixing its dead eyes on the killer?' Abberline moved quickly. Grasping Turton by the arm, he called out, 'Mr Lloyd, help me take Mr Turton to the next room. We must act quickly while the corpse is still fresh.'

Turton let out a howl of terror. 'What be I to do? What be I to do? I ain't got the stomach to see the dead brought back to life!'

'Don't fret, Mr Turton.' Abberline dragged him towards the door.

'It will be over in a few minutes. Though prepare yourself for the sensation of the dead man running his fingers over your face. They do that, you know? Murder victims want to feel the face of the man who took their life.'

'Oh, please, sir, Mr Abberline. Don't do this to me. I confess. I did it! I stabbed the man. I took his ring, and his wallet, and his watch!'

'Where are they?'

'At the home of my uncle. 20 Furlow Avenue. That's the truth. You'll find the knife wrapped in a bloody rag. It's what I used. So help me. I'm telling the truth!'

'I'll prepare a written confession,' Abberline told him. 'You shall sign it.'

'That I will, sir. Gladly. Please, sir, do not bring the dead man back to life.'

Abberline tapped on the door. Instantly, it opened to admit a pair of towering men in uniform. To Thomas, these constables seemed as tall as oak trees, just as strong too.

'Constables,' Abberline began, 'put Mr Turton back in his cell.'

The constables hauled away the trembling, sobbing man.

After they'd gone, Thomas Lloyd stared in astonishment at Abberline. 'The eyes of the dead containing images of murderers? Resurrecting corpses with electricity? Surely this isn't possible?'

Abberline allowed himself a grim smile. 'It's absolutely *im*-possible.'

'The photograph?

'I asked the police photographer to concoct the image. He added a small photograph of Turton's face to the enlarged photograph of what is, I admit, my eye. The phrase is "superimposed", I believe.'

'A trick picture?'

Abberline nodded. 'I trusted the photograph to loosen the man's tongue. It turned out I had to invent the story of bringing the dead back to life as a last resort.'

'You used blatant trickery to extract a confession?'

'Yes.'

'Was that necessary? After all, you have witnesses that place Turton in the public house on the night of the killing.'

'I have only one witness. An unreliable one, who couldn't remember if he saw Turton last night or the night before. The description given was enough to suggest that Turton had been in the Black

Horse at some point recently. But that would be insufficient for a conviction. Therefore, I pretended that detectives have new techniques that will identify a killer.'

Thomas felt a good deal of indignation. 'Is that kind of deception right and proper? You lied to the man. You frightened him into believing that a corpse would identify him as the killer.'

'Turton has violently robbed people in the past. Always there has been insufficient evidence – the case against him breaks down and he walks free. As from now, that thug is no longer a danger to the public.'

'He will hang.'

'Yes, he'll go to the gallows.'

'All because of the trick you played on him? Won't that trouble your conscience?'

'It would, if Turton is executed purely because of his signed confession. But remember, he has told us where he's hidden the murder weapon, along with his victim's possessions. They'll be identified as belonging to Mr Foster by his widow. Won't that be sufficient evidence to prove that Turton killed the man and stole from him?'

'Yes, but hardly orthodox detective work, is it?'

'I agree, friend Thomas.' Abberline's smile was a warm one. 'But until science can actually help a murder victim speak again I'll have to rely on my wits to ensure that killers are brought to justice.'

'Then you'll permit me to write a newspaper story about what just took place?'

'Ha, the photograph and my tale of resurrecting the dead? Absolutely not, Thomas.' He tapped the side of his nose. 'I might have to use that little story again on another suspect.'

'It looks as if my book about you will be a very slim one.'

'A book? What's all this about a book, Thomas?'

'I'll tell you later. However, you sent me a telegram, saying you wanted to see me?'

'Yes. I shall be going on a trip. Would you like to accompany me? That is, if you haven't change your mind again about shadowing me?'

'No, I haven't changed my mind, Inspector, so where do we go?'

'To the Kingdom of Faxfleet.'

'Faxfleet? I've never heard of the country. Where on earth is it?'

'You'll find out soon enough, Thomas. Now, if you'll give me a few minutes, I'll write out Turton's confession. Then we shall have the satisfaction of watching him sign it.'

*

The hour or so following Turton's dramatic confession became something of a rush. Abberline told Thomas to meet him at King's Cross Station at noon. Their train left at twenty minutes past twelve. Thomas sent a telegram to his editor, explaining that he was embarking on a new case with Abberline, and that stories for the newspaper would follow soon. After that, he returned home to pack a few essentials, including a fistful of fresh reporters' notebooks and a dozen new pencils. Mrs Cherryhome saw it as her Christian duty to provide for her lodgers. She parcelled up a loaf of just-baked bread, a thick slice of Cheddar cheese, and a wedge of plum cake.

'Mr Lloyd, just you remember that it was only last week when you nearly drowned in that dreadful canal.'

Thomas smiled. 'The memory is still shudderingly vivid in my memory, Mrs Cherryhome.'

'Be sure to eat this on your journey. You still need to restore your strength.'

'Thank you, Mrs Cherryhome, I will. I always enjoy your cake.'

She fussed around him as he put on his coat in the hallway. Her pink cheeks quivered with her customary anxiety when one of her tenants was leaving her safe nest for a while.

'Mr Thomas, where are you going exactly?'

'I don't know, other than it's called the Kingdom of Faxfleet.'

'Faxfleet? It sounds like it might be in Denmark or some such godless place.'

'Inspector Abberline didn't have time to tell me where it is. One of his prisoners, who'd just confessed to murder, tried to do away with himself.'

'Oh, goodness gracious.'

'Tried to hang himself with his own bootlace.'

'What a world we live in.'

'He'll live – until the hangman does a proper job of it.'

'Oh, Mr Lloyd. I shall dream of ropes and gibbets tonight. Now, you take care. Watch out for those folk overseas. I hear they carry Englishmen off to work underground in coal mines where they're never seen again.'

'I shall be on my guard, Mrs Cherryhome.'

'Take a cup of hot brandy at bedtime. It'll protect your stomach from foreign water.'

'Goodbye, Mrs Cherryhome, much obliged for the food. Take care.'

At precisely 12.20 the express train pulled out of King's Cross Station. The powerful locomotive released an immense gush of smoke. The couplings on the carriages groaned and clanked as the engine pulled them northward.

Abberline settled into his seat opposite Thomas. 'We change trains at Doncaster for Hull. After that, we take a boat to the Kingdom of Faxfleet.'

'So, we'll cross the North Sea to the Continent?'

'Hardly that.' Abberline appeared amused. 'The boat will take us upriver from the city.'

'Now I really am baffled, Inspector. You're saying there is another kingdom in the north of England?'

'The Kingdom of Faxfleet is two miles long and a mile wide. The nation has a population of two hundred and eight people, and is ruled over by King Ludwig III.'

Thomas laughed. 'Then the kingdom is nothing more than a whimsy? A joke?'

'Oh, it's real enough.'

'You're saying it's an independent nation, one entirely separate from Great Britain?'

'The Kingdom of Faxfleet exists as long as our own monarch tolerates it. Just over a hundred years ago King George III granted sovereignty of the island to a certain Ludwig Smith. King George also gave Smith the right to call himself a king and to govern the inhabitants of Faxfleet.'

'It all sounds rather peculiar.'

'I shan't disagree.' Abberline chuckled. 'I've been reading about the place. It seems that King George bestowed a kingship on Ludwig Smith after the pair had drunk an enormous quantity of Yorkshire ale. In later years, successive British monarchs were amused by the Kingdom of Faxfleet, and Ludwig Smith. His descendants were allowed to keep the title of King and to continue to rule their island in the River Humber.'

'So, we are on our way to the Kingdom of Faxfleet, which begs the question: why are we going?'

'Scotland Yard has been asked for their help. A murder has taken place on the island, and there have been other attempts to frighten the islanders, and perhaps even kill them.'

'Does your jurisdiction as a Scotland Yard detective enable you to operate legally there?'

'I have been invited by none other than King Ludwig III himself.' Abberline gazed out of the window for a moment. Redbrick houses had given away to green fields where cows grazed. 'All this business about a king ruling a little island in an English river is nonsense, of course, but a murder had been committed, which is a very serious business. What's more, I understand that certain members of our own royal family are interested in this case, and want the murderer arrested as quickly as possible. Now ... did you say earlier that you are collecting the stories you have written about me into a book?'

Thomas told Abberline what the owners of the newspaper he worked for intended. He found it impossible to disguise his annoyance that he would receive no royalties, which, if they had been paid, would have allowed him to visit his fiancée in Ceylon. Abberline was sympathetic. He expressed his hope that Thomas wouldn't be separated from Emma Bright for much longer. After chatting for a while, Abberline took out his case papers in order to study them before their arrival. Thomas balanced his briefcase on his lap, placed a sheet of paper on its flat surface, unscrewed the top from his pen and began to write.

My Dearest Emma,

Once more I am hotfoot in pursuit of adventure. Inspector Abberline has been ordered to investigate a murder that has taken place on a small island in the River Humber. The island is known as the Kingdom of Faxfleet. Imagine! I grew up in Yorkshire, yet I have never heard of the place before.

I miss you very much and dream of seeing you soon. I shall write to you again once I reach Faxfleet and have met its king.

Yours with absolute affection,

Thomas

Thomas Lloyd walked around the island alone. Here he was in the little-known kingdom of Faxfleet. The island was low lying, flat and covered with trees. It sat in the Humber several miles upstream from where the huge river disgorged itself into the North Sea. After the train journey to the city of Hull, a small steamboat had brought them to Faxfleet, which lay about half a mile from the mainland. The spring afternoon had become quite breezy. Winds blowing across the river shook the trees into such fits of loud rustling it sounded to Thomas as if huge apes must be swinging through those oaks, elms and willows.

'Invisible apes in English trees.' Thomas smiled as he jotted down descriptions of the island in his notebook. 'My grandfather always said that I had a "veritable Goliath of an imagination".' His pencil whispered across the paper: *Isle of Faxfleet, ruled by King Ludwig III – two miles long, one mile wide. Curves, almost a banana shape. King's residence stands on eastern tip. Lots of wildlife – otters, rabbits, foxes; all quite tame. Fox came out of long grass to sniff my boots. More like pet dog than wild fox. This is a strange place. Scent of fragrant blossom. Very heady, almost intoxicating.*

Thomas strolled on, following a path by the water's edge. A seal's head popped up from the river to watch him go by. The creature's eyes shone like balls of polished, black glass.

Inspector Abberline had gone to King Ludwig's home to introduce himself. Abberline suggested he go alone to talk to the man about the murder committed here recently. He wished to introduce the fact that he was accompanied by a journalist a little while later. Sometimes landowners and the aristocracy could be decidedly reluctant to have a man from the press on their property. Even if the owner of the island wasn't perhaps a genuine king in the accepted sense of the word, he, Ludwig III, still had the right to order Thomas to leave. So, yes, definitely best to allow Abberline to diplomatically broach the subject of a journalist being here to write about the murder.

Thomas stepped onto the pebble shore. It stretched out perhaps fifty paces before it reached the river itself. He walked toward the water. There the seal amused itself by turning somersaults amid the waves – trying to catch its tail apparently. Thomas laughed softly to himself. He was glad he'd changed his mind. If he had decided to return to regular day-to-day newspaper work he'd probably be sat at a desk back in London, listening to the editor howl bad temperedly at underlings. Here, there was fresh air, the pleasant rustling of trees, the lap of waves on the shore. Simply beautiful. Thomas smiled, enjoying his stroll.

'Hey. You there. Come over here. Quick!'

He turned to see a figure standing on a rock. A remarkable figure at that. Quite amazing, in fact. An individual of around thirty years of age stood on a rock that was about five feet in height and which protruded from the beach some fifty yards away. The figure stared in Thomas's direction while beckoning with astonishing vigour.

'Come here. Please hurry!'

Thomas stared, open mouthed. The figure wore a short crimson jacket. The clothes on its bottom half were amazing. A kilt in pale brown leather reached its knees. From beneath the kilt came a pair of legs clad in loose-fitting trousers, or pantaloons, or ... or ... Good grief. Thomas couldn't decide what the exotic garment should be called.

'Please, sir. You *must* come over here to me!'

A young man? A woman? Thomas shielded his eyes against the sunlight. He couldn't really tell the sex of the extraordinary creature. The stranger wore its black hair very short. The voice didn't tell him if it was male or female either.

The figure cupped its hands to its lips and shouted, 'Sir? Can you understand English?'

'Yes. I'm an Englishman.'

'Then in the name of Jove, run! Come over here at once. Hurry!'

It's a woman. That striking figure that combined a strange blend of femininity and masculinity quite bamboozled him. In fact, he felt strangely dazzled by this exotic apparition in leather kilt and pantaloons.

'Please hurry!' she cried.

'Madam? Are you in danger?'

'No, but you are, sir. You're in danger of drowning! Fly this way. Move those feet of yours as fast you can!'

Such an odd way with words, he told himself. *Such an odd way of dressing, too.* Despite her bedazzling effect on him, he did move briskly across the beach towards her.

'Faster, sir. Faster. The river is licking at your heels.'

This time Thomas understood her warning. The tide had turned. With astonishing speed it rushed across the pebbles.

'Run!'

Thomas obeyed. He ran up the beach towards the large boulder on which the woman stood. When he reached the rock, she bent down, extending her hand towards him. He held out both his hands to help her down, misunderstanding her gesture.

'Here,' she said quickly. 'Take my hand, I'll help you up. My mission of the day is to keep your shoes dry.'

Her way of speaking seemed decidedly odd, yet she smiled brightly. She glowed with good humour. He took her hand. And, dear God, her grip was a strong one. She energetically hauled him up onto the boulder. Even though he strived to do anything as impolite as stare, he couldn't help but notice the narrowness of her waist and a youthful pretty face that glowed with health.

'There, sir.' She pointed at the river. 'The tide dashes in here like a cock after his dainty little hen. If you hadn't run to me the river would have caught you and carried you off.'

'Thank you, miss.' Thomas politely raised his hat.

'Miss, ha! How sweet. Nobody has called me "miss" for years.'

He found himself gazing at her dancing eyes. They caught the light of the sun, and flashed with such energy and charisma. *This remarkable woman is an explosion in human form. Good Lord. An explosion in human form?* Were those appropriate words to describe a young lady? He shook his head, striving to find more accurate phrases.

'You shake your head.' Her shining eyes fixed on his. 'Are you feeling unwell?'

'No, I'm quite well, thank you. I'm just .... erm, swept away by this turn of events.'

'Swept away.' She laughed, holding a hand up to her perfectly formed lips. 'You very nearly were, sir.'

'Erm ... ah ... much appreciated that you, erm ... warned me.' He'd become staggeringly inarticulate. 'Perhaps there's no need to ... erm ...' He raised his hand that was still clasped by hers.

She laughed. 'Oh, it would be just too scandalous for me to be seen holding a stranger's hand on this rock. We don't want to embarrass our friend the seal, do we? He might write an angry letter to *The Times* about the improper morals of the young today.'

'Ah, yes, quite.' Thomas felt the heat in his face as he blushed. She was quite right. Who would see them holding hands? Besides, nothing improper occurred. The lady had held his hand to prevent him from slipping back into the river. He glanced round, now in no hurry to remove his hand from her forceful grip. The river had engulfed the beach in seconds. The speed of sticks and foam moving by told him that the current was dangerously fast here. Already the water had surrounded the boulder, meaning that they now stood on their own little island.

He said, 'Robinson Crusoe – that's who I've become.'

She laughed, amused by his comment. 'And I shall be your Man Friday, loyal companion and servant.'

'Hardly *Man* Friday.'

They both laughed at this so loudly that the seal bobbed in the river, watching them with an expression of what seemed like comical surprise. The woman released her grip on his hand. Not that he would have minded if they'd remained hand in hand on their rock in the river. An island made for two.

'Good afternoon, stranger.' She held out her hand for him to shake. 'My name is Jo.'

He must have reacted with surprise, because she laughed.

'Yes, sir: Jo. My full name is Josephine Hamilton-West. Jo suits me best, however. So it would make me happy if you called me Jo.'

'If you insist.'

'I do.'

'Jo.'

'Thank you, sir.'

'I am Thomas Lloyd.'

'Mr Lloyd.' She dipped her knee, turning her eyes downwards as if she were a shy maiden being introduced to a gentleman at a dance. Jo was clearly play-acting for her own amusement. Despite this, her manner was pleasantly charming.

'Please call me Thomas.'

'Thank you, Thomas. So, what the heck now? Do we bravely swim for the shore? Or sit here in the sun and talk?'

Thomas Lloyd realized that yet another day was turning out to be really quite extraordinary. This morning he'd set out from London – a teeming, noisy, turbulent city that smelt of coal smoke from tens of thousands of domestic and industrial chimneys – and now here he sat on a rock surrounded by water. Fresh air pleasantly caressed his face. He could smell fragrant blossom. The Humber shone as if it had been magically transformed into a river of gold in the sunlight. He heard the musical notes of birdsong, the lap of waves, the splash of the seal as it hunted for fish. Perhaps most extraordinary of all, he sat here on a boulder, surrounded by the incoming tide, with a woman of thirty or so; pretty much his own age. And she was amazing. Jo wore that incredible leather kilt over exotic pantaloons. Her hair was cut short to her head. Her lively, happy eyes watched him with such intensity as he talked, and she had a heart-warming smile that rarely left her attractive lips.

The woman had such self-confidence, too. She spoke to Thomas as if she'd been his friend for years. When she noticed something of interest – a heron catching a fish, or a ship passing by in the distance – she'd lightly rest her hand on his forearm before pointing out what he should see. Thomas liked her. Josephine Hamilton-West had to be one of the most interesting people he'd ever met.

'You like my clothes?' she asked.

'They're quite eye-catching.'

'I bought them in Russia. Cossack women wear these when they go out riding on those fiery horses they have. To ride one of those stallions is like riding a demon.'

'I imagine people stare when they see you dressed like that.'

'I care not one jot, sir.' She spoke in a laughing kind of way that made Thomas smile. 'Besides, here on the island we're all very strange. You know, I have a hat that should be worn with this costume. It looks exactly like a plant pot. I must confess I never wear it at all.'

'And your boots?'

'These are cowboy boots from America. Why are you here, Thomas?'

'I'm here with Inspector Abberline of Scotland Yard. We arrived this afternoon.'

'Inspector Abberline? He's famous.'

'Most famous, perhaps, because he led the search for the murderer of those women in Whitechapel.'

'Ah …' Her face became serious. 'Jack the Ripper. Do you think he'll ever be caught?'

Thomas could only shrug. 'It's now two years since the last Ripper killing in 1888. There have been none since.'

'Then the devil might have taken a knife to his own throat instead of butchering anyone else.'

'However, nobody knows if this so-called Jack the Ripper is male or female, or whether it was a gang of killers working together.'

'Inspector Abberline, I take it, is here to investigate the murder? Poor Mr Feasby, shot from a tree by an arrow.'

'Indeed he is. The inspector is very good at his job. I'm sure the killer will be caught.'

'Good. I don't want any more of my neighbours being shot down like they're nothing more than pigeons sitting on a branch.'

'Why was Mr Feasby in the tree? After all, I hear that he was over eighty years old.'

'We're all exceedingly strange on this island, Thomas. I might be one of the strangest.' She winked.

Thomas wasn't used to seeing a lady wink in such a mischievous way.

Jo continued, 'Very well, the world-famous Inspector Abberline is here to solve a crime. Why are you here, Thomas?'

'I work alongside him.' Thomas chose not reveal his occupation as a rule, preferring to let people assume he assisted the detective. If people knew he was a journalist that sometimes hindered Abberline's investigations. 'I have been doing so for a number of weeks now.'

'You're not a policeman.'

'Oh?'

'When I got hold of your hand to help you onto the rock I felt a callous on the middle finger of your right hand. Here.' Seizing his hand, she turned it to reveal the thickened pad of skin on the side of his finger. 'That's where a pen chafes your skin. You must spend a lot of time writing to form a callous like that.'

'That's very observant of you. Police officers write, however.'

'Ah, you do not have a policeman's eyes. Don't you find that the police always have suspicion in their eyes, even when talking to a friend? It's a habit they form over time.'

'You don't see suspicion in my eyes?'

'No. You are interested in the world around you, which could make you a poet. However, your expression isn't one of dreamy introspection as one would find in a writer of verse.'

'I might write novels?'

'Novelists sit in backrooms, slaving over their dramas and romances. You have a healthy, golden tan. You spend much of your time outdoors. No, Thomas Lloyd, you are a newspaper reporter. I'm certain.'

He said nothing, merely stared at her in surprise. Her deduction had been absolutely accurate.

'Worry not, Thomas, dear. I will not reveal your secret. Besides, I love secrets. They make the heart thrill with excitement.'

Thomas smiled. 'Why are you here on the island?'

'I don't know if you know about what happens on Faxfleet?'

'I know that this is a miniature kingdom, ruled over by King Ludwig.'

'Indeed.'

'And that you have your own laws.'

'But do you know what actually goes on here on this shard in a Yorkshire river?'

'Some farming, I guess. Fishing? Country sports?'

'Many on this island are vividly eccentric. You will encounter exponents of free love. There are anarchists, free-market economists, holy grail hunters, inventors, explorers, artists, philosophers and free thinkers galore – and one wild lady who shamelessly displays herself in a kilt and gaudy knickerbockers.' She slapped her thigh.

Thomas could barely conceal his surprise. 'They are guests of the king?'

'Oh, bonnie Thomas, it's more than that. We compete for the prize.'

'I don't understand.'

'King Ludwig is a philanthropist. He's kind hearted. He has good intentions, and as we all know good intentions pave the road to hell.'

'Are you making fun of him?'

'No, absolutely not.' She placed her hand on his forearm and leaned closer as if she would reveal a secret. 'People write to King Ludwig; they set out their ambitions, whether that is to invent a new machine, compose a symphony, or develop new philosophical ways of living, and a host of other unusual ideas. If our king likes the idea he invites them to live here on the island in order to work on their beloved project.'

'He sponsors scientists and philosophers and the like?'

'Yes, he provides cottages, and these brilliant men and women live here at the king's expense. A host of geniuses toiling in their little houses.'

'You talk as if you mock them.'

'Not mock, sir. Perhaps a little wise to it all. After all, the prospect of free accommodation and a monthly stipend attracts scoundrels, cheats, the deluded and the desperate, as well as honest men and women of vision.'

'How long do they stay here?'

'If the king believes the work has valuable potential then members of his academy might remain on the island at his expense for years. However, if he ultimately decides that the work has no merit then the individual is given twenty-four hours to return to the mainland. Of course, this is a dreadful outcome for some, if they have no money or no other home. If they are sent away from the island then they might only have the poorhouse to turn to.'

'Then there might be an air of tension at times?'

'Absolutely, Thomas. The month of June is a period of great anxiety for us all. That's when the king makes his judgements. If our work is found to be lacking, then we pack our bags and trudge down to the ferry.'

'I see. We are approaching June now. People will worry.'

'People are excited, too. If the king decides an individual demonstrates exceptional promise then they are awarded a gift of ten thousand pounds.'

'A man could live comfortably on ten thousand pounds for many years.'

'And they receive a trophy, too, in the form of a gold shield. Everyone here covets that. There is a lot of rivalry.'

'You said that you live here on Faxfleet.'

'Indeed so. I work on my own project, and have been given a wee house by the king. Soon I will learn whether King Ludwig wishes me to stay or leave the island.'

'You might win the ten thousand pounds?'

'Perhaps I will.' She smiled.

'What is the nature of your work?'

'Ha! Inquisitive, sir, I shall keep that secret from you … for now.'

'Really?'

'The river level is dropping. You see, a bulge of sorts runs upstream when the tide rises; water levels peak for a few minutes, then fall before rising again. We have a moment or two to reach dry land, otherwise we'll be stranded here for a while yet. This way, Thomas.'

They quickly lowered themselves down from the boulder. The water had, indeed, retreated a few yards, and they soon reached higher ground. Soon they were walking along the path that Thomas had followed earlier. Thomas saw a horse tethered to a tree.

Jo patted the horse's nose affectionately. 'Mr Bonaparte, this is Thomas Lloyd. He's come all the way from London. Say hello to Thomas.' The horse made a snuffling sound.

'Jo, it was a pleasure to meet you.' Before he could offer to help her onto the horse she energetically swung herself up onto its back. He noticed that she did not ride side-saddle; hence the short kilt and trousers. 'And thank you for saving me from getting my feet wet.'

'You'd have suffered more than sodden feet. The currents are vicious.'

Thomas recalled the incident where he almost drowned last week, although said nothing of it. He couldn't have told her even if he'd wanted to. She'd slipped the reins from the branch and abruptly galloped away.

She called back over her shoulder, 'Thomas! We shall meet again!'

Thomas made his way back to the king's palace. The two-storey building could easily have been the residence of a country squire. The house appeared to be roomy, comfortable and not particularly ostentatious. Thomas hadn't been in the house; instead leaving Abberline to enter alone in order to speak with the ruler of this little kingdom. Thomas waited on the driveway. The wait didn't seem a long one; in fact, he rather lost track of time. He found himself replaying the moments spent with the lady down on the beach. He recalled the tone of her voice – the music and laughter that it contained, and the way she kept her eyes so attentively on his face. Was she one of these modern women that he'd read about?

'Thomas?'

'Hmm?'

'A penny for your thoughts.'

'I beg your pardon, Inspector. My mind was elsewhere.'

'A happy elsewhere, I dare say. You were smiling.'

'Was I?' Thomas felt his face grow warm. He was blushing. Abberline noticed yet said nothing, so Thomas asked if Abberline's meeting with the king went well.

'It was an interesting one. I'll tell you about it later. For now, though, we need to find our rooms.'

'Aren't we staying in the palace?'

'Palace?' Abberline smiled, amused. 'A fancy name for that house. No, we've been allocated Samarkand Cottage that lies, according to the butler, along that path to our left.'

The path took them through woodland. On the way, they passed by several small cottages. Smoke rose from chimneys. Through the windows of the dwellings figures could be glimpsed, sitting at desks as they worked at something or other. Though what exactly, Thomas couldn't be sure. These people must be the free thinkers and inventors and whatnot that Jo had spoken about: the geniuses that lived here at the invitation of the king.

Abberline checked the cottages' names: 'Nazareth, Athens, Peru, Siam. Ah, here's Samarkand.' He pushed open a gate that led into a small garden.

'The cottage does look a pleasant one.'

'I'm sure it will suit us, Thomas. The king has allocated another cottage for my colleagues. More detectives will be arriving from Scotland Yard in a day or two.'

'There are no locks on the doors.'

'There is no crime here, so I'm told.'

Thomas opened the door. 'Only murder.'

'Our luggage should have been delivered already. We eat in the palace refectory with our neighbours at six. There's bread and cheese to keep us going until then. Also, some letters have arrived for me. They should have been left here, too.'

The front door opened directly into a kitchen. The place had a decidedly rustic feel.

Thomas raised a cloth from the table. 'Here's the bread and cheese. There's a bottle of beer, too.'

'That looks most welcome.' Abberline opened doors off from the kitchen. 'The bedrooms. Our cases are here.'

'And your letters.' Thomas handed Abberline two envelopes.

'Ah, one from my wife. She promised to let me know when she arrived at her cousin's.' He looked at a mark by the stamp. 'An Eastbourne postmark; it seems she's already there. And ...' His voice faded as he stared at the second envelope. The man's expression suggested he expected a snake's head to dart from the envelope to sink its fangs into his hand. 'Oh ... I know who this is from.' With great care he opened the envelope, removed the slip of paper, and then read aloud: *'Dear Inspector, you lord of failure. Two years ago I led you a merry dance through Whitechapel. I chopped them ladies. I left them with their innards on the outward side of their pretty skins. You tried to catch me. You failed, you lord of failure. I walked past you in the street. I sat in a coffee shop close enough for you to touch me. But, my poor lad, you didn't know that I was the Whitechapel murderer, did you now? Well, boss, I'm back. Yours truly from the heat of hell, Jack the Ripper.'*

They ate the bread and cheese at the kitchen table in the cottage known as Samarkand. Abberline declined the beer, choosing water instead. Thomas Lloyd did the same.

'Red cheese. My favourite.' Abberline popped the last fragment of Cheddar into his mouth. 'There's some bread left, if you're still hungry?'

'I've had plenty, thank you.' Thomas's gaze strayed to the letter addressed to Abberline on the mantelpiece. 'Genuine, you think?'

'From Mr Jack the Ripper? I don't know.'

'Does the writing match the other letters supposedly written by the Ripper?'

'Hundreds of hoax letters arrived during the investigation and afterwards. I've never seen the British public so agitated, or excited, by murder before or since.' Abberline dabbed his mouth with a napkin. 'There's a very large box at Scotland Yard full to the brim with letters claiming to be from Jack the Ripper.'

'I wonder how the letter writer knew you'd be here. After all, it is addressed to "Inspector Abberline, The Palace, Faxfleet".'

'That's a mystery easily solved.'

'Oh?'

'There was a report in the *Star*, saying that I would be despatched here to investigate a death. If the writer of that letter read the newspaper then he, or she, knew where I'd be right now.' Abberline reached for his jacket. 'And the reason I'm here is to find a murderer, which is what I intend to do.'

'You will take the letter seriously?'

'It's probably some tomfoolery by someone who should know better.'

'What if it is from the Ripper? What if he starts killing again?'

'Rest assured, Thomas. I'll make a copy of the letter and send it to my superiors.'

'What do you intend to do first?'

'I'll visit the brother of the deceased. He lives at Camelot House, which, I've been told, is nearby.'

'I have to admit to knowing very little about the case. All I know is that a man was killed by an arrow while climbing a tree.'

'Then you don't know that an animal was found nearby?' Abberline glanced at Thomas. 'The creature had the body of a wolf, the legs of a crocodile, and the wings of an eagle.'

Abberline read from a sheet of paper as he walked along a path. Thomas burned with curiosity. He wanted to ask about the creature with the eagle wings, the wolf body and the legs of a crocodile. However, he knew better than to interrupt Abberline when he was reading through case notes, which would, likely as not, have been sent to him by the local police who'd first investigated the case. They soon arrived at a small house; the sign on the gate read 'Camelot House'. Abberline walked up the garden path and tapped on the front door. There was no answer. Thomas looked up at the bedroom windows in case a face should be looking out. Abberline knocked yet again.

Thomas said, 'Looks as if no one's home.'

A high voice came from behind them. 'Good day, gentlemen. How may I help you?'

Thomas turned towards the voice. An elderly man stood there. He was very small, bright eyed, and reminded Thomas of a pixie from a children's storybook. He held, in both hands, a two-headed rabbit. The animal was clearly stuffed. Thomas looked again, and realized that the twin-headed creature was, in fact, a hare.

Abberline spoke briskly, 'Good afternoon. My name is Abberline. I'm an inspector from Scotland Yard. I'm here to investigate the death of Mr Benedict Feasby.'

'Benedict is my brother. Sorry ... *was* my brother.'

'My condolences, sir, on your loss.' Abberline nodded in Thomas's direction. 'This is Mr Lloyd. He'll be accompanying me for the duration of the case.'

'I see. I see. You must forgive me for not shaking your hands. I have been massaging preservative salts into this fellow's pelt – dear old Split-Hares. He'd begun to moult, dreadful mess, fur all over the rugs. My brother likes to keep a clean home. Oh dear, there I go again. He's dead, isn't he, my dear brother? I couldn't use my taxidermy skills on Benedict. The authorities won't let me. In fact, the local detectives became quite agitated when I said I'd like to preserve my brother and sit him on a chair in the kitchen.'

'Mr Feasby,' Abberline said. 'May we step inside and have a chat with you?'

'Of course, of course. This way, sirs. I'll put Split-Hares on his pedestal. He never had two heads when he was alive, of course. My brother and I acquired two dead hares. We split them down the middle from neck to bobtail. Benedict stitched the two halves together. I've never known a man so adroit with a needle. This way.' He opened the door. 'Don't be alarmed by my little zoo.'

They followed Feasby into a parlour. He stood the two-headed animal on a pedestal. A brass plaque fixed to the front of the pedestal read: GOD DOES NOT SPLIT-HARES. Thomas's nose prickled. The place smelt strongly of chemicals – no doubt substances that preserved this array of strange creatures. Straightaway, he saw a large animal in the corner of the room. This was an absolute monstrosity. Quite alarming, really. Possessing the body of a wolf, the legs of a crocodile, wings of an eagle, and very large teeth, it would have struck fear into children. Most disturbing of all were its blue eyes. Thomas realized that glass eyes, of the kind used to replace diseased or injured human eyes, had been inserted into the wolf's skull in order to create an even more disturbing creature. A kind of zoological Frankenstein monster. Around the wolf's neck was a dog collar on which was printed a name: Sir Terror.

When Thomas looked back at William Feasby, he found himself wondering what kind of man rearranged animal body parts into strange creatures. Abberline glanced at the animals. However, he didn't let them distract him from his purpose. As soon as Feasby invited them to sit down, Abberline began.

'You are William Feasby. You have lived here on the island with your brother for how long?'

'Benedict is – was – my twin brother. We were identical. Every time I look in the mirror I see him. We have lived on Faxfleet for eighteen years.'

'Your late brother was eighty-one years of age when he died?'

'Yes, Inspector.'

'This may sound a blunt question, sir. I do have to ask it. Why was your brother, a man of over eighty, climbing a tree?'

'We study nature. My brother visits certain trees every morning to count birds' eggs and chicks in their nests. We believe that the world of human beings is inextricably woven into the animal world. We both love animals. In fact, my brother and I have been vegetarians since the age of seven.'

Thomas knew that, normally, he should not question people in connection with a crime that Abberline investigated (Thomas was present to observe and write about the cases for his newspaper); however, curiosity got the better of him. 'Why do you make these ... these alterations to animals?'

The pixie-like man gave a sudden grin. 'We travel the length and breadth of Britain, giving talks and magic lantern shows; we hope to educate the public about the importance of animal welfare, and the preservation of species in the wild.'

'Yes, but the purpose of the wolf-beast, the one you call Sir Terror?'

'Mr Lloyd, not a single person would attend one of our lectures if all we did was talk. No, sir. We bring along our bizarre circus of beasts. When we do, people rush to our talks by the hundred.'

Abberline nodded. 'You use these stuffed creatures to draw attention to your work.'

'These are our bait. They entice people in to hear us talk about the wonders of nature.'

'You no doubt saw newspaper accounts of your brother's death?'

'Yes, I did. I understand that newspapers all over Britain printed what had happened to Benedict. His passing drew a lot of attention.'

'The stuffed piece that you call Sir Terror was found in the tree that Mr Feasby had climbed. It was that strange aspect of the case, and the fact that your brother was killed by an arrow fired from a bow, that generated so much interest.'

'Yes, I have the newspaper cuttings here.' Feasby opened a drawer; inside were neatly cut out oblongs of newspaper that bore pictures of the beast that Thomas saw snarling silently from the corner of the room.

Abberline nodded. 'You employ these striking exhibits to draw attention to your lectures, which suggests to me that the killer of your brother used the wolf creature to draw the public's attention to the murder.'

'Goodness me. Why would a murderer do that, sir?'

'Forgive me for speaking plainly, Mr Feasby, but if your brother had been murdered with a knife or a hammer, then the London newspapers would probably not have reported his death at all.'

'You mean the killer intended to make this a famous crime? He wanted the world to know about it?'

'It appears so. Did your brother have enemies?'

'Not one. He was a happy soul. He devoted his life to the glories of the animal kingdom.'

'Do you, yourself, have enemies? After all, you say you look exactly like Mr Benedict Feasby.'

'Do you believe that the killer mistook my Benedict for me? Goodness. But I have no enemies, either.' The man's eyes were wide with surprise. 'We keep ourselves to ourselves. We make our exhibits. We study this island's creatures. We have detailed records of species, feeding habits and animal behaviour. Theirs is a rich and complex world, sir.'

Once again, Thomas felt compelled to ask a question. 'You are here at King Ludwig's invitation?'

'Yes, Mr Lloyd.'

'Which means he provides this house at no cost to you.'

For the first time, a flash of anger made the pixie-like man stiffen his backbone and sit up straight. 'Indeed. Indeed! But accommodation in exchange for our research and studies here. The king shares our interest in animals. We earn the right to be on this island. We are no lazy shirkers, sir – no, we are not.' He caught sight of his reflection in a wall mirror. 'Isn't that right, Benedict? You tell the gentlemen that we work hard here on … oh … I'm sorry. I quite forgot. For a moment, I thought I saw my twin brother.' He sighed. 'I am so sorry … what must you think of me? When I saw his … my face … oh …' He lowered his head and wept.

That evening Thomas Lloyd and Inspector Abberline walked through the trees to the house known locally as The Palace. They'd been invited to eat dinner in the company of the king and the other residents of this eccentric little kingdom.

A footman led them to the refectory at the back of the house. This large hall served as the dining room. A table stood at one end of the room. Eight other tables had been set out at an angle from that table as if to echo the pattern of the spokes of a wheel. In that way, everyone could see the people sitting at the head table. Thomas saw that this seating arrangement also removed any necessity for a guest to sit with their back to the king. Thomas presumed that the large, high-backed dining chair, bearing a colourful crest, was the king's seat. The refectory quickly filled with people: perhaps around thirty men and women. Footmen lit candles on the tables. All this appeared routine for the diners. They nodded to each other, some chatted. A footman showed Thomas and Inspector Abberline to their table. A man of sixty or so already sat there. Standing politely, he bowed as Thomas and Abberline went to their chairs.

'Good evening, gentlemen,' he rumbled in a deep voice. 'I am Professor Giddings.'

Thomas and Abberline shook the man's hand and gave them their names.

'Ah. Inspector Abberline.' The professor smoothed down his beard with his hand. 'You are here about poor Feasby. I hope you catch the devil that killed him. The murderer has been terrorizing the island.'

'Oh?' Abberline raised his eyebrows. 'I was given to understand that one crime had been committed? The homicide of Mr Benedict Feasby?'

'I wrote to Scotland Yard, sir. There have been other incidents. Why, just days ago, the scoundrel fired bullets through my study window. Very nearly killed my wife and I.'

'I see. Then I'd like to –' Abberline didn't finish the sentence.

A footman called out, 'Be upstanding for King Ludwig III of Faxfleet.'

Everyone stood. Nobody spoke or moved as the king entered the refectory. Thomas had expected robes, a crown and courtiers. However, a man wearing conventional evening dress walked with due dignity to the top table and sat down in the chair that bore the royal crest. Already standing at the top table was a silver-haired man wearing a red sash across his chest. Thomas judged the king to be perhaps fifty years of age. His grey hair was thinning at the top of his head, and his manner suggested a rather modest authority, which could have been that of a country squire. There certainly seemed to be nothing remarkable about the monarch of this tiny kingdom. King Ludwig nodded at his fellow diners.

The footman barked, 'Please be seated.'

Chair legs scraped across the stone floor as the diners sat back down again. The king poured himself a glass of water, gestured to footmen to begin serving the first course, and then he began to converse with the man in the red sash. The other diners chatted; cutlery clinked as they cut bread from loaves set out in front of them. A decidedly relaxed atmosphere pervaded the room.

That was until the refectory door opened with a loud bang. Everyone fell silent.

And Thomas stared at the fabulous creature in the doorway. The woman wore a gold band that encircled her head. Her dress appeared, at first glance, to be the typical evening wear of a woman of her class. Yet it was fabulously embroidered with birds of paradise; the pattern reminded Thomas of Arabian fabrics he'd seen. Everyone stared at her.

'So sorry I'm late, your highness. My apologies, ladies and gentlemen.' She swept across the room. 'I broke the heel of my shoe and had to dash back to replace them. I beg of the inventors amongst you to invent a lady's shoe with an indestructible heel. Ha! Newcomers!'

Without a hint of shyness or hesitation this formidable and undeniably beautiful woman approached the table where Thomas sat. She waved away a footman who darted forward to help her with the chair. With a robust strength she pulled out the chair. Quickly, she sat down opposite Thomas, grinning as she did so.

She reached for the bread, broke a chunk off and sniffed it. 'Fresh, thank the Lord. I've already met Mr Thomas Lloyd.' She held out her hand to Inspector Abberline. 'I haven't had the pleasure of meeting you, sir.'

Abberline politely stood, bowed and then shook her hand.

'Oh, sir, don't stand on ceremony.' Energetically, she smeared butter onto the bread with a knife.

'Inspector,' began Thomas, 'this is Miss Josephine Hamilton-West.'

'Please do call me Jo.'

'Very well.' Abberline smiled.

'Uh, I've put some butter on my sleeve.' She raised her arm. Her pink tongue darted, licking off the blob of yellow.

Professor Giddings sighed. 'Jo is a veritable whirlwind in human form.'

'Thank you, Prof.' She munched on the bread.

Giddings said, 'Inspector Abberline and his assistant have come all the way from Scotland Yard in London to hunt for the killer of poor Benedict.'

'I know. Thomas told me. Do you have any suspects, Inspector?'

'We only arrived this afternoon,' he said, diplomatically avoiding discussing details of the case.

She said briskly, 'You'll want to interview everyone on the island?'

'We shall see, miss.'

'Ah, you are wise not to reveal your procedures, Inspector. The walls have ears.'

'A whirlwind,' grunted Professor Giddings. 'Then she does blow away the cobwebs from this stuffy lot.' His eyed the other diners.

Footmen appeared with tureens. They efficiently went from table to table, ladling green broth into the bowls.

'Gadzooks! Pea soup.' Jo wore a broad smile. 'I'm so hungry today. Have you finished your book, Professor?'

'A slight delay, child. I regaled the inspector and Mr Lloyd with news of my own unfortunate incident. Namely, that the murderer discharged a rifle at my home. My wife and I were very nearly bloodily slaughtered.' Giddings spoke in a slow, ponderous way. He could have been giving a speech to fellow professors at a university.

Jo spooned soup into her mouth. After swallowing, she said, 'Professor? How do you know that the person who killed Benedict was the same one who attacked your house?'

'Logic demands that this is so. One of us is shot by an arrow. Another of us, specifically myself, is targeted by a rifle. We, on this island, are being hunted down one by one.'

Thomas asked, 'You didn't see who fired the shots?'

'Regrettably no.'

'Probably a poacher from the mainland,' declared Jo. 'We're not liked by the mainlanders. They accuse us of being ridiculous and frivolous. People over the water call this The Mud Pat. They refer to King Ludwig as King Mud.'

Abberline digested the information. 'So there is hostility from those that don't live on the island?'

'Yes indeed, Inspector. Usually they hurl insults. This time, as an act of mischief, one of them fired a couple of bullets into the professor's window.'

'Ah, there is more.' Giddings held up a finger. 'Before the bombardment of my house began ... yes, my dear, nothing less than bombardment. Before the wicked bombardment I noticed that peculiar symbols had been daubed on my window panes. I believe the gunman had an accomplice who marked my home out for attack.'

Thomas frowned. 'You believe the symbols were a secret code to tell the sniper whose house should be attacked?'

'I do, sir. Hear what I'm saying, gentlemen. You officers of the law are here just in time if you are to avert a massacre on this island. We are all at risk. We, any one of us, could be struck down by an assassin at any time.'

Before anyone could comment, the man in the red sash at the top table rose to his feet. 'Ladies and gentlemen. Pray silence. We have begun to feed our bodies. Now we shall feed our minds. Begin the readings. I call on Professor Giddings.'

Jo winked at Thomas. That wink sent a shiver down his spine.

Leaning forward, she whispered, 'Between the courses there are readings. This happens every evening.'

Professor Giddings stood up, stroked his beard, cleared his throat and spoke in the loud, clear voice of someone accustomed to speaking in a lecture hall. 'Tonight, your majesty – ladies and gentlemen – I have chosen several passages from this book.' He held up a brown volume. '*Problems of the Future* by Mr S. Laing. I shall read his essay that deals with the question of wherefrom the sun that heats our earth derives its fuel. As Mr Laing points out, if the sun was made from coal it would burn out in a mere six thousand years.'

Thomas and Abberline exchanged glances as the reading commenced. Thomas realized that this meal would be a protracted one, if essays were served, as it were, between courses. For the next hour they heard a scholarly dissertation on the sun's flames being fed by comets. After the guests had consumed roast chicken and potatoes, Giddings read an essay that predicted a Great War would, one day in the future, engulf Europe.

The professor's voice boomed: 'The nations of Europe are increasing the size of their armies every year. As of this year, 1890, Russia has five million soldiers. Germany's army stands at three and a half million. France three million. The list continues. The inevitable outcome of these grossly swollen armies is war.'

Jo murmured to Thomas so only he could hear, 'Someone has declared war on Faxfleet, haven't they? The first shots have already been fired. And we're in their gun-sights.'

Chapter 8

BREAKFAST ARRIVED AT the cottage known as Samarkand at just after seven o'clock. A boy, pushing a handcart, delivered a wooden box, containing a tureen of hot porridge, a bottle of milk and a loaf of bread. The bread was warm and smelt so delicious that Thomas's stomach rumbled as he carried the box inside. He noted that the boy trundled his cart to neighbouring cottages and delivered the same kind of wooden box, which presumably contained identical breakfasts. The king of Faxfleet took care of his subjects. This porridge, milk and bread might not be the stuff of luxury. It was wholesome, though. Apparently, the meal came free, too, to the inhabitants of this little island in the muddy River Humber.

Inspector Abberline had received a telegram that morning, stating that a local detective from the mainland would meet them at the scene of Benedict Feasby's murder at nine.

Over breakfast Abberline had a confession to make. 'I don't know where the killing took place, though I imagine our neighbours will give us directions.'

Thomas felt as if he should make a confession of his own. The discussion with the stranger a few nights ago still troubled him somewhat. The man in the carriage had explained he and his colleagues had ambitious plans for Great Britain. They wished to introduce reforms that would lead to a better educated and more prosperous nation. After that, the stranger had handed him the gold pin, which Thomas had brought with him. The Order of the Golden Pin. Thomas had given that name, half jokingly, to the secretive group of what he supposed were individuals from the upper echelons of society. Surely, Thomas should reveal what he knew to the man who sat eating porridge in front of him. Thomas very nearly spoke out there and then, telling Abberline everything. However, Thomas had promised that he would not reveal details of the conversation he'd had with the stranger in the carriage.

'Lost in thought, Thomas?' Abberline pushed the empty bowl aside.

'Oh, sorry. I was miles away.'

'Many thousands of miles, I daresay. As far away as Ceylon?'

Thomas smiled. 'Emma is never far from my thoughts.'

'Your fiancée will come home soon? Should I start considering matrimonial presents?' The man's eyes twinkled with good humour.

'I wish I could send you a wedding invitation. The problem is I have no idea when the wedding will take place. Next year, I hope. Though I fear it might be the year after.'

'No word, then, when Miss Bright will be returning to England?'

'Emma's still so busy with her work at the tea plantation. She and her father have cultivated plants that appear to be resistant to disease.'

'Which will be extremely valuable to plantation owners.'

'Absolutely. However, Emma and her father must monitor their tea plants for at least five years before they can be sure that they're immune to blight.'

'Five years?'

'Emma's letter shocked me when I read that experimentation on those damned plants would take so long. However, Emma tells me she won't stay in Ceylon for the full five years. Her father has an apprentice who will take over Emma's duties when she returns. Though she cannot say with any certainty when she will come back to me.'

'I hope it will be soon, Thomas, I really do.'

Thomas felt an air of gloom creep over him – a familiar enough sensation, and a deeply unpleasant one. All too quickly his spirits would fall when Emma's absence from his life occupied his thoughts.

Thomas stood up. 'I'll clear away the breakfast pots. We meet the detective at nine, don't we?'

'And, as I mentioned, we'll need to find our way to the murder scene. Ah, where shall we put this bread? It would be a shame to let it dry out. I've not tasted bread as delicious as this in a long time. London bakers add china clay to make their bread so white. Knowing I'm eating what amounts to be dirt dug from a quarry tends to blunt my appetite.'

A search of the pantry yielded a ceramic container. Both men decided this would be just the thing to store the loaf. With the bread safely harboured, they pulled on their coats, donned their hats, and set out into the breezy spring day.

The cottage that King Ludwig had allocated to Inspector Abberline and Thomas for the duration of the investigation formed part of a sequence of a dozen or so cottages. They passed Professor Giddings' home. This would be the one whose windows had been shot out a few days ago. The glass must have been replaced for there was no sign of damage. The white-bearded man couldn't be seen. Thomas heard a scholarly voice, however.

From inside the cottage came the sound of Giddings reading aloud in deep, rich tones: 'But, after all, Constantinople remains the chief difficulty. Unless some arrangement can be made respecting it, it must remain a constant source of antagonism between Russia and Austria ...' The voice faded as the pair moved away from the cottage. Thomas saw that William Feasby stood in the garden of his dwelling. A large monkey sat on a chair on the lawn. Feasby groomed the animal with a brush. The monkey's ears had been replaced with the outstretched wings of a bat. Its face had been freakishly moulded to resemble that of a human being. In fact, Thomas thought the monkey resembled (possibly libellously) the present Archbishop of Canterbury. The monkey had been expertly preserved after death. It sat resting its chin on its hand as if deep in thought. A sign fixed to the chair read: *THIS IS LORD ECHO – HE APES THE PHILOSOPHY OF OTHERS.*

Thomas murmured to Abberline so Feasby wouldn't hear: 'Another of the grotesque Feasby exhibits.'

Abberline nodded. 'I daresay they'll give children nightmares.'

Presently, Thomas and Abberline reached a man dressed in workman's clothes; he used a scythe to cut long grass at the side of the path. Abberline spoke to him, asking if he knew whereabouts on the island Benedict Feasby had been killed. The gardener gave directions, pointing along the path. Abberline thanked the man and they continued walking. Soon they left the cottages behind. Thomas judged that apart from the royal palace the little cottages clumped here and there among the trees were the only buildings on the island. There were no roads, only dirt tracks and pathways.

Abberline's own thoughts must have been running on a similar track to Thomas's. 'A funny little place, this, isn't it?'

'It strikes me that this kingdom is nothing more than a trivial plaything of the ruling classes.'

'Yet the kingdom has existed for a century.'

'I suspect it exists because English monarchs saw it as a joke kingdom – one that exists within their own kingdom – and for reasons that escape me regard it as amusing.'

'If we view this "country" with a forgiving eye we can say at least it provides a place for inventors, philosophers and free thinkers to work.'

'True.'

Abberline raised an eyebrow. 'You don't think worthwhile work is done here?'

'I'm not saying that. What strikes me as peculiar is that the king invited scientists and academics here to work on their projects, and they are given free accommodation and wages, yet every year they have to convince the king that they are making progress. If they fail to persuade him they are, they are simply thrown off the island.'

'And there is the business of the cash prize awarded every year, along with the trophy.'

'Which must foster competition among the other academy members.'

Abberline gave a wry smile. 'There is nothing like competing with acquaintances for an award to bring out the worst in people.'

'How so?'

'I'll give you an example. When I was a young constable I was called to a vicious fight at a village hall. The local people had held what was supposedly a friendly contest to decide who grew the best rhubarb. Judges were appointed. A day was chosen for the competition; gardeners took their rhubarb to the village hall to be judged. All went well until the winner was announced. Immediately there was uproar. There were accusations of favouritism; allegations of cheating, sabotage, and all kinds of skulduggery. Neighbours and friends who'd got on well with each other for years shouted insults at one another, punches were thrown, judges were pelted with rhubarb. When I arrived the place resembled a battlefield.'

'All because of a rhubarb contest?'

'Such a turn of events sounds comical. After all, why should a man become so angry because he's told that his neighbour's rhubarb is better than his? And why should it infuriate him when that neighbour, who he liked just an hour ago, is awarded a little scroll tied up with ribbon?'

'Human nature. The quality of the rhubarb would reflect the man's status in society.'

'Exactly. Contestants didn't feel as if it was their plants being judged as superior or inferior to those of their neighbours. They sensed, deep down, that they themselves were being judged. That's what aroused such violent emotion. Old pecking orders were upset.' Abberline paused where two paths crossed. 'If something as humble as rhubarb can start fistfights, then what happens here when the lifework of ambitious individuals is judged? What is the reaction on this island when King Ludwig awards that prize of ten thousand pounds? How does the man in Cottage A feel when the man in Cottage B struts home in a cocksure way with a bag of gold coins in his hand?'

'Then you think there is intense rivalry here?'

'That wouldn't surprise me at all. Every time I eat rhubarb pie I remember the carnage in that village hall. What does surprise me, Thomas, is that blood hasn't been spilt before over the king's competition.'

'So, Benedict Feasby might have been killed by a rival?'

'I wouldn't rule it out. Now ... it pains me, a detective, to admit this. I think we're lost.'

The breeze blew harder; leaves rustled, swished, fluttered. The entire island appeared to be sighing.

Abberline checked his pocket watch. 'Three minutes to nine. It won't look well if a Scotland Yard man is late meeting the local police. They'll think we've turned up late to deliberately insult them.'

They continued walking. Almost immediately a horseman appeared at the next bend in the path in front of them. Thomas blinked. *No – correction – make that horsewoman.* The rider wore her striking leather kilt again.

'Whoa, Napoleon.' She reined the horse to a stop. 'Good morning, sirs.' She beamed. 'Lovely morning for a stroll.'

Abberline raised his hat. 'Good morning, miss.'

'Do please remember to call me Jo.'

Thomas said, 'We're looking for where Mr Feasby was killed.'

'Oh, you're almost there, dear Thomas.'

Abberline spoke pleasantly. 'Would you direct us there, Jo? We're meeting a detective from the mainland.'

'I'll show you. There's space to walk alongside me. Don't linger behind Napoleon, he's prone to kick.'

'Thank you,' Abberline said.

She urged the horse to continue walking. 'I hope you find your suspect. It's disconcerting to share Faxfleet with a murderer.'

'If he hasn't fled,' Thomas pointed out.

'He? Why can't the killer be a woman?' Jo glanced down at Thomas. 'Women are capable of murder, too. Isn't that right, Inspector?'

'That is true,' Abberline said.

Thomas shook his head. 'Feasby was shot out of a tree by an arrow. A woman wouldn't have the strength to draw back the bowstring and fire an arrow with such penetrative force that it could kill a man at that height in a tree.'

'Really, Thomas?'

With that, she drew an archer's longbow from the opposite side of the horse. Thomas hadn't noticed the bow until that moment. She took an arrow from a quiver, and in one swift moment drew the arrow back until the bow was almost bent double, then she released the string. The arrow cut through the air at a tremendous speed. After fifty yards it slammed into a tree trunk where it embedded its point deep in the wood.

'Would that have brought a man down, gentlemen?'

Thomas felt his jaw drop with astonishment.

Abberline looked at her shrewdly. 'Yes, that arrow could have killed a man.'

'Oh, dear. Now you will accuse me of killing poor Mr Feasby. After all, I have a bow and arrows, and know how to use them. Are you looking for blood on my hands, Thomas? After all, you are staring at me very strangely.'

Abberline spoke matter-of-factly. 'I will need to speak with you, miss, in the light of what I've just seen.'

'Good thing, too. I approve. Of course, you must interview all the residents here. Nearly all of us own longbows. We enjoy our little archery tournaments every Sunday afternoon. The winner gets a scroll.'

'Do you hunt animals with the bow?' Abberline asked.

'No. I wouldn't kill God's creatures with this: not for a gold pin.'

'A gold pin?' Thomas thought about the gold pin in its case back at the cottage. Was Jo hinting she was in some way connected with the Order of the Golden Pin (as he'd named the organization of mysterious strangers)?

'Oh?' She looked amused. 'It's just a turn of phrase. I wouldn't do so-on-and-so-forth for a gold pin.' She pointed at a gap in the bushes. 'Poor Mr Feasby was found just through there. If I'm not mistaken, I can see the man you are due to meet. Good day, gents.' She galloped away.

Abberline turned to Thomas after she'd gone. 'Tell me if I'm being overly inquisitive, Thomas. Why does that astonishing woman refer to you as "Dear Thomas"?'

'I really have no idea, Inspector. In fact, I was just thinking the very same thing.'

The time was precisely nine o'clock when Abberline approached a well-built man of around forty, who wore a suit of greenish tweed. The man had a broad, pink face adorned with a blond moustache that had become stained near the lips from smoking, which he did now. A black cigar jutted from his mouth.

Abberline held out his hand. 'Detective Constable Stainforth. Pleased to meet you. I'm –'

He removed the cigar from his mouth. 'Inspector Abberline. Yes, I recognize you from your pictures in the newspapers. Very honoured to meet you, sir. I'm a voracious reader of articles pertaining to yourself.'

The big man vigorously shook the inspector's hand.

Abberline nodded his thanks. 'This is Mr Lloyd. He'll be assisting me.'

'Mr Lloyd of the *Pictorial Evening News*. It is you, sir, to thank for those most informative and exciting depictions of Inspector Abberline's cases. I confess, sir, I've cut out those stories and made quite a scrapbook from them. I read them to my children on a Sunday night, and they hang onto every blessed word.'

'Thank you,' Thomas said. 'I'm glad you enjoy what I've written.'

'Enjoy? It's more than enjoy, Mr Lloyd. They inform us. They educate ordinary folk and policeman, alike, in modern detective work.'

'Ah, quite,' Abberline said. 'Perhaps you would tell me what you know about the killing of Mr Feasby.'

'It will be an honour, Inspector. Please step this way. Mind that mud. It'll go to your very ankles. Now ... see this tree? Over a hundred feet high, wouldn't you say, sir?'

'Yes, perhaps even a shade taller than that.'

Stainforth's face grew a deeper pink. Thomas surmised the man was excited to be in the presence of Inspector Abberline.

Stainforth said, 'This is absolutely the most bizarre case I have ever investigated. Normally in Hull, we deal with drunken sailors who bash each other with bottles and carve each other with knives. Feasby's death is ...' He searched for a word that would impress Abberline with his eloquence. 'Feasby's death is Byzantine. By that, sir, I mean elaborate, complicated and mysterious.'

'Would you tell me what you think happened? I'd value your opinion.'

'You would, sir?' Stainforth grinned with delight. Being asked for his thoughts on the case by a detective of such stature as Abberline was clearly hugely important to him. 'In the early hours of the morning, Mr Feasby climbed that very tree. Up and up he went. As he ascended he made notes in a book about the birds' nests he saw. He was a man who studied the natural world with ... with scientific zeal. As Feasby climbed, I believe he saw a stuffed creature that had been placed up there on a branch. I suspect that the animal, which belongs to Mr Feasby and his brother, was left up there to catch his attention and draw him from the cover of the thick branches so that the bowman would have a clear shot with his arrow. So, we might picture this in our mind's eye: Mr Feasby counting eggs in nests and noting down his findings, then he sees the stuffed creature, which he and his brother have named Sir Terror. You might have seen it, sir. It has the body of a wolf and eagle wings.'

'Yes, we have, Detective. Please continue.'

Stainforth puffed out his chest. This was obviously a proud moment for the man, and Thomas could imagine that for the rest of Stainforth's life he would tell people about the day he helped Inspector Abberline solve a baffling case of murder.

'Inspector Abberline, the arrow struck Feasby in the ribcage. He fell from the branch where the wolf thing had been fixed. He struck the ground close to that muddy patch. The depression caused by the impact is still visible. The victim died instantly, as the fall resulted in a great number of broken bones. Also the arrow point had pierced the man's heart.'

'Has the arrow been preserved?'

'Yes, sir. I have it here.'

Stainforth hurried to the tree where a cardboard tube leaned against its trunk. He tipped an arrow out from the tube, and passed it to Abberline. The feather flights of the arrow were white. The long shaft still remained smeared with a reddish brown material – no doubt Feasby's blood.

Abberline examined the arrow. 'The head of the arrow is missing. Do you have it?'

'Yes, sir.' Stainforth pulled an envelope from his pocket. He gave it to Abberline.

'Thank you.' Abberline removed the arrowhead that had savagely punched through the ribs of the unfortunate Mr Feasby. 'Ah ... unusual.'

'Why unusual?' Thomas asked.

Abberline held the small piece of metalwork up to the daylight. 'The arrowhead is barbed. See the two sharp sections that point backwards in the shape of a letter V. Most arrows you find these days are used in competitive archery. The heads of such arrows are simply smooth points so they can be easily pulled out of the target.'

'A barbed arrow is used for hunting.' Stainforth was keen to make a useful contribution to the conversation. 'An arrow with a barb like that might be used by a poacher hunting rabbits or deer.'

'Exactly.' Abberline returned the arrowhead to the envelope. 'The barb means that the arrow can't be pulled out easily if the animal runs through foliage. A barb's designed to remain embedded in an animal's body ... or, in this case, a man's chest.'

Stainforth added eagerly, 'And the killer used the stuffed creature as bait to lure Feasby along the branch and out into the open.'

'Thank you.' Abberline nodded. 'I will make a note of your theory, Detective. I have to say that I agree with your conclusions.'

'You do?' Stainforth smiled happily. 'I am gratified that I've been of help, sir.'

'Has the ground hereabouts been searched?'

'Yes, sir.'

Abberline crouched down by the patch of mud, which measured perhaps five feet in length by two feet or so in width.

Abberline gazed at the mass of wet dirt. 'There are hoof prints here.'

'Aye, sir, I suppose horse riders follow yonder path and pass over this spot to avoid the low branches.'

'The hooves must go in by a good six inches or so.'

'I expect they do.' Stainforth wiped at a trickle of perspiration running down his jaw. He looked uncertain of himself now, not sure what Abberline was suggesting.

'Thomas, will you hold my coat?' Abberline slipped the garment off and handed it to Thomas. 'I think it's time I got my hands mucky, don't you, Thomas?'

'It's proved very useful before, Inspector.'

Stainforth wrinkled his nose as Abberline plunged his right hand into the mud. The hand squelched downwards until it vanished from sight into that brown mass.

'Inspector Abberline,' he said, 'is that quite necessary? You'll get yourself all filthy.'

'It's in the depths of filth where we often find vital clues.'

'I see, sir.'

Abberline worked his hand through the mud; his eyes were closed as he used his sense of touch to conduct the search.

He murmured, 'If an object had been discarded or has fallen into the mud then a horse's hoof could have pushed it down out of sight.'

'We made a very thorough search,' Stainforth told him, not wanting to appear lackadaisical. 'Went over every inch of ground, we did. With a bloodhound, too. They can sniff out a human hair in a field.'

'Bear with me. Ah ...' Abberline pulled a rusted bottle top from the mud. He flung it aside. 'I think we can safely say that's been lying here for years.'

His hand was coated with mud. Nevertheless, he plunged his fingers into that glutinous, sucking mass of wet dirt. Diligently, methodically, he worked his way from one side to the other before moving his hand slightly and repeating the process, working across the breadth of the mud patch. He gave a sudden grunt. Quickly, he pulled out his hand. Thomas saw a bead of red appear on his fingertip.

'You've gone and jabbed yourself with a thorn,' Stainforth said.

'Not a thorn,' Abberline told him, pushing his hand back down into the dirt again. 'It was this.' He pulled out a slender object that was perhaps barely two inches in length.

'What have you got there, sir?'

Abberline snapped a dock leaf from its stem and wiped the object. 'We shall soon find out. There.' Abberline held up his find.

Thomas stared in astonishment. 'A pin. A gold pin! My good God! And is that a pearl fixed to the end?'

Thomas Lloyd returned to the cottage where he and Abberline were residing during the course of the investigation. The local detective, Stainforth, had already left for the ferry, which would return him to the mainland. Thomas watched as Abberline washed the gold pin in the kitchen sink. The pin had come to light when Abberline had searched the patch of muddy ground near where Feasby's corpse had been found.

'There's no way of telling yet if the pin belonged to Feasby, or the killer, or neither of them.' Abberline dried the pin on a towel. 'This might be a coincidental find; then again, it might be a vital clue on which the case hinges.'

'William Feasby might know if the pin belonged to Benedict.'

'Might?' Abberline held the glittering object up as he examined it. 'A solid gold pin with a pearl at one end? William and Benedict were twins. They lived together in the same small cottage. Surely William would have noticed this in his brother's lapel?'

At that moment, Thomas sensed a hint of suspicion in Abberline's tone. *Or maybe I'm feeling guilty,* he thought, *because I've seen a pin exactly like that before. The man in the carriage had one when he spoke to me. The stranger who followed me along the street had one. And I have the same type of gold pin as well.* Thomas smiled, attempting to hide his discomfort.

'You're right, Inspector. William Feasby would have seen the lapel pin before if it did belong to Benedict. Perhaps both brothers have the same kind of pin.'

'What makes you say that?'

'Oh ... well ... the pin seems something like a badge. Perhaps worn by members of a club or society.'

'You may well be right. That's sound thinking.' Abberline held the pin to the light. 'I don't see the name of a goldsmith or a hallmark.'

Thomas pictured exactly the same kind of pin, tipped with a pearl, in its case at the bottom of his bag in the bedroom. At that moment, he grew angry with himself. If he hadn't agreed to keep that conversation with the aristocratic stranger a secret he could simply tell Abberline he owned an identical pin. Half jokingly, he'd referred to himself being enrolled in the Order of the Golden Pin. Why, he'd even received a letter from the Prime Minister of Great Britain, praising his newspaper articles. Thomas had been honoured to receive a letter from such an exalted figure. He realized that his vanity had been flattered. Dash it all. Now he felt infuriated that he'd given his word to keep the entire damn business a secret. As Abberline studied the pin, Thomas wanted to blurt out the truth. Yet he knew he couldn't. That letter from the Prime Minister effectively gagged him, didn't it? If the truth came out that he'd revealed a confidence, his reputation would be shattered into a million pieces. Nobody would ever trust him again professionally. That meant his career as a journalist would be over.

'Thomas? Are you feeling ill?'

'No ... why?'

'You're staring at this pin as if it's going to explode.'

'Ah, I beg your pardon. I was picturing how the pin might have fallen from Feasby's clothing when he fell, and how it might have been trampled into the mud by passers-by.'

'As long as you're not unwell. Remember that unfortunate incident in the canal. I sometimes worry that I've rushed you back to work too soon.'

'I'll be fine, Inspector.'

'You nearly drowned.'

'Thank you for your concern. I am fully recovered.'

'I consider you my friend. I'd hate it if you weren't your usual healthy self.'

Thomas smiled. 'I feel perfectly hale and hearty, and looking forward to helping you with this case.'

'That's good to hear. Now ... please take care of this.' He handed Thomas the pin. 'I'll go to the palace to speak with Ludwig. As owner – or ruler, I should say – of Faxfleet, I will need his permission to interview his staff and the islanders.'

Thomas watched Abberline from the kitchen window as the man hurried along the path in the direction of the palace. Meanwhile, the dilemma of whether he, Thomas Lloyd, should reveal what he knew about the gold pin churned like bad food in his stomach. He fetched the pin that he'd been presented with by the stranger and laid it beside the pin that Abberline had found in the mud. Yes, identical. Did Benedict Feasby belong to the secret society? And was Benedict's twin brother, William, a member, too? Dash it all. More than anything Thomas longed to confide in Abberline. Surely there could be no harm in it. Thomas placed the pin that Abberline had found in an envelope and put it in a cupboard. The gold pin that had been given to him by the stranger, he replaced in its little case and tucked it away at the bottom of his bag.

'By heaven,' Thomas told his reflection in a wall mirror. 'I'm going to tell Abberline everything, and to hell with oaths of secrecy.'

He then paced the kitchen and rehearsed what he'd tell the man. He'd leave nothing out. He'd describe the aristocratic figure who'd spoken to him in the carriage. He'd produce the letter from the Prime Minister, which he carried in his pocket. Just then, the door burst open. Thomas started with surprise.

Abberline stood there, panting. 'He's done it again. The Ripper's back in Whitechapel. Another woman's been murdered.'

Inspector Abberline had rushed into the cottage with news of a killing in the East End slums of London. After that startling revelation, the detective got busy. Thomas pictured an eager hunting dog, straining at its leash, as he watched Abberline gathering case notes from the table, and pulling on his overcoat. Thomas, meanwhile, had news of his own to reveal. He'd decided to tell Abberline about the gold pin he'd received from the stranger last week. Thomas would tell the detective everything.

'Inspector, the gold pin. I've been thinking about this, and I wish to discuss something with you.'

'Thomas? Would you pass me the envelope on the shelf? The train tickets should be in there.'

Thomas handed the envelope to Abberline. 'You're returning to London?'

'Yes, this very minute. I must examine the scene where the woman was murdered.'

'I've made a pot of tea. I rather thought we could discuss the gold pin you found.'

'Ack, these are the outbound tickets. The return tickets must be in the other envelope. The one under the vase.'

'Inspector. There's something you need to know.'

Abberline gripped Thomas's arm – a warm and friendly gesture. 'I'm sorry, Thomas, the gold pin will have to wait until I get back. It's vital I make a forensic examination of the murder victim. A Mrs Ruth Verity was found with wounds consistent with those of the other Ripper victims. I need to make a judgement whether the killer is one and the same.'

The man grabbed the envelope and checked the train tickets.

Thomas had been determined to reveal how he'd received his own gold pin that was identical to the one found where Benedict Feasby fell from the tree. Yet the expression on Abberline's face, which was a potent mingling of excitement and horror, deflected Thomas from speaking about the pin. Instead, he asked, 'Your colleagues think that Jack the Ripper has struck again? After an interval of two years?'

'It appears so.'

'Do you wish me to go with you?'

'No, please stay here, Thomas.'

'I shall need to write about your investigations in Whitechapel.'

'I'll give you a full account when I get back.'

'When will that be?'

'No more than two or three days. I must hurry, Thomas.'

'Tell the ferry to wait.'

'The ferry could wait, yes, but the tide won't. If it drops any lower I'll be marooned here until tomorrow. And ...' He gave a small shrug. 'I must examine the body of poor Mrs Verity. If I conclude that she's a new victim of the Ripper then I must launch an investigation to catch the devil. This time I will call in the army and search every building in Whitechapel.' Abberline's eyes gleamed – this was a man caught up in the white-hot passion of the hunt for his prey.

Thomas made one last forlorn attempt to reveal what made his conscience burn so uncomfortably. 'The pin. It's important.'

'It is, my friend. And thank you for reminding me that I shouldn't rush off without mentioning something vital. I'd like you to do something for me.'

'Of course.'

'Don't mention the gold pin to anyone.'

Thomas felt a thrill of surprise run through him. *Does Abberline know that I have a pin, too?* 'Of course, Inspector. I promise to tell no one.'

'Ah, excellent. Though I do want you to reveal its existence to one person. I'd like you to take it to William Feasby and ask him if he recognizes it. But make the man swear that he won't tell anyone else about the pin.'

'Of course, but why?'

'That little pin could be the dynamite that blows open the case. We should keep its existence secret for now, because we might need an element of surprise when we question our suspect – whoever that might be.'

'You can trust me, sir.'

'I know I can, Thomas. I trust you with my life.' He checked his watch. 'I must hurry. Cheerio, and take care!' With that, Abberline rushed out of the cottage. He held onto his hat with one hand; his coat tails were flapping.

Thomas called after him: 'Catch him, Inspector. Catch the Ripper.'

Fifteen minutes later, Thomas knocked on the door of the cottage that housed the menagerie of stuffed animals. The door opened to reveal William Feasby, the pixie-like man with the bright, darting eyes. Thomas noted the man's fingertips were blue. Sharp chemical odours spilled from the interior of the cottage to prickle Thomas's nose.

'Mr Feasby. May I have a word with you?'

'Come in, Mr Lloyd, come in!' The man spoke in a lively, good-humoured way. 'Find yourself a perch on the sofa there. Forgive me, I must keep working, otherwise my brush will dry.'

Thomas sat down on the sofa. Everywhere in the room there were stuffed animals. The creatures had been moulded in such a way that they took on the form of monsters or animal men. In one corner was the monkey that resembled a famous archbishop. Nearby was the monstrosity called Sir Terror. A wolf's body had been adorned with eagle wings; its legs replaced with crocodile limbs, and its eyes, made of glass, resembled those of a man. Thomas knew the creature was nothing more than dead skin, fur and modeller's wire – nevertheless, the vicious-looking Sir Terror sent shivers down his spine.

William Feasby sat down at the table. Immediately in front of him was a line of hens' eggs in little wire holders. Just beyond the eggs, a large free-standing mirror had been placed on the table. The looking-glass reflected William Feasby's face back at him. The man picked up an artist's brush and continued his work, painting the eggs a bright shade of blue.

Feasby explained: 'I am preparing these eggs for a tableau, which I will take on my next lecture tour. I shall preserve several crows, and replace their heads with dolls' heads of men and women. I wish to present them as angels of the devil that lay eggs containing the evils that plague our world – ignorance, hunger, war, injustice.'

'I see,' Thomas said, though in reality he didn't completely understand the metaphor of satanic angels with the bodies of birds and the heads of people. 'The public will be astonished to see what you are creating.'

'Astonished? Yes, I believe so. It's my most sincere hope, moreover, that my audience will have their minds stimulated to the extent that they ask these questions: why is there hunger, why is there war, why is there injustice?' He dabbed blue paint on the next egg. 'I must continue the work my brother and I started when we were still boys.' He gazed into the mirror, smiling. 'Isn't that so, Benedict?'

'Mr Feasby?'

'Oh, you will think I am quite capsized in the head. Barmy. Potty. Fit for the madhouse.' William Feasby chuckled as he gazed into the mirror, nodding as if agreeing with a comment he'd just heard. His expression became serious all of a sudden and he sighed. 'No, I'm not insane. I'm bereaved, sir, forlorn. And feeling the burden of loneliness – something I never experienced before my brother's death. But now …' He sighed again as he gazed at his reflection. 'You will be wondering about the placing of the mirror like so?'

'No, sir. Where you stand a mirror is your prerogative.'

'Benedict and I were twins. Identical twins. Nobody could tell us apart. Oh, the jokes we'd play when we were younger on our friends and family, pretending to be each other. We quite bamboozled folk with our capering.' He reached out to lightly touch the reflection on its cheek. 'I loved my brother, bless his soul. So you see the purpose of this mirror, Mr Lloyd? We used to work like this, facing one another across the table. Now, even though he is dead and lying in his grave, I still can. I look at that reflection and tell myself it is my dear Benedict. See, he is alive there in front of me.' William Feasby smiled at the reflection, which, of course, instantly smiled back. A smile full of warmth and affection. 'For years, we playfully hoodwinked people into believing that they spoke to my brother when it was really me, and vice versa. Now, sir, I play my prank again. But I perform it on me. I deceive myself that my brother is alive and sits here painting eggs. Because if I don't –' He glanced at Thomas ' – the pain of losing Benedict is too much to bear. I fear that grief would snap me in two.' He smiled back at the mirror. 'Isn't that so, Benedict, old boy? Now, come on – make haste – we must finish painting these eggs before we skin our crows.'

After such a heartfelt confession of grief by William Feasby, any comment from Thomas would seem clumsy. Thomas, therefore, sat quietly. The clock ticked on the mantelpiece. The sound of Feasby's paintbrush on the eggs became a light whisper. Sunlight fell through the window onto a rug, which bore a pattern of gold lions depicted as either lying on their stomachs, sphinx-like, or running through a lush, green jungle. The tick of the clock receded. The sound of the paintbrush merged with Thomas's respiration. His arms felt incredibly heavy. He saw William Feasby smiling and nodding at his own reflection in the mirror.

Thomas closed his eyes. When he opened them he realized he sat in the horse-drawn carriage again with the thin gentleman. The stranger's bald head gleamed as he studied Thomas's face. The gold pin, tipped with a pearl, burned with the brightness of the sun. The man pulled the pin from his lapel. Its gold shaft was as long as a dagger blade. That's when the carriage walls began to run with blood. Rivers of crimson poured down the windows. Abberline sat beside the man. He said nothing, merely gazing at Thomas.

The stranger uttered, 'Thomas Lloyd. What if you were the demon Jack the Ripper? What if you, the killer, were in the presence of Inspector Abberline all along? What would he say when he discovered that his friend was Bloody Jack, the slayer of Whitechapel's women.'

Abberline took the pin from the stranger, leaned forward, and drove the point into Thomas's neck.

Thomas gasped. He found himself squinting against the bright sunlight. He clutched his neck as a stabbing pain made him wince.

'It seemed such a shame to wake you.' Feasby continued painting the eggs. 'It's this blue varnish. The vapours can go to one's head. Can send one to the land of nod in a trice. Fftt.'

Thomas rubbed at the crick in his neck. He must have slept with his head at an odd angle. 'I do beg your pardon. I shouldn't have fallen asleep like that: most ill mannered of me.'

'Sir.' Feasby raised his eyebrows as if surprised by the apology. 'The fumes of this, sir.' He picked up the jar of varnish. 'I should be apologizing to you. It's remiss of me not to leave the door open to blow away the vapours. They've sent me to sleep before. And I must confess they make me dream like the devil himself paints pictures inside my head. Did you dream, sir?'

'Ah ... no dream that I recollect.' Thomas decided against being sidetracked into talking about dreams with this decidedly quirky fellow. Besides, he had an important matter to discuss. 'Mr Feasby. What I will say next might appear unusual, but trust me, please.'

'Then say away, sir, say away.'

'I will show you an object.' He pulled an envelope from his pocket. 'First, however, I must ask you not to mention to anyone what you are about to see.'

'And why is that?'

Thomas thought he saw both the stuffed wolf and the monkey turn their heads towards him. Those fumes were potent indeed. They befuddled his senses.

'Mr Feasby, do I have your permission to open the door? The fumes from that varnish are quite potent, aren't they?'

'Open away, sir, open away. Fresh air would be welcome.'

Thomas opened the door. Cool air gusted in. He took a deep breath and immediately felt clear-headed once more.

Thomas asked, 'Will you swear not to reveal what is said here, or tell anyone what I show you?'

'You still not have told me why it is so important that I should keep my lips sealed.'

'I beg your pardon. I felt quite lightheaded for a few moments.' He inhaled the fresh air. 'I ask you to keep this between ourselves because Inspector Abberline does not wish the killer of your brother to know the nature of our investigation and what clues might have been found.'

'I see. So you believe poor Benedict's murderer is still on the island?'

'It's possible, although we can't be certain, of course.'

'Hmm. Then you have my promise, sir. I won't breathe a word of this interview to anyone ... although I might share it with this gentleman here.' He nodded at the mirror.

'I daresay sharing a confidence with your reflection would present no problems.'

'Now, sir, proceed with the interview.'

Thomas pulled the gold pin out of the envelope, revealing it to the man for the first time. He carefully watched Feasby for a reaction. The man registered nothing, other than the mildest of surprise.

Feasby gazed at what Thomas held. 'A pin plus pearl. Understated adornment, it must be said.'

'Have you seen this pin before?'

'No, sir, I have not.'

'Or one like it?'

'Never.'

'Did your brother ever mention owning a pin like this?'

'He would have told me if he had.'

'Would you like a closer look?'

'That won't be necessary. My eyesight is excellent.'

'Thank you, Mr Feasby.'

'Is that all, young man?'

'Yes, and I'm grateful for your time.'

'Back to my eggs, then, for another coat of blue.'

Thomas glanced at the stuffed animals in the room. They were bizarre creations indeed. He wondered how long before the devil's angel tableau appeared here. It occurred to him that a satire of such angels laying eggs full of evil might be considered blasphemous in some quarters. However, he didn't comment. Instead, he carefully replaced the pin in the envelope.

Feasby glanced up. 'Where did you find the pin, sir?'

'Did I say that it had been found?'

'Come to think of it, you did not.'

'I can't really say any more about the pin, Mr Feasby. That would be something Inspector Abberline might or might not reveal when he returns.'

'Understandable. The art of detection is mysterious, though, isn't it?'

'It can be, sir. Good day.'

Thomas left Feasby to his eggs. What an extraordinary individual, Thomas thought, unable to decide whether the man was a gifted visionary or simply eccentric. He took a path that led to the water's edge, intending to dispel whatever remained of the varnish fumes from his lungs. By this time, the tide had already retreated, exposing mounds of mud in the River Humber. A few barges with dark red sails drifted downstream. Thomas supposed that Abberline would soon be riding the train south to London where he'd begin his hunt for Jack the Ripper. Thomas wished he'd gone, too, for the Ripper murders were the most infamous crimes in the world. As luck would have it (bad luck, that is), he was confined to this little island while his newspaper colleagues and, far worse, his rivals on other papers, would be penning reports of what would likely be the most sensational case of the year. In his mind's eye, he could see those dramatic headlines: JACK THE RIPPER STRIKES AGAIN! ABBERLINE INVESTIGATES!

'Ah, dear Thomas, you've returned to the place where we first met.'

Thomas glanced round. There was Jo, wearing the short leather kilt with those exotic pantaloons. She smiled happily.

'Good morning, miss.'

'None of that miss business,' she scolded. 'Call me Jo.'

'Of course, Jo.'

'Thank you, Thomas.'

'It's a lovely fresh day. The sunshine's most welcome, too.'

'Oh, Thomas. Let's fling aside polite talk about the weather. Here.' She stepped forward and boldly linked arms with him. 'Come with me.'

'Where?'

'I'd like you to meet someone.'

'Oh?'

'The king of this microscopic country. You've not spoken to him yet, have you?'

He shook his head.

'Then come with me, Thomas. I'll introduce you to His Transcendent Majesty.'

Thomas walked with Jo along a woodland path. In that light, effervescent way of hers, she explained that 'His Transcendent Majesty' was how the male monarchs of Faxfleet were referred to in the charter that granted Ludwig's family the kingship of the island. They emerged from bushes onto a broad lawn that led up to the rear of the palace.

King Ludwig stood with a tall, young man of about twenty-five.

The young man wore his shirt-sleeves rolled up to the elbows. The hard bulge of muscle in his forearms was plain to see. He carried a longbow in one hand. Slung across his back was a quiver full of arrows.

Jo stepped forward, smiling pleasantly; the woman radiated self-confidence. 'Your highness, I don't believe you've been introduced yet to Mr Lloyd.'

The king nodded, smiled, and held out his hand for Thomas to shake. Thomas sensed that the welcome wasn't just polite but had genuine warmth.

'Mr Lloyd. Very pleased to meet you, and delighted that you are staying with us.'

Thomas said how honoured he was to meet the king. Even so, his gaze strayed to the young man who carried the archer's bow. Thomas couldn't help but visualize 81-year-old Benedict Feasby tumbling out of the tree with an arrow embedded in his chest.

King Ludwig gestured for the bowman to step forward. 'This is my eldest son, Richard.'

Thomas shook hands, almost flinching at the power of the young man's grasp. Richard wore a more serious expression than his father. He seemed to find greeting Thomas to be a tedious chore rather than a pleasure. Thomas wondered if he should refer to Richard as Prince Richard, seeing as he was the king's son.

Jo, however, was at ease with the prince. 'Richard, how are you finding the new bow?'

'Much better than the old one,' he said in a friendly fashion. 'At least this one hasn't snapped like a rotten twig.'

'Ha, you don't know your own strength, Dicky.'

The young man smiled. 'Will you practise with me this afternoon?'

'Yes, and I shall beat you, because my archery skills are superior to your brute strength.'

'A bottle of port says I will beat you, Lady Jo.'

'A bottle of port it is.'

Richard clearly liked Jo and it was only with reluctance that he said, 'We have a little tournament today. I best go re-join my team.' He nodded in the direction of a dozen or so men and women who stood near circular targets at the far end of the lawn. They all carried longbows.

After he'd trotted away, King Ludwig said, 'Would you stroll back to the palace with me, Mr Lloyd?'

'Of course, sir.'

Jo smiled. 'I'll say goodbye for now, gentlemen. I have my thesis to write.'

King Ludwig watched her stride back towards the forest. 'A remarkable woman, isn't she, Mr Lloyd?'

'She is indeed, sir. The leather kilt she wears would turn heads if she were to walk down a street in London.'

'I imagine so, Mr Lloyd. Now, what do you think of my little kingdom?'

'It's remarkable. I never even knew of its existence until Inspector Abberline told me.'

'I'm proud of my academy here. I believe that its inventors, artists and philosophers will contribute greatly to the advancement of mankind. Or does that sound vain of me?'

'No, sir.'

'But it is under threat. The academy faces nothing less than danger.'

Thomas understood this as a reference to the murder of one of the academy members. 'The killing of Mr Benedict Feasby was an evil act. I'm confident that Inspector Abberline will find the murderer.'

'You misunderstand me, Mr Lloyd. The threat to the academy doesn't come from an assassin. It is in danger of being ignored. Gradually, the work here, by some of the greatest visionaries of our time, is starting to be considered irrelevant by universities and other academic bodies.'

'I see.'

'I have to say, Mr Lloyd, that British scientific and artistic societies are becoming dismissive, even scornful, of the work of my academy's members. Such brave ideas are born here on Faxfleet: ideas that will make this world a better place. Professor Giddings, for example, believes that the British Empire will not survive unless our dominions overseas are represented in parliament. Therefore, he proposes that each country within our empire will elect a Member of Parliament. Therefore, India will have a representative, Australia will, and so on. Grievances will no longer be bottled up to fester until there is revolution. Our empire will remain intact.'

Thomas wondered why he was receiving what amounted to be a lecture. Nevertheless, he nodded politely. 'I have met Professor

Giddings. He strikes me as a man of remarkable intelligence.'

'He is, sir. He is!'

'The professor said that his house was fired upon recently. Windows were broken. He and his wife had to take cover.'

Instead of responding to this statement, King Ludwig paused at the open doorway of an oblong building attached to the palace. Organ music came from inside.

Ludwig indicated that Thomas should go inside with the words, 'This is the family chapel.'

Thomas stepped in through the doorway. The chapel was large enough to seat forty or so people. An altar stood at one end beneath a stained glass window. Moses was depicted in coloured glass carrying the Ten Commandments. A youth with a very white face sat at the organ. He played the hymn 'Amazing Grace', mouthing the words as he did so.

Ludwig spoke quietly so as not to distract the musician. 'That is my youngest son, Tristan, twenty-two years of age. He has played the organ at York Minster many times.' Ludwig nodded back in the direction of the open doorway and they stepped outside again. 'As you see, Tristan and Richard are quite different in temperament. It's difficult to persuade Richard to come indoors. He'd rather practise archery, or sail his boat on the river. On the other hand, we have a devil of a time persuading Tristan to even put his head out through a doorway. He's devoted to his music. Just last week he sent a whole parcel of hymns he's composed to a publisher in London.'

Thomas smiled. 'Often families can be composed of opposites rather than like-minded souls.'

'I agree, Thomas. I agree. Now, a devilish business, wasn't it? Who would fire a gun at Professor Giddings' home? The fellow and his wife could have been killed.'

'It's possible that whoever killed Mr Feasby is responsible.'

'Very likely, I shouldn't wonder.' The big man ran the palm of his hand over the top of his balding head as he thought about this. 'I have an awful feeling that the devil will attack us again before long.'

'Do you have any men that patrol the island with guns?'

'I have my gamekeeper, and the island's residents are on the lookout for strangers. You see, everyone here knows everyone else. A stranger would be noticed immediately.'

They approached a door that led into back of the palace.

'Perhaps,' Thomas said, 'it would help if the houses had locks on their doors?'

'We pride ourselves on having no crime on the island. Nobody has ever locked a door on Faxfleet in more than a hundred years.'

'Perhaps bolts could be fitted until the culprit is caught. Then if –'

Ludwig interrupted so quickly it seemed he wanted to get something off his chest. 'I specifically asked Scotland Yard to send Abberline here to investigate the death of Feasby.'

'That was wise, sir. Inspector Abberline is the best detective in the world.'

'You truly believe that?'

'Yes.'

'But he never caught that Ripper fellow.'

'No, that is true. Nevertheless, his record for arresting criminals is extraordinary.'

'Well ... I don't doubt his competence for one moment. But I'm pleased that Scotland Yard sent Abberline, because that has delivered the real prize to me.'

'In what way, sir?'

'You, of course. You are the prize, Mr Lloyd.'

Thomas stared at Ludwig in surprise by this unexpected twist in the conversation. 'How can I be the prize, sir?'

'You are a first-rate newspaperman. The articles you write are quite brilliant.'

'Thank you.'

'I wanted you here on the island. You are the detective's shadow and you will write about the murder case he will investigate?'

'Yes.' Thomas had become wary. He cast his mind back a few moments to when Ludwig bemoaned the fact that his academy wasn't being taken seriously by the academic and artistic world at large. Thomas guessed that he was about to be recruited (or should that be press-ganged?) into publicizing the work of the academy in such a way that it would win the public's approval. Thomas disliked being tricked into becoming the Faxfleet Academy's champion – someone who would praise it in the newspapers in order to gratify its patron, namely King Ludwig III.

Ludwig flashed charm and smiles as he patted Thomas on the shoulder. 'Anything your require, Thomas, and I shall see that you are amply supplied. Ha! And you shall be my guest at the top table at dinner tonight. I have some excellent Chablis I would like you to taste.'

'Thank you, sir. That's most generous.'

'Mr Lloyd. Go wherever you wish on the island. Interview whoever you wish, too. I want you to write about what you find here for your newspaper readers and show the entire world that this little realm is populated by a race of geniuses.' He pulled out his pocket watch and flipped open its gold cover. 'I must go and talk to my land agent. More tedious aspects of life intrude: rent reviews, property audits and such-and-such. I look forward to chatting with you over dinner tonight, Mr Lloyd. Cheerio.'

The big man marched away with an air that suggested he had Thomas safely tucked away in his pocket. That he only had to pull Thomas out again to obediently do his bidding.

Thomas frowned. He certainly wasn't going to become a puppet of King Mud (as some called him). Nevertheless, now that Ludwig had given him permission to go wherever he chose on the island and to interview its inhabitants, he decided to do exactly that. Thomas returned to the cottage to collect his reporter's notebook and pencils and then set out to explore the island.

Thomas strode out along a woodland path heading north. Sunlight shone down through the branches. The breeze caused a soft whooshing sound that slowly rose and fell. He came upon rows of cottages here and there. These were where members of the Faxfleet Academy were housed – the artists, philosophers, inventors and scientists. Thomas reached the northern tip of the island. To his surprise he found a waterside village here. This was clearly a community of fishermen and their families, living in log cabins. Nets had been hung out to dry. Small boats rested on the beach above the high-tide mark. A dozen women, wearing long woollen skirts and shawls, smoked clay-pipes as they peeled potatoes and chatted to one another. Occasionally, one would call to children playing on the beach.

Thomas took the trouble to appear nonchalant as if simply enjoying a stroll. The women peeling potatoes stopped talking when they saw him, immediately realizing he was a stranger.

He smiled and politely raised his hat in greeting. 'Good afternoon, ladies. Lovely weather, isn't it?'

They nodded back and continued peeling the gleaming white

spuds. Although they could hardly be described as hospitable, they didn't seem overly suspicious of his presence.

'I'm a guest of the king,' he said conversationally to a woman with long silver hair. 'I didn't realize there was a village here?'

'We're only here spring and summer,' she said in a no-nonsense way. 'We go back to the mainland come October. Fishing isn't much to speak of when it drops cold.'

Smiling, he nodded, and continued his stroll. A dog barked at him. One of the women told it to shut up, using some very colourful language. The dog ignored her and darted at Thomas. She threw the potato she was peeling at the dog, although it came closer to Thomas's head than that of the dog. He glanced back, wondering if that had been deliberate. However, she shook her fist at the mutt and seemed genuinely irked that it was bothering the stranger. At that moment, the dog lost interest in him. It began to eat the potato.

He moved along the shore to where a fisherman loaded a rowing boat with empty baskets. The man's suntanned face was almost dark purple in colour. He wore a sleeveless leather jacket over his woollen jersey.

Conversationally, Thomas asked, 'Is this a salmon river?'

'Not for me, it isn't. I'll be taking mussels and crab out of there.' He nodded at the river. 'The others go for skate and whiting.'

Thomas didn't want to usurp Abberline's role and begin asking questions. After all, he wasn't a policeman and Abberline wouldn't approve if Thomas blunderingly attempted his own investigation. Nevertheless, if he engaged the fisherman in conversation he might pick up some useful facts. After all, Thomas was mindful that King Ludwig's Academy would be expensive to maintain and he did wonder how it was funded.

Thomas looked at the cabins. 'The king provides accommodation for the fishermen?'

'Provides? Rents more like. Would you pass me that oar?'

Thomas picked up the heavy wooden oar and handed it to the man.

Thomas said, 'Is the fishing good in the river?'

'Fair.'

'This is freshwater?'

'Yonder wet-stuff's briny.'

'Tidal currents must make your work hard.'

'You get used to it.'

'At least you don't have the dangers of the open sea.'

'We've got the dangers of the river instead.'

'Does the ferry take your catch to Hull?'

'Aye.'

'Would you sell me some mussels?'

'Aye.'

'How much?'

'Penny a pot.'

'Do you have a bag to put them in?'

'You bring the pot, mister. I'll put them in that.'

'They're big mussels.'

'Aye.'

Thomas knew that most Yorkshire men spoke as little as possible. If they could communicate with a one-word response then that's what they would do.

'Have you fished from the island for a long time?'

'Aye.'

'The cabins look new.'

'Ten years old.'

'Oh? Is that how long you've been here?'

'Look, mister. Why not say what's on your mind?' The fisherman picked up a basket full of mussels. The shells were a glistening blue-black.

'Oh, nothing's on my mind as such.'

'Seems it to me.'

'I'm a visitor. I wanted to get an impression of life here on the island.'

'Well, make the most of it. Won't be here for much longer.'

'You're saying the island won't be here for much longer?'

'I just said that, didn't I?' He sorted through the mussels, picking out those that were open and throwing them behind him onto the beach. The dog arrived to sniff optimistically at them: another meal seemed to be arriving in its direction. The man stood up straight, scratched his bristly jaw, and nodded at pieces of timber, jutting up out of the water about fifty yards offshore. 'See the sticks?'

'Yes.'

'That was our jetty. The village stood close by. Ten years ago the whole lot was washed away, along with a good chunk of the island.

That's why the cabins yonder are no more than ten years old.'

'That must have been a devil of a storm.'

'Not so much the storm's doing, mister. The Admiralty's been dredging the river in a fierce way for the last twenty years. Fiercer and deeper they go. They've ripped up the riverbed so big steamships can go upstream to Goole. What they're doing is changing the flow. This island's now being eaten away by the water. Shrinking ... dwindling.' He snapped his fingers. 'In another thirty years all this'll be water. Faxfleet will be gone for good.'

This was quite a speech for the fisherman. In fact, he looked disgusted with himself for using so many words. To many a Yorkshireman, being garrulous is a repellent quality. He returned to stirring shellfish with his suntanned hands. He threw more open mussels onto the beach. These were the dead ones that wouldn't be good to eat. The dog decided otherwise – it began to crack the shells with its teeth.

Thomas thought about what he'd heard. 'Then the king will, one day, lose his kingdom?'

The man didn't reply. He picked out a small crab from the basket and dropped it onto the beach. It scuttled toward the water's edge. The dog gave chase, then retreated when the crab turned on him with its pincers.

'It was shocking to hear that Mr Feasby had been murdered. Shot from a tree by an arrow.'

'Here.' The fisherman handed Thomas a little basket filled with the mussels he'd been sorting.

'Thank you. I'm afraid I don't have any money on me.'

'Pay me later.'

'That's very trusting of you.'

'A gent like you won't diddle me for a pennorth of shellfish.'

Without another word he pushed the rowing boat down the beach to the water. The dog chased the crab as far as the river's edge, then stopped dead as the crab vanished into the waves.

'Thank you again,' Thomas called after him. 'And goodbye.'

The man paused. 'Mr Feasby was all right. He loved creatures. I don't know why, but he did. He fixed yonder dog's leg when the daft thing got itself bit by a seal.'

'The dog looks fine now.'

The fisherman gave a nod. 'I hope you catch whoever it was that killed Mr Feasby.'

'How do you know I'm looking for the killer?'

'Because you came snooping.' He slid the boat into the water and climbed in. 'No need to look amongst us fisher-folk for the murderer. We liked old Mr Feasby. You should do your snooping among the king's guests in their little cottages. Some of those gentlemen and ladies are so crooked they couldn't lie straight in bed.' He sat down on the boat's seat and began working the oars.

With the words ringing in Thomas's ears, he carried the basket of mussels back towards the cottage that would be his home for the foreseeable future.

Before Thomas Lloyd reached the cottage he encountered a striking figure on the shore. A man of about fifty stood with his foot resting on a boulder as he plucked strings on a violin. Tied to his leg above the knee was what appeared to be a wooden board on which was pinned a page of sheet music. The man was tall and as thin as a broom handle, or so it seemed to Thomas. The stranger appeared to concentrate so ferociously on plucking the strings of the violin that his face had become fixed in an extraordinary scowl. Every so often he'd stop picking the instrument's strings, remove a pencil from behind one ear, and then add musical notes to the paper attached to his leg.

Thomas decided not to interrupt the man. He quietly walked up the beach, intending to take a woodland path.

The man had closed his eyes while moving the pencil in the air as if it was a conductor's baton. Suddenly, he opened one eye. He fixed it on Thomas.

'Mr Lloyd, how does the day treat you thus far?'

'It treats me very well, thank you,' he said, responding to the man's quaint greeting. 'Good afternoon.'

The musician tucked the pencil behind one ear. 'Mr Lloyd, we have not met. I saw you at dinner in the refectory. You were in the company of the Scotland Yard detective.'

'Inspector Abberline.'

'Yes, Abberline!' He briskly advanced towards Thomas while holding out his hand. 'Pleased to make your acquaintance, sir.'

'And I also.' The handshake was a decidedly twitchy one, hinting that the man was animated with an overabundance of nervous energy. 'I beg your pardon. I didn't mean to interrupt your work.'

'And such fascinating work it is, sir. You see, I create music. However, instead of deriving melodies from that cauldron of cliché used by so many other composers, I listen to the sounds of nature. The air moving through the trees. The lap of waves on a beach. Such as now! I've absorbed the sound of those little ripples striking lightly against the pebbles. I replicate the sound like so.' He picked at the strings; the sound echoed the waves washing against the stones. 'That's where I draw inspiration for my music.'

'I see.'

'My name is Virgil Kolbaire. I have been composing my music on this island for eight years. The king has been so pleased with my compositions that he has extended my stay each year.'

Thomas sensed the man was eager to state his case as if he required Thomas's approval and endorsement. 'You must have produced a considerable body of work in that time, Mr Kolbaire.'

'I compose a symphony each year, which I dedicate to King Ludwig. I also write opera, and nocturnes for the violin.' He plucked a string to underline the point.

Thomas carried the basket of mussels in one hand. He realized that the smell coming from the fisherman's basket was a pungent one. Kolbaire didn't seem to notice. Seemingly he wanted to reveal important truths.

'You know, Mr Lloyd, this is a crucial time of year. Soon, members of the Faxfleet Academy must present a selection of our work to King Ludwig. He judges our output. He then decides who remains here and who is despatched.'

'I imagine that such a judgement is trying. It must prey on the minds of the academy members.'

'Indeed it does, Mr Lloyd. Mark my words, many people on this island will be lying awake at night worrying – worrying that their time here is coming to an end and they will be sent back to the mainland.'

'Do many leave each year?'

'There are over thirty members living here. A dozen will be exiled, as it were. Some people do not know the meaning of hard labour. They will end up in the poorhouse, or sleeping at the side of the road.'

'Then the stakes are high.'

'Ha!' The man vigorously gestured with the violin. 'I've seen people come and go. They arrive with such cocksure optimism. They leave on the ferry as broken-down relics. Their faces wet with tears.'

'You make this sound like a cutthroat business.'

Kolbaire's eyes blazed with excitement. He actually seemed to enjoy describing the sad exit of academy members that had failed to please the king. 'It is a cutthroat business. Men and women scheme here. They puff up their chests and pretend they are geniuses. But next month you will see dejected people ride that ferry back to the mainland. Their dreams in tatters, their hopes dashed – ha! – all their pretence of greatness stripped away.'

'As you've been here for eight years, Mr Kolbaire, I doubt if you fear being cast out, as it were.'

'I do not fear that one jot, sir. I have my beautiful music.' His thin fingers plucked the strings very fast so that they sounded like drops of rain striking a tin roof. He nodded towards an area of higher ground where the forest met the shore. 'Just look at Manvers over there. He's painting landscapes day and night. He frittered his year away drinking too much, talking too much. Now he's trying to catch up. Ha! He'll be on the ferry with his tail between his legs. He'll end up shovelling manure for a living. Mark my words.'

Thomas saw a figure dressed in a white linen suit sitting at an artist's easel, where he feverishly brushed paint onto a canvas.

For a while, Thomas listened as Kolbaire spoke in that quick, nervy way of his. The musician swiftly listed every member of the academy and dismissed each one as deluded, workshy or a charlatan. The only praise he heaped on one fortunate individual was himself. Kolbaire eagerly explained that he was a unique genius. And, moreover, he was the most distinctive and celebrated of composers.

Thomas did find himself tempted to ask why he'd never heard the name Virgil Kolbaire before. However, he decided that it would be wisest for him to absorb whatever information he could. That way, he could help Abberline more effectively when he returned.

Kolbaire appeared satisfied that he'd completed his character assassination of his neighbours. He nodded, smiled, and wished Thomas a pleasant day. Thomas recognized the hint that it was time to leave. He said goodbye to Kolbaire and walked away with his basket of mussels. He'd only offered to buy them from the fisherman in order to encourage the fellow to talk. Now he must decide what he should do with this quart or so of shellfish that were becoming smellier by the minute.

*

Thomas Lloyd arrived at Samarkand Cottage to find two strangers standing by the door. Thomas immediately guessed they were policemen. He'd worked with Abberline long enough to recognize a detective, even though they wore the everyday kind of clothes an office worker or businessman might wear.

'Good afternoon.' Thomas walked through the garden gate. 'Do you wish to speak with me?'

Both men were solidly built. They wore thick woollen overcoats and bowler hats. One had a red moustache, the other a black moustache.

The one with the red moustache spoke bluntly. 'I'm Detective Constable Sutton. This is Detective Constable West. We're here from Hull CID to assist Inspector Abberline.'

'Inspector Abberline is back in London.'

'We know.'

'I'm Thomas Lloyd. I've been working with Inspector Abberline.'

'We know who you are, sir,' said West in a standoffish way. 'You're a journalist.'

'Can I help you, gentlemen?'

'We're staying in the cottage next door. We'll be investigating the death of Feasby while Inspector Abberline is away.'

'I'll do whatever I can to assist you.'

'That won't be necessary,' Sutton told him in a ponderous way. 'We just wanted to let you know that we're here on the island and we'll be taking care of things.'

'That way,' added West, 'you can continue with your story writing.'

Sutton looked down his nose at Thomas. 'Rest assured we shan't distract you from your work. Good day, sir.'

Both men raised their hats politely, yet their expressions suggested displeasure at something they'd found squirming beneath a rock.

Thomas had experienced this kind of suspicion from police officers before. Even contempt. Many policemen distrusted the presence of a newspaper reporter in their midst. They preferred to keep journalists at arm's length as a rule, seeing them as meddlers, or worse, someone that might portray them in a disagreeable way in a newspaper story. Thomas wished that Abberline would return soon. Meanwhile, all he could do was wish the detectives a good day and carry his basket of mussels into the cottage.

*

Thomas Lloyd sat down to write about what he'd discovered on the island. Partly this would help Abberline in his investigations when he returned but the notes would also be useful when he came to report on the murder case for his newspaper. After half an hour's intensive writing at the kitchen table, Thomas stood up, took the basket of mussels out of the sink, and placed them on a bench outside. The smell had become overwhelming. He opened a window and returned to the table.

So far, he only had general information – the geography of the island, its ruler, King Ludwig III, and his academy comprising thirty-three members. He'd been able to confirm Abberline's suspicion that the academy was nothing less than a boiling pot of intrigue, envy and downright fear. Academy members would soon have to submit samples of their work from their past year's residency on the island, whether that be paintings, musical compositions, inventions or scientific or philosophical essays. No doubt there'd be supporting presentations, too, where members would describe what they'd achieved during the preceding year as well as outlining plans for the next twelve months' work. Eventually, the king would deliver his judgement. Ten of the academy members would be informed that their tenure here had ended, and they'd be effectively booted off the island. Thomas looked at the word 'booted' in his notes. Was that too vulgar and violent a word? No, he decided it was quite apt. Although the act of 'booting' was metaphorical, academy members failing to meet King Ludwig's expectations were given just hours to pack up and go.

Thomas turned his attention to the murder of Benedict Feasby. There were no obvious suspects. Facts relating to the case were minimal. All that was known for sure was that Feasby had climbed the tree one morning in order to check birds' nests. There were no witnesses to the death (other than the killer). The assumption local police had made was that the stuffed wolf with the eagle's wings had been stolen from the Feasby household and had been left on a branch. Feasby had noticed the creature, prompting him to move from dense leaf-cover into the open. This allowed the killer a clear shot with a longbow. The arrow had struck Feasby in the chest. By the time he hit the ground, he was probably already dead. Abberline had later found the gold pin – this was identical to the one given to Thomas by the stranger in the carriage a few days ago. Thomas also noted that Professor Giddings, who lived just a couple of cottages away from Thomas, had been forced to take cover when a gunman had fired bullets through the window.

Thomas wrote: *Who would have a motive for killing Benedict Feasby and attempting to shoot Professor Giddings?* He thought about the intense rivalry between academy members. He jotted down: *A member of the academy wishing to dispose of rivals?* Which, when it came down to it, might possibly be *all* the academy members. Every single one seemed to be nervously eyeing each other, wondering who would stay, and who would be expelled. Also, there was the matter of the ten thousand pounds, awarded to the member who impressed Ludwig the most.

He considered the murder weapon: an arrow fired from a longbow. It seemed that most of the academy members, their families, and the king's son enjoyed archery. Each one could have let loose the fatal arrow. He recalled Jo, the striking woman in the leather kilt. She had expertly fired the arrow from the back of her horse. She was an academy member, although he didn't know her field of work. He tried to visualize her shooting Benedict Feasby out of the tree. Thomas shook his head. No ... that wasn't likely. In fact, when he did think about Jo, he found himself sitting there, smiling, as he pictured her face. With a shudder of guilt, he replaced that mental image with one of his fiancée out in Ceylon. He pictured Emma helping her father in the tea plantation.

'Shellfish,' he declared. 'I'll boil them.' It would be another four hours until dinner (he recalled he'd been invited to sit at the top table with Ludwig). 'I'll boil the mussels and eat them now.'

He found a large pan in a cupboard. A spirit burner stood by the sink. He could boil up the pan of mussels and treat himself to a late lunch.

Thomas carried the mussels to the beach. They remained tightly shut in the basket, meaning that they were still alive. After standing by the pan, readying himself to tip the creatures into the boiling water, he decided he had no appetite for them after all. Thomas crouched at the water's edge, where he tipped the mussels into the river. No doubt they'd find their way back into whatever murky, aquatic place they called home.

At that moment, he heard voices. He glanced along the beach. There was the violinist again. He used that novel system of employing his lap as a writing slope: a board, with paper, tied to his thigh. A little further away, the landscape artist still painted. Neither men appeared to be shouting.

The voices came again: loud enough to scare birds from the trees. Thomas walked along the beach, carrying the empty basket. In the next cove he saw the two detectives, Sutton and West. They talked to a fisherman who stood by a wooden frame over which nets had been draped. The fisherman was no doubt from the community based at the northern tip of the island. Thomas, initially, would have described the policemen as talking to the fisherman but in reality they were confronting him. They spoke loudly. One grabbed hold of the man's arm. The other detective jabbed his finger into the man's chest as he spoke.

Thomas walked towards the three men. When Sutton grabbed the fisherman by the lapels of his jacket and shook him, Thomas shouted, 'Hey!'

West grunted. 'This is nothing to do with you, Mr Lloyd.'

Thomas knew he couldn't turn a blind eye to this. 'Talking to the man is one thing, bullying him is another matter entirely.'

'Go back to your cottage, Mr Lloyd. This is police business.'

'Is intimidation and rough-housing the man how you conduct police business?' Thomas took another step forward. 'While I'm here I am the eyes and ears of Inspector Abberline.'

'Sir,' growled Sutton, 'we need to question everyone on the island.'

'Will you manhandle King Ludwig when you question him?'

Sutton glared at Thomas. The man seemed to be getting ready to deliver more rough treatment. However, West shook his head. Without another word, the two detectives trudged back in the direction of the forest.

The fisherman sighed with relief. 'Thank you, sir. They'd have started to dust my chin with their fists if you hadn't come by.'

'You will be questioned by the police again, no doubt. But not so roughly.'

The man began to adjust the nets over the wooden frame. 'I beg your pardon, sir, and don't wish to appear ungrateful, but I need to set my nets before the tide comes in.'

Thomas nodded and said his goodbyes before leaving the man to finish work on his fish trap. Thomas concluded that the two detectives had been ordered to conduct tough and even menacing interviews in the hope that information about whoever had killed Feasby could be scared out of the working folk here. No doubt the police didn't consider any of the island's upper-class residents to be the murderer. In fact, Thomas suspected that the head of the local police would be satisfied with a quick arrest and it didn't matter one way or the other whether the person arrested had actually committed the murder or not. The chief constable was probably under pressure from local politicians to make sure that someone was promptly caught and convicted.

Thomas returned to the cottage to be alone with his thoughts. Now that he'd released his intended meal back into the river, he cut a slice of bread, a hunk of cheese, spooned pickle from a jar, and sat down at the table to eat. He knew full well he'd made the two local detectives angry. How long would it be before they devised a way to pay him back?

'Has he gone?'

'No, he's still there in the lane.'

'What's he doing?'

'Checking his coat pockets.'

'Careful, Ivy. Don't let him see you.'

'Ah, he's going now. Striding ... striding .... like he's lord of the world.'

'Well, he won't be back till late. He can't stop us now.'

Ivy turned from the window where she'd been peeping out at Professor Giddings. Her silver hair glinted in the sun as she tilted her head. 'Maude? Why doesn't he like you taking a sherry or two? It's very healthful, any doctor will say so.'

'Oh, my dear husband does have these thoughts, you know.' Maude Giddings clearly felt it safe to venture forth with the bottle of sherry on its tray, flanked by a pair of tulip-shaped glasses. 'Those notions get lodged into his brain. Stick there like limpets to a rock.'

'Very fixated, your husband.'

'Last year he took something fierce against walnuts. Wouldn't have them in the house. Even the word "walnut" distressed him.'

'Oh?'

'Something to do with the nut being shaped like a brain inside a skull.'

'Goodness gracious. How peculiar. Wait. Let me open the door for you.'

'With him being a professor, he thinks deeply.'

'A bit too deeply for my liking, Maude.'

'Now, now, he's a very nice man.'

'Yes, I expect you've a lot to thank him for.'

'What do you mean by that?'

'I'll move these things so you can put the tray down.'

'Careful, Ivy. Those are his Constantinople papers.'

'No harm done. I'll put them on the sideboard.'

'You said I had a lot to thank Charles for? Hmm?'

'Oh, let's not fall out. We've time for a drop of something warming before supper.' She glanced back at her sister and met her ferocious glare. 'Dad always said you could give a look that'd curdle milk. At this rate you'll sour the sherry.'

Primly, Maude straightened her back. 'I had my home taken away when poor Frank passed. Forty-six years old I was, and me a widow. They turned me out the week after I buried him. I'd still be living in a pauper's shack if it wasn't for Professor Giddings.'

'Like you say, Maude, he thinks deeply about things. He looked deep into you and saw a person he cherished, even though you ...'

'Even though ... what?'

'Even though you were of a lower class.'

'Yes. Yes, he did. A wife couldn't have a better husband.'

Ivy smiled at her sister. 'We'll drink a toast to your Charlie.'

Maude smiled back. 'Yes, all right. 'Ere, don't go spilling any sherry on his papers. He'll have our guts for garters.'

The two sisters toasted Charles Giddings. Ivy downed the glass in one and then held it out for more. Maude filled the glass again.

'You don't have any gin, do you, Maude? I mean, for later?'

'Sherry will be quite sufficient.'

'We might as well finish the bottle.'

Maude raised an eyebrow. 'Thirsty?'

'It's good to see you again after so long, Maude. I feel celebratory. Spree-ish.'

'I'd hate it if Charles found us tipsy. He dislikes inebriation.'

'As much as he's disgusted by walnuts?'

Ivy realized that the walnut comment had tripped off her tongue much too quickly. She waited for her sister to erupt with anger.

Maude looked at her very directly. The corner of her mouth twitched. A second later, laughter burst from her lips.

'Walnuts, indeed. You're a devil, Ivy Kellet, an absolute devil.'

Both laughed, enjoying each other's company. Ivy quickly took the opportunity to top up both their glasses – to the brim this time.

'Oh, you will get me tipsy. Brrr ...' Maude rubbed her arms. 'Why – it's gone so chilly in here.'

'Goodness, the papers are blowing. Who let the draught in?' Ivy plonked a vase down on the professor's Constantinople essay to prevent it from fluttering away.

'That's odd.' Maude frowned. 'I'll be right back.'

Maude quickly left the room. Equally quickly, her sister emptied her glass. She'd refilled it by the time Maude returned.

'Kitchen window wide open,' she declared. 'Letting in a hurricane. It's a wonder it didn't blow the fire clean out of its grate. Now, I really must have some supper or I'll be drunk as a lord.'

'The meal's all ready. The rice can be eaten cold. S'nicer like that.'

Maude smiled happily. 'Rice, the Calcutta way. My, I haven't eaten that in years.'

'Then there's no time like the present. I'll bring the bottle.'

The two sisters made their way to the kitchen. The fragrant aroma of spices filled Ivy's nostrils as she lifted the lid from a tureen and stirred the rice and its bright speckling of exotic herbs. Maude set out plates and cutlery on the table. Both women sat down and Maude began to eat. Ivy topped up the glasses. She wanted to enjoy the drink before eating any of the rice. After all, food soon blunts the charming effect of alcohol. They chatted in a lively way about this and that. Ivy told Maude that she and her husband planned to take over a small tavern in Bridlington by the harbour. Maude laughed and commented that the profits would be poured down her throat. Ivy chuckled, too, not taking offence at the clear hint that she was an inveterate tippler.

Maude had begun eating hungrily. Now she picked at the food, a frown on her face.

Ivy paused. 'Anything wrong?'

'Hmm?'

'Too much spice?'

'Rice the Calcutta way. It's not how I remembered.'

'Oh? I used the same recipe.'

'Ouch. The heartburn it's given me.'

'Water?'

'No ... no. I think I'll go and lie down. I feel quite at odds with myself.'

Maude stood up quickly and left the kitchen.

Ivy called after her: 'I'll just clear the plates first and then I'll come up and see how you are.' Ivy sniffed the food. 'I hope the chicken wasn't off. I'll never hear the end of it if I've given her a case of the doings.'

As she put the tureen on the little table by the sink, she heard a loud thump from upstairs.

'Maude?' She hurried into the hallway. 'Maude, are you all right?'

A faint voice echoed from upstairs. 'Ivy ... will you come up? I think ... I'm quite ill.'

Ivy hurried up to Maude's bedroom. Maude was trying to climb to her feet from where she'd clearly fallen on the floorboards.

'Uh ... Ivy ... my stomach's burning.'

One glance at Maude's grey face told Ivy that her sister wasn't at all well.

'Difficult to breathe ... Oh, it hurts.'

'Maude, best come downstairs.'

'Don't think I can.'

'Once you're out in the fresh air you'll be right as rain. Here, give me your arm.'

Ivy helped her sister to stand. Carefully, she pulled Maude's arm around the back of her own neck, then held her so Maude's face rested against the side of hers.

'Away we go, Maude,' Ivy told her. 'We'll be outside in a trice.'

By the time they reached the bedroom door Maude couldn't walk. Ivy had to all but carry her. And when they reached the top of the stairs, Ivy was panting with exertion.

'Ugh ... I do feel rotten.' The words came from her sister's mouth in a slurred mumble. 'Stomach's on fire. Ah, it's sore.'

'Here are the stairs. Let me get you down them in one piece. Uh, try and take the weight on your feet while I catch my breath.'

'Sorry ... can't. Legs all ... like ... uh.'

Ivy felt her sister's breath in her face as she struggled to carry her down the steps. The exertion was terrible. Ivy felt breathless. Her chest tightened so much it became a struggle to inhale. What's more, the strain of carrying her sister made her lightheaded. She managed to descend one step... then another ... and another. Then ....

'Maude. I'm exhausted. I can't – can't catch my breath. Need to sit for a while. There. I'll lower you down. Uh ... we can sit for a moment. Side by side. Oh, my throat's burning.'

'I'm sorry, Ivy.'

'It's not your fault, dear. If I can just ... rest a wee while. The fresh air ... that's what ... uh ... I do feel odd.' Her sister's head felt so heavy on her shoulder. 'Maude? Don't fall asleep ... not ... here on the ... the steps ... I ... I don't think I ...'

Ivy's head lolled forward. When she opened her eyes it was dark. A voice called through the door.

'Mrs Giddings? Is all well?' A man's voice. 'May we come in?'

'Hello ... I ...' Ivy's head spun. She was conscious of her sister's head resting on her shoulder. 'We're ...' She began to cough.

The door swung open. Two large men, carrying candles in glass jars, entered. Both looked up in surprise at Ivy and her sister sitting there.

'We're detectives,' one said. 'Can you say what happened to you?'

Ivy's throat felt as if it was on fire. Nevertheless, she managed to croak, 'This is my sister ... Mrs Giddings. We've taken poorly.' She closed her eyes as vertigo engulfed her.

She heard the men talk for a while then one said, 'This doesn't look right. Bolt the door. There might be someone else here in the cottage.'

Ivy drifted in and out of consciousness. She couldn't be sure but she thought she heard the sound of clumping feet as the two men searched the cottage. She opened her eyes as a man's face loomed towards her, lit by the candle in his hand.

'We'll soon have you out in –' He coughed '– two shakes of a lamb's tail.' He squeezed past the two of them on the step and went upstairs.

The second detective stood at the foot of the staircase. 'Anyone else up there? Can you –' A sudden fit of coughing prevented him from finishing the sentence.

'Uh ... it's close in here. No air.' These words came from the detective behind her. 'Come on, ladies, let's get you outside.'

'Did you hear that, Maude?' Ivy whispered. 'They're going to carry us into the garden.'

'Uh?' Maude tried to raise her head from Ivy's shoulder. 'Who is ...'

'Don't worry. You'll be ... right as rain.' Ivy closed her eyes for a moment. When she opened them again she wondered if she'd been asleep. 'You know, Maude ... I came here in the hope you ... you'd help buy me the tavern in Bridlington.'

'Oh?' Maude answered softly. 'Tavern ...'

'Nice place it is ... views of the sea ... you can visit any ... any time you want. You and the professor.'

'Yes.'

Ivy licked her dry-as-dust lips. With an effort, she focused her eyes on the man standing at the bottom of the stairs. He seemed to be thinking about something important, because he didn't move. He just stood there, staring at the banister rail. From just behind her came a loud thump. The stairs shook. She managed to turn her head. For some reason, the second detective had sat on one of the higher steps behind her. He gazed downward into his lap. Ivy looked back at the other man. His expression was strange, quite blank, dreamy, and he kept coughing then grimacing. He attempted to climb the staircase, making swimming motions with his arms, as if trying to do the breaststroke through the air. Almost straightaway he seemed to lose his balance. He grabbed at the banister for support, missed the rail, and fell face down onto the stairs.

How strange, Ivy thought. *Why can none of us stand? Those two men were perfectly healthy when they came into the cottage. Is this island bewitched? Will we sleep for a hundred years?*

Ivy managed to take a deep breath. 'Maude. I will carry you outside myself. I will ... I promise ...'

Her sister muttered some words but Ivy couldn't make out what they were. Not that it mattered, because her own body felt so heavy now as sleep crept over her and her eyes slowly closed.

Thomas Lloyd knew he must remain polite and friendly as he ate dinner at the top table in the palace refectory that evening. He occupied the seat beside King Ludwig. He applauded after Virgil Kolbaire played his latest composition on the violin. He attentively listened to Kolbaire's lecture on a new form of Aeolian harp: a device that transformed the breeze into musical notes. Thomas did all this because he knew that, in effect, he was Inspector Abberline's representative. Abberline would depend on the goodwill of the people here in order to efficiently continue his investigation into Benedict Feasby's death. Thomas, however, resented the fact that Ludwig expected him to write glowing reports of the academy for the *Pictorial Evening News*.

Thomas listened to more music by Kolbaire, played on the piano. This was after the soup bowls had been taken away and before the arrival of the mutton stew. The tunes appeared quite complex to Thomas, and he doubted if he would hold the melody in his head for long. At last, after a long evening, the final glasses of port were consumed. Thomas walked back through the forest in the company of Professor Giddings and the stunningly beautiful Jo. Night had fallen by this time. They each carried an oil lantern. Every so often, the light revealed a badger or a fox on the path ahead of them. Jo walked lightly, her charisma even seeming to outshine the three lamps.

'Professor,' she said, 'will you present your book to the king at the next assessment?'

'Ah, my dear, if only I could. I shall give him a copy of the manuscript. The other copy, fate willing, should have reached my publishers by then.'

'Jo,' began Thomas, 'you haven't told me about your line of work yet.'

'No, my dear Thomas, I have not.' She beamed. 'I know ... rather than tell you, I shall give you a demonstration tomorrow.'

'You make it sound so mystifying.'

'Your sense of anticipation will heighten your excitement.'

Professor Giddings chuckled. 'You tease the poor fellow, my dear. Can you not give him the slightest hint?'

Jo grinned. 'Thomas must wait and see for himself.'

'I hope he won't be shocked,' Giddings said.

'Oh, I dare say he will be absolutely flabbergasted. He won't have seen a woman present ... ha, I nearly said too much.'

They walked along the track that led to the cottages. Jo wished them good night and headed towards the cottage she occupied (and occupied it alone as far as Thomas knew). However, instead of walking through the gate, she paused, raised the lamp, and frowned.

'Isn't that Mr Feasby sitting on your garden fence, Professor?'

'Why ... upon my soul it is.'

Thomas saw William Feasby perched on the top rail of the fence.

The man kept his gaze fixed on the front door of Professor Giddings' cottage.

Giddings hurried forward, the light from the lantern glinted on the cottage windows. 'Mr Feasby? Anything amiss?'

Something about the man, sitting there in the dark, was unsettling enough to send shivers down Thomas's spine. He glanced at Jo. She wore an expression of deep concern. Clearly the woman sensed that there had been a worrying turn of events. As they approached Feasby, he shielded his eyes against the brilliance of the lamps.

'Feasby, old chap,' Giddings said. 'What on earth's happened?'

'Good evening, Professor. I can't really say, but there is decidedly strange activity afoot. I am quite puzzled and afraid.'

Professor Giddings hurried through the gate. Feasby lightly hopped down from the fence and followed.

'Has something happened at my house?' asked Giddings.

'Yes. Something very peculiar.'

'My wife should be at home with her sister, Ivy. Why are there no lights on in the house?' He tried to open the door. 'And why is this door locked?'

He stood back in order to look up at the bedroom windows.

Jo lightly rested her hand on Feasby's arm. 'Can you tell us anything at all?'

'I stepped out into my garden for some fresh air. The lacquer I used on a lizard skin had made me quite dizzy. I saw two gentlemen in long coats approach the Professor's house. I knew these men to be detectives. West and Sutton.'

Thomas looked through the downstairs windows. His light revealed that the living room was empty. There were candles on the table. Not one had been lit.

Feasby continued: 'The two detectives knocked on the door. No one answered. The detective with the red moustache saw me and asked if I knew if anyone was home because they wished to interview all the local residents. I said that Mrs Giddings never ventured out during the evening, and that her sister had come to stay. This perplexed the two men because it was dark by this time and there were no lights in the house.'

'My dear Lord.' Giddings looked worried. 'What happened?'

'Well, this is the strangeness of it all. The men opened the door, and went inside. One immediately came back out again and said to me, "Please stay where you are. I might need to call on you to help us." With that, he went indoors, closed the door. I heard a bolt being drawn.'

Jo raised her eyebrows. 'I didn't think any of the cottage doors could be locked or bolted shut.'

Professor Giddings tried the door again. 'My wife insisted on a bolt. She didn't like to be alone with the door unlocked when I was at the palace.'

Thomas looked in through the other windows. His lamp revealed nothing but rooms with nobody in them.

Thomas asked, 'How long is it since the two men went inside?'

'Oh, forty minutes at least.'

'How did they see, if it was dark?'

'They carried candles in glass jars. They must have been without lanterns so they improvised.'

'Oh, this is very alarming.' Giddings' eyes were wide as he stared at the locked door. 'Why is it so dark in the house? What's happened in there?'

Thomas put his ear to the door. 'I can't hear anything. It's absolutely quiet.'

Feasby shuddered. 'I don't like this, I don't like it one little bit.'

'Stand back,' Thomas said.

He kicked the door as hard as he could. It remained locked tight. He kicked again. This time the door flew open.

Giddings rushed to the open door.

'Wait!' Thomas grabbed hold of the man, stopping him. 'Let me check first.'

'My wife is in there. She might need me.'

Jo whispered, 'Please let Thomas check first.'

Thomas slowly entered the cottage. He shone the light along the hallway, revealing it to be deserted. Then he looked up the staircase.

He froze. An extraordinary sight met his eyes. Two women were halfway up the stairs. They lay back with their arms around each other. The two detectives were there as well. One sat on a step, with his back to the wall, near the top of the staircase. This was West. His head hung down and the bowler hat was on his lap. The other detective lay face down on the stairs near the bottom. The way his arms were raised above his head suggested that he'd slipped partway down the stairs. All four people were unconscious. Thomas quickly retraced his steps.

Giddings, meanwhile, had entered through the doorway. 'Great Scott! What has happened to them?'

The man would have rushed upstairs if it wasn't for Thomas. Giddings was well built and strong. Thomas, however, managed to haul the man out through the doorway and onto the path outside.

Giddings roared, 'Let go! I must help my wife!'

'No. You can't go in there.'

'I must.'

Jo held onto Giddings' arm. 'Please wait out here.'

'Didn't you see? My wife is ill. Let go of me.'

He tried to force his way back to the house. Both Thomas and Jo held onto him.

'Professor,' Thomas panted. 'Stay out here.'

'My wife needs me.'

'If you go back in there, your wife will kill you!'

'Kill me?! Are you insane?'

'I think I've seen this before. There is poison involved. And poisonous gas.'

Giddings stared at Thomas in astonishment. 'Poisoned and gassed? I don't understand.'

'Please wait here. I will go in and see what can be done.'

This time Giddings did stay as Thomas returned to the house.

Thomas held up his hand. 'Jo, you stay outside, too.'

'You will need my help.'

'No.'

'I will come. I will help you. I promise you that, Thomas.'

'All right. Whatever you do, don't breathe the air inside the house. Hold your breath as if you're swimming underwater. Understand?'

She nodded.

'Open the windows,' he said. 'When you need to breathe again come outside before taking another breath. That's important. It's a matter of life or death.'

'I understand,' she told him. 'Ready when you are.'

'All right. Three, two, one.' He took a deep breath and rushed indoors.

He darted into one room to open the windows, while Jo entered another. Jo returned outside to breathe. Thomas's lungs were burning yet he ran upstairs, picking his way past the motionless figures.

The small window at the top of the stairs didn't have a section that opened. Picking up a vase from the sill, he smashed the glass. By the time he ran downstairs his lungs were on fire. He darted out onto the lawn where he released the air from his lungs in a gush and inhaled deeply.

A moment later, he approached the door again. 'Are you ready, Jo?'

'Whenever you are.'

'Hold your breath again. The gas might not be clear yet. We'll move the man closest to us. If we can, we'll bring him out here onto the lawn.'

'I'm ready.'

'If you need to breathe come back out here. Even if you have to drop the man.'

They hurried indoors. The detective was immensely heavy. In the end, they could only move him by taking hold of a foot each and dragging him outdoors onto the lawn. Thomas examined the man's face in the lamplight. The skin was covered in red speckles. It wasn't blood, it was the colour of the flesh. His lips were blue. He hadn't so much as grunted as they'd dragged him.

They returned to the house. Removing Mrs Giddings and her sister was much easier as both were slightly built. Thomas and Jo, however, struggled to move the second detective. It took three attempts to shift him downstairs. At one point, Jo let out her lungful of air. Before she could stop herself she'd inhaled. Her eyes began to water. Thomas picked her up and carried her outside.

'I'll be fine,' she protested.

'Stay here. See if you can rouse them.'

Thomas held his breath again. This time he managed to haul the second detective outside. Feasby and Giddings helped him drag the man away from the house. Soon all four victims were laid in a row upon the grass. Sutton muttered, opened his eyes. A second later he passed out again.

Thomas sucked in a huge lungful of fresh air. He glanced across at Jo, who knelt beside Mrs Giddings. Jo shook her head.

'I'm sorry,' she said. 'Mrs Giddings has gone. And so has Ivy.'

Professor Giddings ran his hands across his head. 'What happened? You said poison.'

Thomas breathed deeply. 'I've seen this before. If someone is poisoned with a compound of phosphorus and aluminium, it can kill anyone else that comes near.'

'How?'

'The compound reacts with liquid in the victim's stomach, which produces poisonous gas. When the victim is moved, they – it must be said plainly – belch poisonous gas. It can kill anyone nearby.' He knelt down beside Sutton. 'It seems as if either Mrs Giddings or her sister was poisoned with the compound. One tried to help the other downstairs. One of them succumbed to poison, the other died as a result of the gas. The two detectives saw them lying on the stairs. They went in to help but were overcome by the fumes, too.'

Jo said, 'The men are still breathing.'

'Nothing can be done for Mrs Giddings and her sister?'

Jo shook her head.

Professor Giddings fell to his knees and wept.

Moonlight shone down on the trees. The mantelpiece clock in Samarkand Cottage struck midnight. King Ludwig sat at the kitchen table. He stared at his hands as he knitted his fingers together. This was a worried man. Jo sat on a chair opposite him. Thomas Lloyd went to check on the two detectives. Sutton had been put in his bed. West occupied the bed that Abberline used when he'd first arrived here. Of course, Abberline had no need of it now. He was back in London on the trail of Jack the Ripper.

West muttered in his sleep. He didn't answer when Thomas asked how he was. However, his respiration appeared normal. The red mottle had vanished from his face along with the blue tint of his lips. Thomas was confident that the man would recover. Sutton had opened his eyes when Thomas had gone into the bedroom.

'Is Billy alive?' Sutton asked in a rasping voice.

Thomas guessed that Billy was West's first name. 'He's asleep in the next room.'

'He will recover?'

'Yes. I'm sure of it.'

Sutton gave a loud sigh. 'I'm so weak. I … I can't get events straight in my mind, sir. We went to the Professor's cottage to interview him. The lights were out. When I opened the door …' He coughed and immediately winced as if his throat was sore. 'I opened the door, sir. I saw them lying on the stairs. The two ladies. They lay in each other's arms. What happened, sir?' His expression became troubled. 'Billy and I examined the ladies. Then we found we couldn't move ... it was like we were suddenly drunk. Then that's all I knew until I woke up here. There's poison ... the door opened ... there they were. Eyes. I remember two staring eyes. My mother called me down to the coal cellar. My old dad ... he'd fallen ... I should have stayed back ... way back when ...'

Thomas tried to soothe the man. 'Rest. Everything is all right.'

'My old dad. He fought in Egypt. Said scorpions could dance right over your face at night ... when you were sleeping.' He wiped his face. 'Sir. Scorpions ... will you get them off, sir?'

'There are no scorpions. Try and sleep.'

He began to mutter like his colleague in the next room. Thomas waited until his breathing became regular and he seemed to be sleeping normally before returning to the kitchen where Ludwig and Jo sat.

Thomas said, 'Jo, I should escort you back home. You shouldn't be here without a chaperone.'

'Don't worry about me, Thomas.' She gave a tired smile. 'Thank you for your concern.'

Ludwig stood up. 'I'll make tea. A large pot should suffice for an hour or so.' He glanced at Thomas and Jo as if he suspected they were going to protest. 'A king can make a pot of tea, you know.'

He busied himself filling a kettle before setting it on the spirit burner. Almost two hours had elapsed since Thomas and Jo had brought the four people out of the nearby cottage. Mrs Giddings and her sister were dead. Ludwig's domestic staff had taken the bodies to the palace. Professor Giddings had followed the sad procession through the wood, wringing his hands as he went. Thankfully, the two detectives showed signs of recovery. Thomas hoped there would be no permanent damage to their lungs. He'd not liked West and Sutton. They appeared thuggish and dull-witted – in fact, the very kind of policemen that belonged to the past, not to the modern world of detection. However, the pair must have experienced plenty of thuggery in the dockland areas of Hull. They were accustomed to meeting force with force. Thomas realized he shouldn't have judged them so harshly.

Ludwig spooned tea into a teapot. 'Thomas, Jo – your actions were heroic tonight. You saved the lives of those two policemen.'

'Thank you, sir.' Thomas said.

Jo added, 'Not that I felt particularly heroic. We did what had to be done.'

'What an evil night,' Ludwig said. 'Imagine – it is possible to poison someone and then for the poison to generate toxic fumes that can kill people who approach the victim. I still find it hard to understand that such a thing could happen.'

Thomas said, 'That's the nature of poisoning with a compound of phosphorus and aluminium. It reacts with liquid in the victim's stomach.'

'You've seen this before?' asked Jo.

'I once reported on the death of an undertaker. A farmer had committed suicide by swallowing the same compound. When the undertaker worked on the body, gas leaked from the corpse's mouth and nostrils, and the undertaker was killed, too.'

'But here?' Ludwig shook his head as if unable to believe what had happened tonight. 'The wife of one of my academy members dies in her own home in such bizarre circumstances?'

Jo shuddered. 'Decidedly bizarre.'

'Suicide?' ventured the king.

'I can't say,' Thomas replied. 'However, it seems to me that one of the women swallowed the poison, either deliberately or someone else had added it to her food. When she collapsed upstairs in the cottage the other woman tried to carry her downstairs. Perhaps she believed that fresh air would revive the victim.'

Jo shuddered again as if feeling the touch of something icy on her backbone. 'It's all too easy to picture one sister trying to rescue the other. She'd carry her in such a way that the unconscious woman's head was on her shoulder. All the time, lethal vapours would be streaming from the victim's mouth, which the other woman would inhale. By the time they were halfway down the stairs both would be overcome – one by poison, the other by fumes.'

Ludwig stared at the kettle as it began to boil. 'Feasby shot from a tree. Mrs Giddings and her sister poisoned to death. The newspapers will cover their pages with this story. The academy's reputation will suffer. Confound it.'

Thomas watched the monarch of the tiny kingdom of Faxfleet pour boiling water into the teapot. Ludwig appeared to have devoted his life to the academy. *In fact,* Thomas told himself, *he's clearly obsessed with it*. The sudden deaths on the island were of secondary importance as far as Ludwig was concerned. Thomas found that distasteful ... no, he was disgusted. Three people had died.

Jo touched Thomas's hand. 'Would you like anything to eat?'

'No, thank you.'

'Sir?' she asked Ludwig.

He shook his head. 'That's kind of you, Jo. In truth, I feel sickened tonight.'

For the next thirty minutes they said very little. They drank cup after cup of tea in a detached kind of way. Jo's eyes were distant. Thomas realized that she probably could think of nothing else but tonight's events. Thomas's own mind was full of images that flashed with a terrible brilliance. He kept seeing the four victims in his mind's eye. Two women lying dead on the stairs. The two detectives, unconscious. Inevitably, he recalled the time recently when he fell into the canal – drifting down through the black waters, unable to breathe. Death waiting with open arms. Tonight Death had succeeded in taking the two women.

Jo lightly touched the back of his hand again. 'Tired?' she asked.

'My body feels like a lead weight, yet my mind's racing. I keep seeing them in the cottage again. Lying there.'

'Me, too.' She stood up from the table. 'I will try to sleep, however. I'll go home, unless you need me any more tonight?'

'I don't think we can do anything until morning.'

Ludwig nodded. 'Try and sleep, Jo. That will help settle your mind.'

'Then I shall bid you good night, gentlemen.'

Thomas said quickly, 'I'll walk you home.'

'Oh, that's not necessary. It's just a moment's stroll away.'

'I insist,' Thomas told her. 'There's a real danger that there's a murderer on the island.'

'Then I accept. Thank you.'

Ludwig opened the door for her. 'Shut all your windows, and do what you can to bar the door.'

Thomas added, 'Everyone here should fix locks and bolts to their doors. The practice of leaving them unlocked should be stopped.'

'I agree, though with a heavy heart.' Ludwig sighed. 'I'll order strong bolts, and have them fitted in all the houses by tomorrow night.'

Thomas stepped into the garden with Jo. He carried a lantern to light their way. Carefully, he looked around him. He saw no one, certainly no lurking stranger that might commit murder (although his imagination supplied him with plenty of images of assassins lying in wait with knives and pistols). The moon shone down onto the lane. He saw its light playing on the river in the distance.

Thomas said, 'Put a table behind your front door. Pile plates onto it. If someone opens the door that will send the plates crashing. That will tell you there's an intruder.'

'Thank you. I will.'

'Keep your bow and arrows nearby, too.'

'You care about my safety, don't you, Thomas?'

'Of course. I wish you weren't spending the night alone in your cottage.'

'Oh?'

Thomas glanced at her. The woman's eyes shone brightly in the moonlight.

'Ssss.'

Thomas spun round at the sound of the hiss.

'Mr Feasby. I didn't see you there,' Jo said in that pleasant way of hers. 'You rather startled us.'

'I'm sorry, Jo. The bald truth of it is I cannot sleep.'

Thomas said, 'Would you prefer to come to my cottage, Mr Feasby?'

'Thank you, Mr Lloyd, that is most kind. However, I shall stay here. I feel as if I should keep watch on my neighbours tonight.'

Thomas held up the light to reveal the man who was over eighty years of age. Thomas wanted to applaud his courage and his care for the people who lived nearby.

'Mr Feasby, I shall join you in a moment,' said Thomas, 'if I may?'

'I would welcome that, sir.'

Thomas continued walking along the lane with Jo. They'd only taken a few steps when Mr Feasby said:

'We are being exterminated, aren't we? Everyone on this island, one by one, is being murdered, and we can do nothing to stop it happening again.'

Chapter 9

A MIST LINGERED that following morning. Thomas stood on the jetty as the boat steamed away in the direction of the mainland with the two bodies on board. They would be taken to the hospital in Hull for a post mortem examination. That would determine which woman had swallowed the poison, and which had been killed by poisonous gas leaking from the mouth of the corpse. The detectives West and Sutton had boarded the ferry, too. Thomas watched them sitting, round-shouldered, with their heads hanging forwards. They were recovering from inhaling the toxic fumes. They were still weak, however. The pair would go to hospital, too, though it was likely that they would be allowed home within a matter of hours. The ferry also carried one of King Ludwig's footmen. He would deliver a letter to the police asking for immediate assistance on the island.

Thomas decided to take a stroll, relishing the fresh air as he did so. Just the thought of holding his breath in that gas-filled cottage last night made his throat feel unpleasantly tight. He watched seals hunting for fish in the shallow water near the shore. From further out in the river came the lowing of foghorns as ships moved through the mist. He'd slept for around five hours last night after standing guard with Mr Feasby in the lane that ran by the cottages. They'd seen no one. If anything, the hours after the removal of the bodies to the palace had been peaceful ones. Early that morning King Ludwig had organized a search of the island. The fishermen from the island's northern tip, along with the other inhabitants of the island, arranged themselves into groups, armed with cudgels, axes, rifles, longbows and kitchen knives. Two groups worked their way along the beaches. The other groups attempted to form a line across the narrow island before moving from the south to the north in the hope they could trap the killer. The density of the forest meant that to keep everyone in sight so no assassin could slip through wasn't easy. Thomas knew that it would require a large number of police officers, together with bloodhounds, to conduct the search properly.

The ferry returned later that morning. Day-to-day life had to continue, of course. The boat carried a cargo of fresh milk, eggs and other foodstuffs. The boat also delivered the morning papers and a sack of mail. Ludwig arranged for the newspapers to be handed out at no cost to the islanders. When Thomas's copy of the *Yorkshire Post* arrived at the cottage, he took the paper down to the beach where he found a rock to sit upon.

He leafed through the newspaper, reading about a fire that had destroyed a theatre in Wakefield. An escaped bull in Pontefract had knocked over market stalls before being trapped in the back yard of a tavern. Huddersfield's mayor pledged funding for a new bridge over a canal. Thomas's heart lurched when he saw the headline INSPECTOR ABBERLINE BAFFLED BY LATEST WHITECHAPEL MURDER. Thomas read the first few lines of the news report. *Inspector Abberline, the detective who led the hunt for the murderer known as Jack the Ripper two years ago, has returned to pursue the villain again. Mrs Ruth Verity was found in a derelict house on Tuesday. She'd been murdered. The killer had used a knife to disfigure her body.*

Thomas sighed. Part of him wished he was back in London, shadowing Abberline as he searched for the Ripper. He also realized that he needed to continue gathering information about the island and its population. Yet he felt as if nothing would progress substantially here until Abberline was back on the island. He returned to the cottage and wrote a letter to Abberline, telling him what had happened in the Giddings' household last night. Once he'd sealed down the envelope, he returned to the jetty in time to see the arrival of the ferry. This time it brought six policemen in uniform together with three detectives. Thomas felt enormous relief at the arrival of the police. The population of Faxfleet would feel much safer now.

He handed the ferryman the letter, which would be posted on the mainland. After that, he strolled back in the direction of the cottage. Groups of islanders passed by as they returned from their search, which had found nothing at all. Even so, Thomas looked into the eyes of each man and woman and wondered if they harboured a grim secret. Competition for both the prize and the opportunity to remain on the island as part of the academy was fierce. Was one of the academy members trying to eliminate their rivals? At that moment, every single one of those people looked suspicious to him. They were all ambitious. They had so much to lose if their year's work was considered to be inferior to that of their neighbours. If they were judged to be failures they would be evicted from their rent-free cottage and the island within hours. Was it possible that one of these men or women was the murderer?

The sun shone by midday. Thomas sat on a bench outside Samarkand Cottage. The local detectives from Hull came and went from the house where the deaths had occurred last night. The detectives interviewed Mr Feasby, Jo and Thomas.

'I'm not a member of the king's academy,' he'd told them, 'I arrived here with Inspector Abberline.'

They nodded, wrote down what he'd said in their notebooks, then asked him if he'd seen any strangers on the island. On this occasion, Thomas realized he was being treated as a member of the public, not a participant in the investigation. Thomas didn't see that there would be anything to be gained by trying to become part of the detection team. Therefore, he sat on the bench, making notes, while keeping his own eyes and ears open.

At one point, a detective emerged from Professor Giddings' home. Thomas clearly heard the man say to a colleague: 'We've found it. It was in the bowl of rice.'

Thomas felt pretty confident that the 'it' referred to by the detective was the poison. So, the poison had been put in a rice dish? Thomas made a note.

Jo rode up to the garden gate on her horse. 'Good morning, Thomas. How are you?'

'Good morning. I'm fine, and you?'

'Bad dreams, Thomas, I had plenty of those. I've never been in a house filled with poisonous gas before.'

'Would you like a cup of tea?'

'I'm afraid I can't. I have to deliver my prospectus to Ludwig. Cheerio, dear Thomas.' With a flash of that brilliant smile, she waved, then urged the horse into a trot.

Thomas watched the woman ride away. Once again, she wore

the short leather kilt and what appeared to be pantaloons in white silk. She really was extraordinary. A crackling, dazzling firework of a human being. He mulled the word she'd used: 'Prospectus'. That must be something to do with the academy members' annual submission of their work to King Ludwig. No doubt the prospectus would be assessed along with examples of Jo's work. He wondered if Ludwig would approve of her work, whatever that work was, and permit her to continue living here, or whether she would be sent back to the mainland. He hoped she'd win through and stay.

'Telegram. Telegram for Mr Lloyd.'

Thomas looked up. 'Inspector?' He rose to his feet, smiling. 'Hello. I didn't know you would be coming back so soon.'

He opened the gate for Inspector Abberline, who carried a leather case in one hand and an envelope in the other.

'Welcome back,' Thomas said warmly. 'It's good to see you.'

'Thank you, Thomas, and good to see you.' He smiled. 'Here's your telegram. I can tell you what's written here because I wrote it. I sent the telegram first thing this morning but I caught up with it on the way.' He shrugged. 'Communications with this island are slow, to say the least.'

'And I sent you a letter with news of last night's events. Though I daresay it won't reach your office at Scotland Yard for another day or so yet.'

'You're referring to the death of Mrs Giddings and her sister?'

'You've heard?'

'The ferryman told me as we made the crossing.'

'I'll give you a detailed account. Firstly, though, you might like to put your things in the cottage.'

'Oh, they can wait, Thomas,' he said good-naturedly. 'Besides, it's best to hear what happened while it's still fresh in your mind.'

Thomas gave as thorough a report as he could about the events of the previous evening when he, Jo and Professor Giddings found Mr Feasby outside the cottage. Abberline listened carefully as Thomas revealed how they'd found four figures on the stairs – two dead, two unconscious. In a matter-of-fact way, he described how he and Jo had held their breath each time they went inside the cottage to retrieve the men and women. He finished his account with the information that he'd overheard just a few minutes ago, that the detectives had identified a bowl of rice as the source of the poison.

Abberline digested what he'd heard for a moment. 'Use of the phosphorus and aluminium compound as a poison is extremely unusual.'

'Indeed, murderers often use our old friend arsenic.'

'Hmm, the so-called inheritance powder. Arsenic as a murder weapon is so commonplace that newspapers wouldn't report its use at length. But death by such an exotic compound that was used here yesterday is so rare, and the fact that it led to three people being gassed will guarantee front-page news far and wide.'

'I'm sure reporters will be clamouring for the story.'

'Especially as two policemen almost died. And, even more dramatically, the men were rescued by you and the young lady. A heroic story like that will make the pair of you famous.'

'We did what anyone else would do in the circumstances.'

'But the newspapers will shout out the story to the world. The poisoning and the rescue will be discussed over dinner everywhere from a poor hovel to a rich man's castle.'

'You think that the method of poisoning was chosen deliberately to draw the public's attention?'

'Just as Mr Benedict Feasby was shot from a tree by an arrow.'

'Then the killer is attempting to make their work famous?'

'It looks like that.'

'Are they striving to be as famous – as infamous – as Jack the Ripper?'

'Which leads to my own ferreting about in Whitechapel.' Abberline gave a rather sad smile. 'Shall we go indoors? I could do with a wash and brush up, and then I'll tell you what happened to me and my hunt for loathsome Jack.'

A boy arrived at Samarkand Cottage. He wore a brown apron and pushed a wheelbarrow on which was balanced an easel and a blackboard. The boy had shiny black marks on his forehead and chin. He rolled the wheelbarrow up to the door where Thomas was levering off his boots.

'Sir,' he said to Thomas. 'I've been told to bring this board and easel. There's a bag of chalk, too.'

Thomas guessed that Inspector Abberline had asked for the loan of these items. He preferred to order his thoughts about a case by chalking salient points on a board.

'Thank you.' Thomas gave him a penny.

The boy's eyes lit up as he took the coin. 'Ta, sir,' he said, using 'ta' (rhyming with 'tar'), the local slang word for 'Thank you'. 'I'm the lad that cleans boots at the palace. Would you like me to put a bit of a shine on those for you?' He nodded in the direction of the boots that Thomas had levered off. The lad clearly saw more of Thomas's money coming his way. He pulled a cloth and a tin of boot polish from a huge pouch sewn onto the front of the apron.

Inspector Abberline appeared in the doorway. 'You could give mine a polish, if you would?' Abberline handed him a pair of shoes that still had a bright sheen.

'Ta, sir!' Straightaway, he sat on the bench with the shoes on his lap. He vigorously applied polish. Some of the polish had clearly found its way onto his face earlier.

'My name's Abberline. What's yours, young man?'

'Wilf.'

'A pleasure to meet you, Wilf.'

'You, too, sir.'

Thomas followed Abberline back into the cottage. 'Your shoes looked perfectly clean to me, though I suppose you have an ulterior motive for having the boy polish your shoes?'

'Boys like that have a knack of seeing and hearing plenty. He'll know a lot about what happens locally. In fact, he probably knows secrets about the islanders.'

Thomas smiled at Abberline's knowing glance. Thomas then collected the easel and blackboard from the barrow. Meanwhile, Wilf buffed Abberline's shoes until they glinted as if they'd been freshly varnished. The boy had also managed to get more boot polish onto his face and earlobes.

Thomas set up the easel and board in one corner of the kitchen. Abberline had sliced some cheese and bread and set it out on a pair of plates.

'I think we could do with stoking up on some food while we work.' Abberline fished pickled onions from a jar.

Thomas had to ask a question that had been preying on his mind. 'Inspector, tell me if I'm being nosey. Have you received any more letters?'

'From bloody Jack?' He shook his head as he sat down at the table. 'Despite the murder of Mrs Verity prompting a huge amount of newspaper stories, he's kept quiet.'

'Are you certain that the recent murder in Whitechapel was the work of the Ripper?'

'Too early to say.' Abberline stared at the bread and cheese on his plate as if he'd abruptly lost his appetite. 'I can tell you what I know so far. Mrs Ruth Verity arrived from Poland as a little girl. She was raised by hardworking and honest parents in Plymouth. When she was twenty she married a George Verity. They moved to London where he bribed officials in order to obtain a contract for a new road. George Verity went to prison. He's still there. Mrs Verity went to live in a lodging house in Chelsea where she made an honest living repairing watches, a skill she learned from her father. This week her body was discovered in a ruined house in Whitechapel.'

'The body had been mutilated?'

'Yes.' Abberline avoided looking at the food. 'Face and torso slashed by a sharp blade. Wounds resembled those found on some of the Ripper victims of two years ago. Facial injuries were especially similar to the way that Elizabeth Stride had been cut.'

'Then it is the Ripper. You had a letter from him threatening to start killing again. A few days later the body was found.'

'I can't leap to conclusions, Thomas.'

'So there is something unusual about this case?'

'Very sharp of you, Thomas.' Abberline's face crinkled into a grim smile. 'The autopsy revealed that the woman's lungs were covered with an orange stain.'

'Residue from smoking tobacco?'

'Iron oxide.'

'Iron oxide? How?' Thomas shook his head in bewilderment. 'How on earth can lungs be stained with iron oxide before they've been removed?'

'The police surgeon believes that Mrs Verity drowned in water where there's a substantial iron content. You've seen streams and rivers that are a distinctive orange.'

'She was drowned by the killer?'

'I can't reach that conclusion yet. It does suggest, though, she was immersed in iron-rich water, which she inhaled as she drowned. Then the body was removed from the water, washed, dressed in clean clothes, before being delivered to a derelict house in Whitechapel. That's where the cuts were inflicted.'

'I see. You think it might be a hoax?'

'A gruesome hoax, Thomas.'

'But it could be an attempt to torment the police by making them fear that Jack the Ripper is back.'

'Yes, Thomas. I think you might be right.'

'And someone went to a lot of trouble to do that. It wouldn't be easy to procure the body of a recently deceased woman then move it around London without being noticed. A carriage must have been involved, along with, as likely as not, more than one person.'

Knuckles tapped the doorframe. 'Sir? Mr Abberline, sir?'

'Ah, Wilf. My shoes.'

'All done, sir.'

'They look splendid.' Abberline pulled several coins out of his pocket and handed them to the boy.

'Blimey, sir. Thank you. Do you want any more boots shining up?'

'No, thank you.'

Wilf headed back to collect his barrow from the path.

Abberline followed him outside. 'Wilf? Have you worked at the palace long?'

'Three years, sir. I'm fourteen next week.'

'You must see plenty of the academy members come and go.'

'Oh, aye. They come across the water from the mainland all smiles. Everyone gives me a shilling here and a shilling there for my help.' He clearly saw an opportune moment to underline the notion that his services were invaluable and were to be rewarded with coins aplenty. 'Then if the king decides they're not up to much – then *kush!*' He swung his foot as if kicking an object out of the way. '*Kush!* Off they go, back to the mainland. Sometimes they're shouting, and cursing, and angry at being chucked out. Other times they're sad as sad can be and weeping. It's something to behold, Mr Abberline.'

'I can imagine.'

'And another thing, sir. They have games. The strangest sport you've ever seen. I bet you ...' Wilf's voice instantly faded when he glimpsed a figure leave a cottage just along the lane. The colour drained from his skin. His eyes widened with shock. Just the sight of Jo terrified the lad.

'What's wrong?' Thomas asked.

'That lady.'

'Miss Hamilton-West?'

'Let me hide indoors, sir. I don't want her to see me.'

Thomas laughed in a bemused kind of way. 'Why ever not, Wilf?'

'I'm scared of her. She hurt me.'

The boy crouched down on the garden path, in the hope that Jo wouldn't notice him.

'Nip into the kitchen,' Abberline told him. 'She won't see you there.'

Wilf dashed into the cottage. The expression of terror on his face alarmed Thomas. *Why is the boy so frightened of Jo?*

Jo strode along the lane, carrying a longbow. Did the boy think she'd fire an arrow at him? The sudden turn of events bewildered Thomas.

'Oh, hello there.' Jo smiled in that bright way of hers. 'Did you have an interesting trip to London, Inspector?'

'Interesting and informative.'

She appeared in a hurry so continued walking. However, she called out, 'Thomas, dear. We're having a competition this evening, archery on the palace lawn. You're welcome to join us. You, too, Inspector.'

Thomas and Abberline thanked her and said they'd come along.

'Cheerio, gents.' With that, she vanished into the trees.

A moment later, Wilf's boot-polish-mottled face appeared. 'Has Lady Jo gone?'

'Yes.' Abberline smiled to put the boy at ease. 'All clear. You're safe.'

'Thank crikey for that!'

Thomas watched the boy as he hurried to his wheelbarrow. 'Why are you so frightened of the lady? She's very pleasant.'

'You don't know what she did to me! Just seeing her makes my blood run cold.'

'Why? What did she do?'

'I must go back to the palace. I'll get a right yelling at if I'm not back in time to do the saddles.' He picked up the handles of his barrow and trundled it away at a run.

'Well, upon my soul,' murmured Abberline. 'What do you make of that?'

'I can't believe that Jo would hurt a child.'

'Wouldn't you, Thomas? I didn't have you pegged as a naïve man.'

Thomas felt uneasy. He'd formed an impression of Jo as being a cheerful, friendly woman who would be kind to adults and children.

Now … well, he felt as if the rug had been pulled from beneath his feet. He couldn't help but ask himself what kind of suffering she had inflicted on the boy to make him so terrified of her.

Inspector Abberline had regained his appetite. Earlier, when he'd been talking about the murder of Mrs Verity, and her injuries, he'd been unable to eat. Now, however, he finished the plateful of bread and cheese. Thomas ate as well. It would be a few more hours until dinner at the palace refectory. After they'd eaten, Abberline went to the blackboard, set upon its easel in one corner of the kitchen. There, he chalked the names of the three people who'd died recently on the island. For now, this case would be the one that he'd devote his time to. Presumably, his colleagues at Scotland Yard would continue to investigate the death of Mrs Verity.

Abberline stood beside the board. 'I've been looking into the independent nature of this island,' he said. 'There's a copy of the royal charter at the British Museum. King George III granted Ludwig Smith the right to be the Royal Sovereign of Faxfleet. Today's King Ludwig is the eighth monarch. He created his academy thirty years ago with the intention of allowing what he calls "gifted and exceptional individuals of vision" to pursue their studies in art, science and philosophy.'

Thomas nodded. 'There are thirty or so current members, which receive a monthly allowance, and free food and lodgings, so it's a considerably expensive exercise.'

'Good point. Which leads to this question: how does the king afford the upkeep of his palace and the academy?'

'There's a fishing village in the north of the island. A man there told me that they pay the king rent.'

Abberline chalked the name 'Ludwig' on the board. Beneath that he wrote 'Landlord'. 'It might help if we create a clear picture of the king and his financial situation.'

'Income from the fishermen's rents won't amount to much.'

'Agreed. However, I discovered the real backbone of his income. The royal charter allows Ludwig to create a total of twenty-five senators. He sells each title for ten thousand pounds.'

'Quite a sum.'

'The really clever part is that any man becoming one of Faxfleet's senators doesn't have to pay the British government income tax or excise on imported goods. Instead, they only pay about a third of what would be their usual British taxes to King Ludwig. He's been very astute by selling the senator titles to some very wealthy men. They're pleased because they save vast amounts on income tax. Accordingly, this scheme has made Ludwig a very rich man.'

'Meaning he can gratify his passion for running the academy.'

'An academy that breeds envy and rancour amongst its members.'

'I've seen evidence of that.' He told Abberline about meeting the composer on the beach and how he'd listened to the man's gleeful criticism of his neighbours. 'And soon Ludwig will judge their work and decide who will stay and who will leave.'

Abberline chalked the words: *Academy + Rivalry = Murder?*

Thomas said, 'There's no evidence that academy members have killed each other?'

'No. But there is evidence that people on the island have resorted to violence in the past. I've checked the police records in Hull. Twenty years ago, two inventors fought a duel because one accused the other of stealing his design for an oil pump. They decided to settle the argument with pistols. Fortunately, it rained when they tried to shoot each other. The gunpowder in the pistols had become damp and wouldn't fire. On another occasion, a painter and a sculptor fought a duel with swords. When the painter wounded the sculptor in the arm the painter fainted at the sight of blood.'

'Nobody actually died?'

'No. It does demonstrate that emotions among academy members become inflamed. Arguments flare up. There are fights. Stones thrown at windows. Rivals attempt to sabotage the work of others. So –' Abberline held out his arms '– how long until a desperate man, or woman, resorts to murder?'

For the next hour, Abberline and Thomas discussed what they'd discovered about the island. Thomas knew from previous investigations that Inspector Abberline believed it essential to create a firm base of background information before he built his case: hence his research of the royal finances and history of the academy.

Later, as Abberline covered the blackboard with a towel to hide what was written there from prying eyes, he paused. 'Oh. Just another point about the charter that grants independent sovereignty to Faxfleet. It stipulates that the kingship will only continue to exist as long as the island exists.'

Thomas raised an eyebrow. 'Coincidentally, I was speaking to a fisherman recently. He told me that the river's current has been changed by dredging. He's certain that the island is getting smaller. Gradually, it's being washed away, and Faxfleet will be gone in thirty years.'

'Interesting. Which means that one day the Kingdom of Faxfleet will dissolve along with the island, and the royal line will come to an end.'

'Along with a huge annual income. What now? Shall we begin interviewing the islanders?'

Abberline smiled that knowing smile of his. 'Or we could go and watch some archery instead.'

The archery contestants gathered on the palace lawn. There were about thirty of them. They fired arrows at targets fixed to the same kind of easel that Abberline had borrowed. Abberline and Thomas exchanged glances as arrows powerfully thudded into the targets. Contestants were aged anywhere between fifteen, perhaps, to mid-seventies. They were either members of the academy or their sons and daughters and so on. Thomas knew what Abberline was thinking. The archers were skilled. Any one of them could have fired the fatal arrow that brought Benedict Feasby crashing down from the tree. Thomas glanced across at William Feasby. The twin of the dead man sat on a tree stump with his knees drawn up near his chin as he watched the competition.

Servants, meanwhile, carried trays, bearing glasses of sherry, from person to person. Jo marched across the lawn to Abberline and Thomas.

'I'm so glad you could make it.' She beckoned a servant. 'The sherry's very good.'

Thomas and Abberline took a glass apiece.

'Will you test your luck with the bow, Thomas?' she asked.

'I don't think I will. I've never fired an arrow in my life.'

'You should try,' she told him firmly. 'In fact, you should try everything once.'

Abberline smiled pleasantly. 'I daresay that should not include theft or murder.'

Jo laughed. 'Yes, I should say try everything once within reason.'

Thomas had something to get off his chest, although he

approached the subject obliquely. 'We had a visit today from a young lad called Wilf. He was most keen to earn some money by polishing our shoes.'

'Yes, he does boots at the palace. He's quite an imp.'

'You mean he can be mischievous?'

'Are you trying to lever some information from me, Thomas?'

'It would be prudent to know if he can be trusted.'

'With your footwear?'

Inspector Abberline took a sip of sherry. 'It might be useful to have a reliable lad who can run errands while we're here.'

'Yes ... Yes.' Her eyes narrowed. 'I know what this is about. Wilf's told you about the terrible injury I inflicted upon him.'

'What injury?' Thomas was shocked. 'What did you do?'

'Oh, the usual type of brutal assault that scientists inflict on their specimens.'

'You're making fun of us,' Abberline said.

'Yes, I am, aren't I?' She grinned. 'Yet another demonstration of my cruel nature.'

'What did you do to the boy?' Thomas felt himself becoming angry.

'I will make my confession, gentlemen. I study phrenology, together with its relationship to the ancient ape-like creatures that were our ancestors.'

Thomas stared at her in surprise. Her bizarre statement left him flabbergasted.

She continued. 'In short, gentlemen, I'm attempting to categorize and predict human behaviour by studying the shape of people's skulls. Phrenology has its doubters but I firmly believe it is scientifically valid.'

'How did this result in you hurting Wilf?'

'Ha. He has been telling you quite a tale, hasn't he? The little scamp.' Jo tasted her sherry. 'Delicious. Well, I promised Wilf a shilling if he would let me shave his head. You see, I wanted to take detailed measurements of his skull. I also asked if he would consent to having a plaster of Paris cast made of his head. The shilling appealed to him so much he agreed. I shaved away the hair, made the measurements – in the presence of a chaperone, I should add. All went well until I started applying plaster of Paris to his forehead. He believed, mistakenly, that I'd cover his face with the stuff and choke him. He panicked. Got plaster of Paris in his eyes, which meant he couldn't see. Even so, he tried to dash from the cottage. Instead, he ran into the door, and ended up with two marvellous black eyes. He's never forgiven me.'

'I see.'

'I gave him a shilling for the examination and another shilling in compensation. But he still thinks I plan to asphyxiate him with plaster of Paris. Now, will you arrest me, Inspector Abberline?'

'That won't be necessary, miss.'

'Ah, then let's celebrate my escape from justice with another sherry.'

The moon shone on the trees that grew thickly on the island. Thomas Lloyd lay on the bed, gazing through the window. The moon tended to be reddish and bloated in London, due to the distorting effect of smoke pouring from a million chimneys. Here, in the clear air, the moon burned with a hard, bright light, as sharply delineated as a new silver coin.

Thomas replayed the events of this evening in his mind. He'd gone along with Inspector Abberline to watch the archery contest. Jo had revealed how she'd hurt – accidentally hurt, that is – Wilf, the boy whose job it was to clean boots at the palace. Jo had revealed something surprising. She studied the science of phrenology. Or, more accurately, that should be the *discredited* science of phrenology. Abberline, now fast asleep in the next room, had declared quite forcefully on the walk back to the cottage: 'Why on earth is an intelligent woman like that wasting her time on crank ideas? Phrenology is nonsense. No scientist or doctor worth their salt believes in that foolishness anymore.'

Thomas tried to muster up what he knew about phrenology. A German doctor in the 1700s had developed a theory that the human brain developed bumps and protrusions according to the personality and intelligence of the owner of that brain. In effect, the brain moulded the shape of the skull, just as a foot moulds the shape of a leather shoe. According to phrenologists, a cruel person would develop a bony ridge beneath the skin above their ear. An especially charitable person would produce a bulge at the top of their brain which, in turn, would form a corresponding bulge in the top of the skull. In effect, phrenology supposes that the brain possesses a geography like a country, and just as towns, hills and rivers can be drawn on a map, so the human traits of kindness, jealousy, religious zeal, friendship and so on can be mapped out on the human head. Phrenologists could, or so they believed, determine an individual's intelligence, personal characteristics and intellectual abilities (or lack thereof!) by measuring the head, and by running their fingers over the bulges, ridges and curves of the skull.

Thomas gazed at the shadows of tree branches thrown onto the wall by the moonlight. He agreed with Abberline. Jo demonstrated a keen intelligence. She brimmed with confidence and sheer gusto. A human whirlwind. Nevertheless, even though she had succeeded in becoming a member of the academy, she had, for some peculiar reason, decided to study a subject as bizarre and absolutely worthless as phrenology.

He found himself picturing Jo running her fingers over the heads of her fellow islanders. Carefully mapping out skulls, assessing people for their artistic and intellectual abilities as well as their emotional geography. Thomas wondered how it would feel if she mapped his own skull. What would her fingertips feel like as they explored the surface of his head? What could she divine about his personality? Would she revise her estimation of him as a man? Did he have qualities that she'd admire?

He closed his eyes and her smiling face filled his mind's eye, growing bigger and brighter, until he drifted away to sleep, and he dreamt of them both standing on a beach where they waited for a ship that would take them away forever.

The local phrase for it was 'first on'. Wilf always liked to be 'first on' the beach as the tide went out. The thirteen-year-old crept through the cottage, which he shared with other boys who worked in the palace or the stables. Quietly, not wanting to wake the others, he pulled on his boots and a big cap that almost covered his eyes, and lifted the latch on the door. Outside it was dark beneath the trees. The moonlight couldn't penetrate the masses of branches.

When it was low tide Wilf baited hooks and attached them to boulders with lengths of string. The tide would return, submerging the hooks in five feet of water. All being well, a few fish would hook themselves there and Wilf could collect them. He had to do this quickly when the tide retreated, leaving the fish high and dry, otherwise gulls would eat his catch.

Wilf moved through the darkness beneath the trees. Every so often a shaft of moonlight would pierce the branches to light a little patch of dirt ahead of him. He saw mice scamper. Once an owl flashed by his head, startling him.

Wilf headed through the darkness in the direction of the beach. Soon he realized that something, or someone, followed him. A foot scrunched on dry earth. Wilf knew only too well that people had been murdered on the island. He walked faster. Behind him, there was a rustle of bushes. Whoever followed him now walked faster. Wilf began to run. Footsteps thudded behind him, becoming quicker and quicker. Wilf raced along the path; however, he couldn't see in the dark. A twig caught his cap and flicked it off his head. He didn't pause. He ran faster. The next second, the toe of his boot caught a fallen branch and he fell forward, sprawling.

He glanced back. And there, passing through a beam of moonlight, was a hooded figure with eyes that burned at him. The face was covered with a white cloth. When he saw the figure raise its arms he realized that it had no hands. Instead, metal hooks protruded from the sleeves – the hooks were sharp. Murderously sharp.

Wilf scrambled to his feet and pelted along the path towards an iron gate. Beyond the gate lay the beach. He seized the gate in order to swing it open. The instant he touched the iron bars there was a blue flash. Sparks. A loud crackling sound. Pain flashed along his arm. Wilf screamed. The next thing he knew he was falling backwards … after that, he knew nothing. Nothing at all.

A youth of around sixteen years of age usually brought containers of hot porridge to the cottages. This morning he didn't arrive at all. Thomas Lloyd stepped out into the garden. Birds sang in the trees. Clouds floated across a deep blue sky. He reached the end of the garden path, and all the while his empty stomach told him it was breakfast time. What had happened to the boy who delivered the porridge and fresh milk?

Just then, William Feasby hurried along the lane. His eyes were bright with tears. The little man, who was over eighty years of age, moved with astonishing speed.

'Mr Feasby,' Thomas called out, "is anything wrong?'

'Oh, Mr Lloyd. Dreadful news! The boy who does the boots.

Young Wilf Emsall. I found him lying out in the wood last night. Quite still. Eyes closed. Oh my ...' He hurried along the path to his own cottage. 'It's murder. I'm sure it is.'

'Wilf has been killed?'

'I found him. I'd been out counting foxes and badgers – plotting their nightly toing and froing. I tripped over Wilf's body.'

'Mr Feasby, Inspector Abberline will need to hear about this.'

'Oh, another murder, Mr Lloyd. It has brought back what happened to my own dear brother. I am most upset.'

'I'll fetch the inspector.'

'No, sir. I cannot be interviewed. I'm much too distressed.'

Tears were pouring down William's face. He threw open the door to his cottage before vanishing inside. Thomas rushed back indoors to find Abberline lacing up his shoes – the very shoes that Wilf had polished yesterday.

Thomas heard the tremor in his own voice as he said, 'Inspector, Wilf has been murdered.'

Thomas Lloyd and Inspector Abberline hurried in the direction of the palace. Barely five minutes had passed since Thomas had heard the news of another death from William Feasby. Abberline decided that rather than trouble the distressed man now he should visit the king and discover what had happened from him instead.

Thomas saw Ludwig standing at the door of a cottage in the palace yard. The man rubbed his forehead as he stared at the ground, clearly deeply worried.

Abberline approached him. 'Sir. I've just heard that there has been another murder.'

'Wilf,' Thomas added, his heart pounding as the horror took hold.

Ludwig took a moment to emerge from what seemed nothing less than a prison of his own anxiety. 'Oh? Mr Feasby told you?'

'Yes, he said he found the body last night.'

'Wilf is in the cottage.'

Abberline said, 'I must examine the body immediately.'

Then Ludwig did the strangest thing. He smiled. 'Examine the body? You may do more than that, Inspector. By all means, go talk to him. He's eating his breakfast.'

'Mr Feasby said that Wilf was dead.'

'So we all believed. We brought the boy back here and laid him out on a bench in the barn. After that, Mr Feasby rushed off in a state of distress. He'd no sooner gone than Wilf gave a loud shout and sat up.'

'Thanks goodness!' Thomas sighed with relief. 'The thought of a child being murdered ... '

Abberline frowned. 'Do you know what happened to the boy?'

'Fainted. That's my guess.' Ludwig shrugged as if the subject had already become irrelevant. 'Boys sometimes faint,' he added vaguely. 'They outgrow their strength. Now, if you'll excuse me, I have letters to write. I'm striving to persuade Britain's universities to recognize my academy. Unfortunately, they regard us as mere hobby artists and dabblers in science.' He shook his head. 'Please do call on Wilf. I'm sure he'll be excited to receive visitors.' King Ludwig swept back across the yard.

Thomas glared at the man as he vanished into the palace. 'He was worried about his academy, not about the boy's health.'

'I don't see there's any harm in wishing the lad a speedy recovery.' Abberline walked towards the cottage.

'You think that Wilf might have been poisoned, like Mrs Giddings?'

'It would be a breach of my professional duty if I didn't check on him.'

Abberline knocked.

A voice rang out from inside: 'Why don't you come in? Stop knuckling the bloody wood!'

Abberline entered the cottage. Thomas followed. Wilf sat at the kitchen table, spooning in great mouthfuls of porridge. Milk dripped down his chin. When he saw who it was he jumped up, startled.

'I'm sorry, Mr Abberline. I swore because I thought you were Bertie tapping on the door to annoy me.'

'Why would Bertie do that?'

'He keeps pretending to be the Grim Reaper, sir.'

'That's a cruel joke of Bertie's, especially after what happened to you last night.'

'He pretends to be the Grim Reaper, coming to throw me into the fires of hell.' Wilf shrugged. 'Bertie's only ten. I'm thirteen so I should be able to bear his ribbing.'

'That's very adult of you,' Thomas said. 'How are you feeling?'

'A bit shaky in my legs and arms. You might say that I'm ...' He tried hard to find the right word. 'Tremulous.'

Abberline gestured for Wilf to sit down. 'Don't let your breakfast get cold.'

Wilf was soon spooning the porridge into his mouth again. Thomas realized that if his appetite was that good then it was unlikely he'd been poisoned.

Inspector Abberline smiled. 'Can you remember what happened?'

'Yes, sir. Well, some of it.' He used a sleeve to wipe milk from his chin. 'I was going to the beach to check my fishhooks. I thought I heard feet behind me, chasing me. So I ran.'

'Did you see who chased you?'

'A monk. The ghost of a monk! He had his hood up. I saw big, staring eyes. And I knew the ghost wanted to kill me.' He paused, frowning. 'Though I think the monk must've been in a dream I had after I fell down.'

'Did the monk hit you?'

'No, sir.'

'Did you feel poorly or sick before you fell?'

'I was all right. Never better.'

'Do you know why you fell?'

Wilf gazed into space, trying to remember. 'I reached the gate at the end of the path, just before the beach. I tried to open the gate. Then I started hurting. I fell onto the ground and that's all I can say. When I woke up I found myself in the barn.'

'How did you feel?'

'Shaky. And tremulous … very tremulous. My tongue was sore because I'd bitten it. Look.' He opened his mouth. Somewhere amid smears of milk and oatmeal a cut in the tongue could be made out.

Abberline stepped closer. 'Do you mind if I take a closer look at you?'

'Look as much as you want, sir. You know, your shoes could do with a polish.'

'Call round later, Wilf. You can do Mr Lloyd's boots at the same time. Now, tilt your head forward. Thank you. Would you pull back your sleeves, so I can see your arms? Thank you.'

'I feel all right now, sir.'

'I'm glad to hear it, Wilf. People were worried about you. How did you come to burn your fingers?'

Wilf stared at the small blisters at the ends of his fingers in surprise. 'I don't know. I can't remember getting them burnt.'

A loud knock sounded on the door. Following that, a voice boomed: 'Wilf … Wilf Emsall. I'm here to take you to hell.'

Abberline opened the door to reveal a tiny boy in a brown jacket. 'You'll be Bertie. Or should that be the Grim Reaper?'

The boy's mouth dropped open in surprise.

'Don't be harsh with him, Mr Abberline,' said Wilf. 'He's only ten.'

'I'm sure I played tricks like that on my friends when I was ten.' Abberline smiled. 'Off you go, Bertie.' The boy fled. 'Wilf, try and rest. We'll let Mr Feasby know that you're alive and well.'

'Mr Feasby was very upset,' Thomas told him. 'He really did think you were, well …' That was a sentence that didn't need completing.

'Thank you, sirs. It was nice that you came to see me.'

'Oh.' Abberline paused in the doorway. 'Will you tell us where we can find the gate where you fell?'

They walked along the path until they reached the iron gate.

Thomas said, 'Inspector, you don't think that Wilf simply fainted, do you?'

'He may have done. I'd like to take a closer look where he passed out.'

'And he mentioned a monk that pursued him.'

'Which he then dismissed as something from a dream.' Abberline tapped the gate's bars. They gave a metallic ring.

Thomas examined the ground. 'There is nothing I can see. The ground's dry. There aren't even any footprints. Nothing but grass and leaves.'

Abberline walked along the fence. Occasionally, he stooped down in order to brush stalks of grass with his fingers. At a distance of perhaps ten feet from the gate he picked up a stick, prodded an area of grass then sniffed the end of the stick.

Abberline beckoned Thomas. 'What do you smell?' He offered Thomas the stick.

Thomas flinched. His eyes prickled. 'Some chemical … acid?'

'I think so, too. See the mark in the grass? Probably an acid burn.'

'You believe that Wilf was attacked in some way?'

'Yes, and left for dead. Fortunately, the murderer made a mistake this time.'

'Ah … Wilf had burn-marks on his fingertips. Those were caused by acid?'

'No.'

'Oh?'

'Something else entirely.'

Thomas scratched his head. 'But you think the killer of Feasby and the two sisters somehow forced Wilf to swallow acid?'

Abberline shook his head. 'Look at what's here, Thomas. An acid burn in the grass. Grass stalks have been broken alongside the fence. Now examine the gate.'

'It's an iron gate. An old one, covered by rust.'

Abberline shook his head again. 'Look closer. Examine specific details – don't just gaze at the gate in its entirety.'

Thomas focused his eyes on the ironwork that comprised the gate. Most of the iron was covered by orange rust. However, he noticed three places where the metal shone bright silver.

Thomas glanced up at Abberline, wondering if this is what he'd seen. 'The metal has had the rust filed away in three places. Here on the top bar of the gate near the hinge. Then here, where people grasp the gate to open it, and again there on the edge of the gate.'

Abberline nodded. 'So you see what happened to Wilf last night?'

This time Thomas shook his head. 'No, not for the life of me.'

'Someone set an electric battery down there on the grass ten feet from the gate. A few drops of acid spilt out, burning the grass. Wires were then run along the side of the fence. The killer pushed the wires down into the grass so they'd be out of sight.'

'Breaking grass stalks in the process.'

'For electricity to pass from the wire to a metal surface it should be clean and free of rust. That's why the killer took a file and scraped away the rust down to bare metal. The wires were attached at both sides of the gate.'

'And when Wilf put his hand on this bar to open the gate, the electricity leapt through his fingers, burning the skin.'

'The killer perhaps underestimated the amount of electrical force needed to end a life. The battery was too weak.'

'But it still knocked the boy out.'

'Yes.'

'Mr Feasby thought Wilf was dead, so whoever electrified the gate might have made the same assumption. The killer quickly checked the body then made off.' Thomas stared at the gleaming patches of metal that had conducted the electrical current. 'Although, we should say would-be killer rather than killer. After all, they did not succeed. Thank heaven.'

'I'll use the word killer, Thomas. I strongly suspect that the individual who shot Benedict Feasby and who killed Mrs Giddings and her sister was responsible for this, too.'

'So ... the killer has tried to murder a boy with an electric shock.'

'And so continues a pattern of attacking victims in such an unusual way that it's guaranteed to attract the attention of the newspapers.'

'A killer who's a showman? An extrovert? Is that likely?'

'It is, if he or she wants either notoriety for themselves, or to make this island famous.'

'Why?'

Abberline shook his head. 'I can't say.'

'Ludwig should be informed that an attempt was made to kill one of his staff last night.'

'I agree, Thomas. The local police are still on the island. I'll let them know what happened to Wilf. Would you call on Ludwig?'

'By all means.'

'Ask him to have his footmen tell everyone that they should not go out alone, either during the day or at night. People should travel in pairs at the very least.'

'You believe the killer is still on the island?'

'They might even be stood behind a tree listening to us. We must consider everyone on Faxfleet to be a potential murderer. And everyone is a potential victim, too.'

'The murderer's going to strike again soon, aren't they?'

'Yes. They have a mission to kill. And to kill in a bizarre and outlandish way. They are hell-bent on making the world pay attention to this place.'

Thomas started to walk in the direction of the palace.

Abberline softly called after him. 'Take care, Thomas. Keep your wits about you. We have become prey.'

Life went on. The River Humber lapped the little island, shrinking it day by day. The sun warmed its green forest. The man in the lane copied birdsong on his violin. Professor Giddings worked on an essay, reading it aloud in grave, booming tones that stated the importance of the continued existence of the British Empire. Jo galloped by on her horse in a hurry. Her eyes were flashing diamonds. Mr Benedict Feasby sat cross-legged on the lawn outside his cottage. He plucked feathers from a dead peacock. He repeated 'Life goes on' softly to himself over and over. Inspector Abberline fiddled with the garden gate. He opened it, shut it. Slapped his hand down on its top rail. Scotland Yard's most famous detective was deep in thought. King Ludwig's gardeners went from cottage to cottage with a wheelbarrow full of bolts, which they fitted to doors. As they worked, they sang a music hall song that seemed to involve a bizarre procession of men visiting Mrs Shaddock in Shadder Alley. The gardeners' smiles grew wider as the rhymes got ruder. Inspector Abberline closed his eyes. He stepped smartly forward to the gate and slapped a hand down upon it.

Thomas sat on the garden bench. He was busy writing about the murders here for his newspaper. However, he suspected that the slaying of Mrs Verity in London would mean that his own story would be tucked away in the middle pages. People wanted to read about the return of Jack the Ripper. Thomas's story would be overlooked. Thomas glanced up as Abberline tried to open the gate as quickly as he could.

Thomas aired a thought that preoccupied him. 'The killer here on Faxfleet will be in competition with Jack the Ripper for newspaper coverage. The killer will have to devise a spectacular way to despatch his next victim or he'll be ignored by the public.'

In a dreamy way, Abberline nodded. 'Hmm, I expect so.'

Abberline fiddled with the gate. Jo galloped back along the lane. The violinist imitated the screech of a crow. Mr Feasby stuck peacock feathers into the eye-sockets of a large fish.

Thomas gripped his pencil and wrote in large letters across a sheet of paper:

> THE POPULATION OF FAXFLEET IS INSANE AND MADNESS IS CONTAGIOUS.

Thomas sighed. 'Inspector? Does the gate bother you in some way?'

'Ah, Thomas. Would you help me with an experiment?'

'Gladly.' Thomas walked along the path to the gate.

Abberline stood back. 'Would you open it?'

Thomas opened it.

'Stop,' Abberline said. 'Freeze exactly where you are.'

Thomas stood there with his hand on the part-open gate. 'All this about the gate has something to do with what happened to Wilf last night, hasn't it?'

Abberline raised his eyebrows in surprise. 'Of course. What do you think I've been doing with this gate for the last ten minutes? No! Don't move. Keep your hand on the gate.'

'Like this?'

'Yes. Just stay as you were when you opened the gate. Now ... when you pulled open the gate, what part of your hand touched it first?'

'The palm. Then I hooked my fingers round this section at the top in order to pull it open.'

'Wilf would have needed to pull open the gate last night. From his side of the path it must be pulled open, not pushed.'

'Yes, I think so.'

'Trust me, Thomas, I remember which way that particular gate opened.'

'We already know that the boy opened the gate and suffered an electric shock.'

'But something isn't right. If he opened the gate like you just have, the burns caused by the electricity would have been on the palm of his hand. Wilf's burns were on his fingertips.'

'The position of the burns must have occurred by sheer chance.'

'No, Thomas.' Abberline gave a knowing smile. 'That won't do. Wilf approached the gate in the dark. He couldn't see it clearly. Even so, he must have walked along that path hundreds of times before. No. Wilf was running in utter panic. He wildly snatched at the gate to open it. He was in such a hurry he misjudged the distance. His fingertips came down like this on the iron gate.' Abberline slapped his hand down in such a way that only the ends of his fingers made contact with the gate. 'That's why his fingertips are blistered.'

'Then he was running from someone.'

'It seems so.'

Thomas thought back to what Wilf had told them that morning. 'The boy said that after he passed out he dreamt that the ghost of a monk had chased him.'

'I doubt if it was a dream, after all. The boy was running for his life. Although he wasn't being pursued by a ghost. No ... it was flesh and blood. He was being chased by the killer.'

The post arrived, delivered by Wilf of all people. He declared he was well and asked if he could clean Thomas's boots. Thomas agreed.

Mrs Abberline had sent a letter to her husband. He took it inside to read. Thomas received a package from Mrs Cherryhome, his landlady. It contained a slab of fruit cake and kippers. No doubt Mrs Cherryhome thought that Yorkshire food wouldn't be enough to sustain her tenant. Although it was likely the fish that would become the smoked kippers had been caught by Yorkshire fishermen anyway, and might have arrived through the port of Hull just downstream from here. Thomas cut slices of cake for Wilf and Abberline and himself. Wilf happily munched the cake as he vigorously buffed the boot leather.

Shortly after Wilf left, and Thomas had laced up his now gleaming boots, King Ludwig arrived with his two sons – the eldest son was strong and suntanned, the youngest had a much slighter build and paler skin. The eldest son, Richard, shouldered an old-fashioned musket rifle. The youngest, Tristan, carried a wad of envelopes. Ludwig explained that they were delivering invitations to academy members to meet with Ludwig at a given time in order to deliver a summary of their year's work on the island. This would help determine whether the individual would continue as an academy member, or receive the disappointing news that they must leave.

Ludwig approached Abberline, who'd come to the cottage door. 'Inspector, I hear that the boy's injury last night was caused by an electrical discharge.'

Abberline told him that someone had gone to considerable trouble to prepare the gate. That rust had been scraped off in order to ensure a clean contact between the metal bars and the victim's skin – this was essential in order to deliver an electric shock to the human body.

King Ludwig frowned. 'How could the boy suffer an injury caused by electricity? There is no electrical generator on the island.'

Abberline said, 'The electricity must have come from what might be called a chemical cell or battery. Isn't that so, Thomas?'

Thomas nodded. 'It is possible to make a battery, using bars of metal immersed in a glass or ceramic jar filled with acid.'

'And that creates electricity?' Ludwig sounded surprised. Clearly, he didn't have much knowledge of electrical science.

'The jar must have been a large one,' Abberline added. 'At least a gallon in volume. Whoever built the battery is intelligent. Yet I don't believe they have specialized engineering knowledge, because the battery didn't generate a powerful enough charge to kill a human being.'

'Thank the Lord for that,' Ludwig declared with feeling. He turned to his sons, who stood patiently next to him. 'Richard, you best go deal with the rats. Tristan, would you post the letters?'

Richard sauntered away with the gun over his shoulder. Meanwhile, Tristan left the garden and walked up the lane, delivering envelopes to the cottages as he went. No doubt academy members would feel a pang of anxiety when they saw what those envelopes contained. They'd know the time was coming when they would be judged.

'There's an old mill on the beach,' Ludwig explained, nodding in the direction of his eldest son as he disappeared into the forest. 'That's where Richard is heading. The place is infested with rats. I'm not concerned about the mill itself as it's no longer in use, but rats are using it as their barracks, shall we say? They come out at night and raid your neighbours' pantries.'

'That old blunderbuss is quite formidable,' Abberline told him.

'It is indeed. Richard doesn't even need to load the gun with shot. He merely packs the barrel with powder and discharges it point-blank into the rat holes. Blows the filthy little beasts to kingdom come.'

Abberline watched the gardeners move to the next cottage with the wheelbarrow. 'They'll soon have the door bolts fitted. Your tenants will feel a lot safer.'

'I do hope so, Inspector. By the by, have you talked to the police here on the island?'

'I have, sir. All but three constables will be returning to Hull on the evening ferry.'

'That's a pity. We need men here to deter the swine that's been killing my people.'

'Two more detectives will be arriving from Scotland Yard tomorrow.'

'Of course, I will use my own staff to patrol the island. They'll be armed with shotguns. We might bag the killer ourselves.'

'Meanwhile, Thomas and I will continue our investigation.'

The king sighed. 'I hope one of us catches the devil. I find it hard to stomach that someone would try and electrocute a child. After all, why target a boy who cleans boots?'

'I suspect the killer isn't targeting anyone in particular.'

'Oh?'

'The victim's identity isn't important. The killer's intention is to take lives in a distinctive and unusual way.'

'The man must be insane.'

'That's possible. Which means it will be more difficult to discover their motive. After all, a lunatic might be driven to take a life because the sky is too blue, water too wet, or his mule told him to.'

'Indeed. Who can say what's in a madman's mind?' Ludwig looked as if he had the troubles of the world on his shoulders. 'I'll say good day, gentlemen.'

Ludwig walked back along the lane, his head down, hands clasped behind his back.

Thomas said, 'I didn't realize we'd be joined by your colleagues?'

'The island is too big for the pair of us to cover, Thomas. I've called on some good men, with solid years of experience. They will stay in the next cottage to ours.'

Abberline collected a paper and pen from the house and sat on the garden bench to pen a reply to his wife. The musician leaned against a tree trunk on the other side of the lane to play the violin. Mr Feasby had finished implanting peacock feathers into the eye-sockets of the fish. Thomas supposed that the feathery fish would join the man's bizarre menagerie. Mr Feasby carried the wolf outdoors – the singular creature with the eagle wings and human-like eyes. He set it down on the ground and appeared to begin kissing its back. A moment later, Thomas realized that the man must have been blowing dust from its fur.

A tall man in a straw hat walked past the musician. The tall man carried the boxy shape of a camera under one arm. He called out to the musician, 'Kolbaire! I say, Kolbaire, haven't you done choking that cat yet? It's making a devil of a screech.'

Kolbaire turned furiously on the man. 'Have you done taking photographs of angels?'

Both paused for a moment to glare at each other with nothing less than murderous fury. After that, both men went their separate ways.

Thomas shook his head before saying to Abberline, 'We've been asking ourselves who would kill the academy members? The real question should be which one in the academy would *not* want to kill their fellow members? It strikes me most hate each other with a passion. Come to that, nearly all of them are in ... in the foothills of insanity – if not actually on the mountain of madness.'

'Foothills of insanity? Mountain of madness? That's a quirky choice of words, Thomas.'

'There must be lunacy in the air.' Thomas shook his head. 'I think I'm catching it, too.'

'You must be missing life in the city.'

No, Thomas thought, *I'm missing Emma.* Her absence in Ceylon was becoming even harder to bear. They should arrange a date for the wedding. Engrave that date in stone, if need be. And yet, lately, he found himself thinking about Jo. The remarkable woman fascinated him. When he was in her company he seemed to wear a permanent smile on his face. A happy smile. Thomas tried not to put a certain powerful feeling into words. He tried, but failed. *I'm approaching a crossroads in my life,* he told himself. *I'm going to make a decision soon that will change everything.*

The notion that destiny might be involved in his growing friendship with Jo seemed to be reinforced when he decided to take a walk along the shore. Jo sat on a fallen tree trunk near the water's edge. Perhaps fifty yards from her stood the derelict water mill. This must be the building that the king's son, Richard, had gone to, for Thomas heard the loud bang of a gun.

Jo sat there in her leather kilt, pantaloons, and a black jacket profusely embroidered with scarlet thread. She read pages bound in a file with stiff covers.

He lifted his hat. 'Good afternoon. I won't disturb your work.'

'Oh, this? I'm just checking my report. I have to submit it to Ludwig at dinner this evening. We all do.'

'It must feel like being back at school again.'

She laughed. 'It does, Thomas, and I have done my homework.' She cheerfully brandished the file above her head. 'Twenty pages of my best handwriting, ten pages of diagrams, five pages of supplemental notes and appendices.'

'Then I won't distract you.'

'Dear Thomas, I do so like being distracted by you. Here.' She patted the log beside her. 'Won't you keep me company for a while?'

'Your work? It must be important.'

'It is, it is! You are important, too.' She smiled. 'Besides, I have re-written this document again and again! It shines with perfection. I can do nothing more to improve it.'

Thomas sat beside her. 'Do you think Ludwig will grant you another year on the island?'

'I hope so. Twelve more months here and I'll have gathered enough material to make a presentation to the government.'

'Oh? The phrenology?'

'Don't look at me like that, Thomas.' She spoke warmly despite pretending to be stern with him. 'I know that many dismiss phrenology as a crackpot science. I beg to differ.' She gazed out across the river as a paddle-steamer puffed its way eastward. 'We live in a new world where people like your friend Inspector Abberline must protect society from an entire plague of criminality, otherwise civilization will collapse into chaos. People will be slaughtered in their beds.'

'Police work is demanding, but improvements are being made in detection methods.'

'Yes, but imagine if I could do this.' She reached up and ran her fingers across his forehead. 'Imagine if we could discover whether a person has criminal tendencies just by examining the shape of their skull.'

'You can do that?'

'Don't sound so doubtful, Doubting Thomas.' She laughed. 'I have studied the craniums of hundreds of individuals. I can tell who is predisposed to art, or philosophy, or who will be humane by the bumps, dips and ridges in that bone that encloses the human brain. I can even identify if an individual is likely to become a thief or a murderer.'

'But how do you know that someone will steal or kill before they actually do it?'

'That is the essence of phrenology. It is the science of prediction. Policemen, like Abberline, can use those techniques to discover who is likely to become a criminal.'

Thomas had always enjoyed the woman's company. But now he found her words disturbing. And not just the words. Her ironclad certainty bothered him, too. 'Jo, it seems to me that you're saying that men and women, whom you identify as potential criminals, should be imprisoned before they do anything wrong.'

'That need not happen. Such individuals would be told that they have criminal instincts. Even though their actual nature cannot be changed they could be educated to resist the urge to do wrong. Also, criminal behaviour is very often passed down the bloodline to children.'

Thomas found Jo's philosophy extremely unsettling. With a shudder of distaste, he said, 'So the children of *potential*, not actual, criminals would be treated differently to other children? They'd be sent to special establishments to have discipline instilled in them?'

'That problem wouldn't arise. Men and women who exhibit the skull shape of criminals would be forbidden from having children.'

'My God ...'

'We can no longer produce children in the old ways of our ancestors. We should eliminate chaotic procreation that produces a criminal sub-species.'

'I must say that your ideas overwhelm me.'

'We live in testing times that will demand powerful remedies if society is to prosper.'

'Jo, how on earth do you prevent human beings from producing families? Are you suggesting that you put policemen in their bedrooms?'

A loud bang sounded from the direction of the mill. Richard was clearly determined to despatch as many rats as possible with that musket of his.

Jo's voice was quite gentle. 'Dear Thomas, you are a compassionate man. I like that quality in you. But see what Richard is doing. He's destroying infant rats in their nests. If he did not do that the vermin would breed until there were so many they would overrun the island. They would attack us the moment we stepped out of our homes.'

'Human beings aren't rats. What did you find when you examined Wilf Emsall's skull? Did you discover that he's a criminal in the making? Will he grow up to steal and cut throats?'

'I've made you angry, Thomas.' Her eyes glistened with tears. 'You are so angry you want to strike me down.'

'No, I wouldn't hit you.'

She reached out for his head again. This time she pulled his face to hers and crushed her lips against his.

Chapter 10

TWO O'CLOCK IN the morning – that's when all hell broke loose. Thomas awoke hearing screams. It sounded like a woman shrieking.

'Jo!' he gasped.

He scrambled out of bed to tug on his trousers and boots. By the time he'd rushed from the bedroom he saw that Abberline had already reached the front door and was pulling back the shiny new bolt that had been fitted yesterday. Thomas noted that Abberline was already dressed. *He's sleeping in his clothes,* Thomas thought. *He's expecting another murder.*

Thomas rushed out of the cottage. 'Jo! Where are you?'

A breeze whipped the trees. Leaves streamed into his face. From neighbouring cottages people emerged, holding lanterns. They wore dressing gowns over their nightclothes. Their faces were tight, pale masks of worry.

William Feasby battled against the gales blowing in from the river. 'What is happening?' he cried. 'Is it murder?'

Abberline had managed to light a lantern. He followed Thomas down the path to the lane. Meanwhile, the high-sounding shrieks grew louder.

'Jo!' He ran against the winds that gusted into his face. 'Jo!'

The screams came from ahead of him. But when he heard a female voice call out, 'Thomas!', it came from behind. He turned to see Jo stepping out from her garden into the lane. She held a white kimono around her, the breeze rippling the silk.

Thomas stopped running. 'Jo? Are you all right?'

A piercing scream penetrated his skull. He spun around to see a thin man hurtling towards him. The man held one hand above his head. His eyes bulged in terror. This was the musician, Virgil

Kolbaire. He was still clad in the black evening suit he'd worn for dinner in the palace refectory. The white shirt was now smeared with red marks.

'Mr Kolbaire,' was all Thomas managed to say before the man struck him in the face.

To Thomas's surprise the blow was wet. The man's hand was sopping. Thomas felt the wetness on his left cheek where the blow had landed. Kolbaire howled like a madman. His eyes blazed as they fixed on Thomas's face. The man attempted to strike Thomas again. This time Thomas caught the man's wrist. The hand was just inches from his eyes. Then Abberline darted forward to catch hold of Kolbaire's arm, as well as holding the lantern up to illuminate the scene.

Thomas's gaze locked onto Kolbaire's hand. The first two fingers were gone. Blood streamed from raw amputation wounds.

Kolbaire screamed, 'The devil took them! He doesn't want me to play!'

With a howl of sorrow Kolbaire broke free of both Thomas and Abberline. Thereafter, he fled down the lane. Thomas followed. Within moments, he was pursuing the wounded man along the beach. Gusts of wind blasted the pair. The river had turned white, huge waves raced in to break on the shore. Kolbaire hurtled into the water, shrieking all the time. Thomas realized that Kolbaire was now in danger of drowning, so he waded in after the musician, and managed to grab the man by his jacket.

Kolbaire fought back, trying to punch Thomas with his intact hand, as well as the ruined fist of the other. Although it was almost too dark to see Kolbaire, other than his stark, white face, Thomas succeeded in seizing the screaming man and hauling him back to the shore.

Inspector Abberline arrived, carrying the lamp. There were others there, too, including Jo.

Kolbaire no longer fought. He clung to Thomas like a frightened child. Sobs convulsed him as he cried, 'It's finished ... I am done. I am no more.'

The force of the winds became even more formidable as it grew light the next day. Mr Virgil Kolbaire lay on a sofa in Samarkand Cottage. He was deeply unconscious. Jo had stitched together the open holes where the fingers had once been. She'd then tightly bandaged his hand, using wads of cotton, so the end of his right arm had become bulbous. Thankfully, her medical skills had stopped the bleeding, and no blood leaked through the white bandage.

King Ludwig called early that morning to check on Kolbaire.

Ludwig asked briskly, 'Is his life in danger?'

Abberline shook his head. 'I'm sure he will recover, providing there is no infection.'

Thomas added, 'We should take him to the infirmary in Hull as quickly as possible. A doctor should inspect the wounds.'

'Nothing can be done yet, I'm afraid. The ferry won't run in weather like this.'

'In that case, we'll do our best to take care of him until he can be taken to the mainland.'

'Is it true?' asked the king. 'His fingers were cut off?'

'Yes.'

Ludwig flinched, looking sickened. 'This must be the work of the killer.'

Abberline nodded. 'I have every reason to believe it is.'

'He must still be on the island, then. Boats can't make the crossing when the water is so rough. We have the devil trapped here, Abberline. I'll get my men out and we'll search until we've caught him.'

'Sir –' began Abberline.

'I'll put a bullet between his eyes if I have to.'

Even though Abberline tried to speak with Ludwig, he rushed out of the cottage, jumped onto his horse, and rode away.

'If the killer hasn't left the island,' Thomas said, 'then there's every chance he'll be caught.'

'He? The killer might be a woman. Or there may be a gang of murderers. What worries me is if Ludwig sends out hotheads there's every chance they'll shoot an entirely innocent islander.'

Kolbaire grunted in his sleep. Abberline pulled back the man's eyelid to examine his eyeball. After that, he slid back the man's sleeves to look at both arms.

Thomas asked, 'Have you seen something?'

'The man's pupils have shrunk to tiny dots. He's been drugged. There are no injection marks that I can make out.'

'The killer must have introduced the drug to his food, just as they slipped poison into the meal that poisoned one of the women in the Giddings' household.'

'It's entirely possible.'

'Is the killer changing their aims? The last two attacks resulted in injury, not death.'

'Remember what you told me,' Abberline said. 'The killer must compete with news that Jack the Ripper might be back in Whitechapel. It will take a very dramatic story to divert the public's attention from Jack.'

'There are still three constables on the island. They could mount patrols.'

'They are just three men, Thomas. They can't guard everyone. The cottages are spread out through a mile or so of forest. And then there's the king's palace at one end of the island and the fishing village at the other.'

'Perhaps the academy members could be housed in the palace for the time being?'

'And leave the fishermen and their families to guard themselves? Tut tut, Thomas. I wouldn't have thought you, of all people, would deprive the working class of police protection.'

Thomas felt his face burn. He realized his suggestion had been a careless, slipshod one.

Abberline continued in that mild, understated way of his: 'Kolbaire is still fast asleep. At least the drug is keeping him unconscious. When he wakes, however, the pain in his hand will be hard to bear.'

'Someone nearby might have laudanum.'

'Perhaps you would ask our neighbours if they have some?'

'Of course. I think most of them are awake.'

'Would you ask, also, for brandy? Well, any spirit will do. See if you can get at least half a pint.'

'I think laudanum would work best to kill the pain.'

'No, Mr Kolbaire's fingers ... they must be somewhere nearby.'

Inspector Abberline told Thomas that now it was daylight they should search Kolbaire's home. Thomas had returned with a bottle of laudanum. He also had half a pint of gin in a stoneware jug. Abberline transferred the gin to a clean glass jar with a cork lid. He took this with him to Kolbaire's cottage just along the lane. Immediately, they found drops of blood on the path that led to the front door. The blood trail continued into the kitchen that also served as a living room. Abberline nodded at the sofa where a pillow still lay at one end with a dip in the middle that had been formed by someone resting their head upon it.

Abberline said, 'We both saw Kolbaire at dinner last night. Did he appear as if he was intoxicated?'

'Not excessively. I noticed he did sway a little when he walked.'

'It looks as if he returned home and decided to sleep on the sofa. Perhaps he thought he might be ill in the night and wanted to be near the sink.'

Thomas looked around the room. It was extremely tidy. A neat stack of sheet music stood on a low table. On a shelf was a violin case. Kolbaire was scrupulous in keeping a well-ordered house.

Thomas checked the floor around the sofa. 'There's no blood here. So where was he attacked?'

Abberline went to a sash window. He raised the heavy frame containing the glass and looked out. 'Here,' is all he said before walking outside.

Thomas followed him around the cottage until they reached the other side of the window. Blood smeared the window ledge. More red splashes adorned the outer wall and the soil beneath the window itself.

'Ah.' Inspector Abberline removed the jar, containing the gin, from his pocket. Crouching down, he picked up a red object. 'The middle finger.' He dropped the severed digit into the gin. The hitherto clear liquid turned a cloudy pink. 'And the first finger.' He added the other digit to the spirit.

Standing up, he pressed the cork top back onto the jar. Thomas tried not to look at the pair of objects floating in the gin.

Inspector Abberline took a deep breath. 'Cleanly severed. Perhaps an axe, machete or cutlass. The kind of blade that would cut two fingers clean off in one forceful swipe.'

Thomas swallowed. 'The man plays the violin as well. Or, rather, he once did.'

'Tell me what you think happened. We'll see if our theories match.'

'Mr Kolbaire ate dinner in the palace refectory last night. We were there with the other academy members. Kolbaire left early. He came back here where he lives alone. He ate or drank something that contained a narcotic. He was under its influence when he opened the sash window and looked out. Either something had attracted his attention or he needed fresh air. He leaned forward with his hands out on the ledge like so.' Thomas extended his arms, hands out, palms down. 'The attacker waited nearby, seized their opportunity, and brought an axe or sword or something of the like down hard. The blade cut through the fingers as they rested on the window ledge.' He swallowed hard. 'I suppose it was like hacking meat on a chopping board.'

Abberline examined the window ledge. 'Even though it's partly covered by blood, you can see a fresh cut mark in the wood. The blade went right through flesh and bone before cutting into the ledge itself.'

They returned to their own cottage where, after a while, Kolbaire began to come round. The man shouted loudly when he moved his hand. Abberline poured out a glass of laudanum, yet he asked the injured musician some questions before allowing him to drink the potion that contained opium and wine, for that would quickly render him insensible again. Kolbaire revealed that he'd begun to feel unwell during dinner and had returned home early. He'd lain down on the sofa and fell asleep. He woke up in the dark and needed fresh air because his head was spinning so much. He opened the window and leaned out, resting his hands on the ledge as he did so. That's when he felt a blow to his right hand. He hadn't realized what he'd suffered immediately. He'd closed the window and tottered back towards the sofa. That's when he glanced at his hand. Blood poured from open wounds, and two of his fingers were gone.

'I ran out of the house,' he told them. 'Everything became strange. I couldn't feel any pain. It was as if I'd drunk a bottle of whisky all to myself. Then I don't recall anything else until I woke up here.' His eyes rolled and he wore an expression of anxiety. 'Am I finished, sirs? Will I be able to play my music?' He winced and clenched his undamaged fist. The pain was making itself felt more strongly than ever.

'Here,' said Abberline gently. 'Drink this.'

The man eagerly downed the laudanum in one gulp. He sighed with relief. Soon he was fast asleep again.

A knock sounded on the door. Thomas opened it to reveal Professor Giddings, who stared at the sleeping man on the sofa. Giddings looked so unhappy that he seemed close to tears.

'Inspector Abberline.' He whispered the words. 'I'm here to make a confession. It is all my fault. I am responsible for that man's injury.'

No one spoke after Professor Giddings' stark confession. The white-bearded man remained in the cottage doorway, staring at Kolbaire, who lay sleeping on the sofa. A tiny spot of red had formed on the white bandage around his hand. Giddings then turned his attention to the glass jar that contained a pair of fingers, floating in the pink liquid. Abberline picked up the jar and placed it in a wall cupboard.

At last Abberline did speak. 'Professor Giddings. Tell me everything.'

'Yes, Inspector.' He stepped into the kitchen. 'Kolbaire ... that imbecile ... he infuriated my wife so much that just the sight of him would put her in a bad mood for the rest of the day. She said he was a crook, and couldn't play the violin any better than a monkey could.'

'Go on,' Abberline prompted when Giddings stopped.

'Kolbaire tortured me with that violin of his. He stood in the lane, scraping the strings, making it screech. I will not call it music – I will not. My wife and her sister lay dead in a mortuary, and he continued making ridiculous noises with that instrument of his. It just seemed so unfair, Inspector.' He inhaled deeply. 'When I was in Malaysia I obtained a quantity of drugs used by witchdoctors there. I brought them home as part of a collection of objects from the Orient. Well ... I decided to add a quantity of narcotic powder to Kolbaire's wine last night at dinner. I hoped it would trigger bizarre behaviour. If he caused an unpleasant scene then I reasoned that the king might demand that he leave the island.'

'You put the drug into his wine glass?'

'Yes.'

'That is a crime in its own right,' Thomas said.

'I know. But I hated the man so much. I wanted rid of him.'

Abberline spoke sternly. 'Then you followed him home and cut off his fingers. That way he'd never play the violin again.'

'No, Inspector. I'd never attack a man like that.'

'Who did amputate his fingers?'

'I don't know, sir. It wasn't me. When I returned home I went straight to bed.'

'Can you prove that?'

Professor Giddings shook his head. 'The drug must have lost its power. Perhaps it had grown stale. I'd kept it for months in a box.'

'It did work, but not as quickly as you planned,' Thomas said.

Abberline added, 'The man only became fully intoxicated when he reached his cottage.'

Giddings couldn't take his eyes off the injured musician. 'I put the drug into his wine when he wasn't looking. I admit that. I did not maim his hand. I did not. I would swear on the Bible that I did not.'

'Do you believe Giddings?' Thomas asked the question as he and Abberline walked to the palace later that morning. Storm-winds violently rocked the trees.

Abberline paused. 'I believe I do. Giddings' intention was to drug Kolbaire so that he would behave in a ridiculous way.'

'Then someone else must have discovered that Kolbaire was intoxicated by the drug and used that to their advantage.'

'I think you're right.'

Jo waved a greeting to them as they neared the palace. For once, she was dressed conventionally in a long dress of white muslin. Gone were the cowboy boots and leather kilt. She walked across the lawn in the company of Mr Feasby, and one of the king's gardeners who carried a shotgun. Clearly, Ludwig had ordered some of his staff to act as guards.

Abberline gazed at the woman in white. 'She looks like a bride, doesn't she ... Thomas? You're blushing.'

Thomas shook his head vigorously. 'It's the breeze. It's blowing very hard today.'

'Oh.' Abberline's expression said it all.

Thomas didn't know what to do about Jo. Yesterday, on the beach, she had kissed him. After that, they'd gone their separate ways. Was the kiss an impulsive gesture? Did the kiss mean anything significant? But aren't kisses always significant? Thomas Lloyd found the situation confusing. And when he thought about his fiancée, Emma Bright, out in Ceylon, he felt the crushing weight of shame.

Just then, Ludwig's strapping son, Richard, strode by and Abberline stopped him.

'Good morning,' Abberline said. 'You don't have a microscope I could borrow, by any chance?'

'A microscope?' The young man couldn't have looked any more surprised if Abberline has asked to borrow an elephant. 'I don't have one. I have plenty of guns – pistols, shotguns, rifles.'

'Thank you,' Abberline said politely. 'It's a microscope I'll be needing today. Although the guns might become useful.'

'Just give the word, Inspector. I'll be delighted to help you track down the fiend that's been attacking our people.' The man's eyes burned. He was clearly eager to hunt game larger than the rats he'd been shooting yesterday.

Thomas said, 'You don't know where we could borrow a microscope?'

'Oh, my brother has that kind of thing. Telescopes, microscopes. If he's not composing tunes, he's looking at the stars.'

Abberline nodded. 'Do you know where we could find your brother?'

'He's busy with one of his string quartets. Sulks like fury if he's disturbed. I'll tell Wilf to bring a microscope to your cottage.' At that moment, he saw the boy wheeling the barrow along a path in the distance. 'Wilf! Wilf! Over here, boy!'

Wilf left the barrow and obediently ran along the path towards them. There'd be a moment before he arrived so Thomas decided this was a good opportunity to broach a subject that had been on his mind for a while. He approached the matter in a conversational way to make it seem like he wasn't interrogating what amounted to be a prince of this little kingdom.

'The winds blew hard last night,' Thomas said, looking at Richard as he spoke.

'The ferry can't run in this weather. We've become Robinson Crusoes, one and all.'

'A fisherman told me that Faxfleet is shrinking.'

'It is, by crikey.' Richard spoke cheerfully, then shouted at Wilf, who was perhaps fifty paces away. 'Sprint, lad! Work to be done!'

Thomas continued, 'I heard that the river is actually wearing the island away.'

Richard didn't seem concerned. 'Thirty years from now Faxfleet will have vanished.'

'Doesn't that bother you?'

'Oh, me and my brother have talked about it and we have an answer. When the island has shrunk to the size of this courtyard we'll build a stone tower. It doesn't have to be a big one. Thirty feet high will be ample ... a sort of lighthouse design. The tower will serve as the kingdom of Faxfleet. The old charter that grants my family kingship of the island states that if the island should disappear then our royal title will disappear with it. But if a tower is built and preserves a bit of ground underneath then Faxfleet will continue to exist forever and a day. Of course, I'll eventually become king at some point.'

Richard chatted in a carefree way. He seemed confident, to the point of being blasé, that he and his younger brother had cooked up a nice little scheme to preserve the royal line, which meant that Richard would inherit a great deal of money, too. When Wilf arrived, panting hard from the run, Richard told him to collect a microscope from a storeroom and deliver it in his barrow to Abberline's cottage.

Abberline patted Wilf's head. 'Are your fingers still sore?'

'I burst the blisters with a pin,' Wilf announced proudly. 'You should have seen the stuff that came out.' He held up his hand, showing them the scabs on his fingertips.

If anything, Richard was impressed. 'Who would have thought that electricity could burn skin like that?'

Thomas said, 'Electricity is largely the same as lightning. And lightning can knock a house down.'

'Just imagine.' Richard whistled. 'It should be possible to hunt animals using electrical power. Beaters could drive deer into wires that contained electricity.' The notion clearly interested him because he seemed to be visualizing such a thing as he wished them good day and headed towards the stables.

Wilf saluted Abberline and Thomas and returned to where he'd left his barrow.

Abberline said, 'Does it strike you that Richard is far more interested in preserving the monarchy's cash income rather than preserving the island and its way of life?'

'A pragmatic young man.'

Abberline headed across the courtyard. 'I think it's time to ask the king to invite the island's population into the palace until they can be evacuated to the mainland.'

'Are you suggesting that the building is turned into a fortress?'

'It will be safer. Mr Kolbaire was at home when he was attacked. As you yourself told me, the killer will need to become even more inventive if they're going to steal the public's attention back from the latest Jack the Ripper murder.'

'Then we'll be under siege?'

'And possibly besieged by a single individual. But they are very dangerous. I dread what the killer will do next.'

*

They were greeted by the butler with an apology – in fact, two apologies.

'I'm sorry, gentlemen.' The butler was a red-faced man with black hair that had been oiled flat to his head. 'The king is interviewing members of the academy. It is the annual assessment.'

'I must see King Ludwig,' Abberline insisted. 'It's important.'

'His royal highness will speak to you at eleven o'clock. I am also to apologize for the fact that you did not receive your mail yesterday. What with the injury to the Emsall boy, our cherished routines were disrupted.' The butler picked up a silver tray on which were a number of envelopes. He held the tray out to Inspector Abberline. 'Will that be all, gentlemen?'

'Thank you.' Abberline scooped the envelopes from the tray. 'Will you inform the king that we shall return at eleven?'

'Yes, sir.'

Thomas and Abberline stepped back out into the blustery courtyard.

Thomas frowned. 'Couldn't you have demanded to see Ludwig? After all, you're a senior Scotland Yard detective.'

'I'm also a foreigner in another country. Due to the whimsical shenanigans of an English king over a hundred years ago, who decided to give one of his friends sovereignty of an island, I'm limited in what I can demand. The only authority I have here is what is granted to me by Ludwig. My hands are tied.'

'If the butler delivered a note written by ... What's the matter?' Thomas had seen Abberline's expression turn grim.

Abberline held up a small white envelope. 'Recognize the writing?'

'Good God, it's from him.'

Abberline slipped the other envelopes into his pocket. He then carefully opened the small envelope that bore reddish marks, blood perhaps. He read the letter aloud. '"Dear boss, Whitechapel got too hot for you, my lad? Did you like the neat blade-work I did on the Missus? Dame Verity never looked so pretty. Did you find her tongue in the kettle by the fire? Ho! Picture me laughing out loud as I pen this merry little note to you. I shall get to work again in Whitechapel, boss. Next time I will double up. Start shedding tears, cos you will never catch me. Yours, from hell, Jack."'

Abberline's eyes burned as he stared at the piece of paper in his hand. Thomas realized that he was focusing all of his hatred on the writer of that vicious note.

At last, Thomas broke the silence. 'It is from him, isn't it? I recognize the Ripper's handwriting from two years ago.'

'He's promising to kill again. There's nothing I can do to stop him.'

Thomas caught sight of the words written by a profoundly evil man. '*Next time I will double up*. He's intending to kill two women next time, isn't he?'

Abberline sighed with regret. 'Yes. And I'm two hundred miles away.'

'Will you return to Scotland Yard?'

'Until the weather improves I can't even reach the mainland, let alone go back to London.'

'If the winds blow themselves out, the ferry will start running again, then you can catch an express train from Hull.'

'No. I won't.' Abberline spoke with absolute certainty. 'My duty lies here. As soon as I can, I'll send a telegram to Scotland Yard about this.' He held up the letter. 'There are plenty of policemen who can guard Whitechapel. It's on this island where people are most vulnerable. Come on, Thomas, we have a killer to catch. And they are probably closer than we think.'

Kolbaire was awake when they returned to the cottage. One of his neighbours had sat with him while Abberline and Thomas had been absent. The neighbour politely bade them good day and left as soon as Thomas and Abberline entered.

'I will play the violin again,' Kolbaire announced grandly. 'If I form a strong enough desire in my mind to do so I will play. I have two fingers remaining and a thumb. They will be sufficient.'

'I'm pleased you are looking to the future,' Abberline told him.

'My hand hurts as if Satan himself chews my flesh.' He laughed. The sound was a shrill one, and his eyes darted nervously to the window as if expecting his attacker to return in order to chop off his remaining fingers.

Thomas said, 'Try and rest. We intend to move all the islanders into the palace until the danger is past.'

'Gathering lambs into the barn before the storm comes. Ha!' Kolbaire's eyes glittered. 'My hand burns. Give me laudanum.'

He rubbed his forehead with his good hand. 'Yes, sir, I should say "please" but there is no *please* about it. I must have laudanum. I need to kill the pain.' He raised the bandaged hand.

'Yes, of course.' Abberline took the bottle of laudanum from the cupboard and poured some into a glass. 'The pain will soon pass.'

Kolbaire drained the glass in one massive swallow.

Abberline spoke gently. 'Mr Kolbaire, I need to ask you what happened last night.'

'You already did. Another glass.'

'No, that wouldn't be wise.'

'My hand still hurts.'

'The laudanum will take a minute or two to dull the pain.'

'Damn you.' A tear rolled down Kolbaire's cheek.

'I am going to ask a number of questions because you might remember something else. A small detail could be of vital importance in discovering who hurt you.'

'Very well.'

'Did anyone leave the palace refectory at the same time as you?'

'No.'

'Did you notice anyone follow you back to your cottage?'

'No.'

'You didn't see anyone outside the palace when you left?'

'Jo, the firebrand lady.'

'What was the lady doing?'

'Jo stood at the far side of the courtyard. She was with Prince Richard. You've seen the way she dresses so provocatively.' He gave a sly glance. 'They are sweethearts. Sometimes he calls at her cottage. You know, she lives alone. Quite alone. And the young prince? Well ... he comes calling.'

'Tell me what happened when you arrived at the refectory last night.'

'Again?'

'Yes, again. It is important.'

Kolbaire described his arrival. How the diners listened to a piano recital before the footmen brought in the soup and so on. Abberline didn't mention Professor Giddings' confession: that he'd poured an exotic drug of some sort into Kolbaire's wine. Kolbaire told them what happened right up until he realized that his fingers had been hacked away. His account of events did not differ from the one he gave earlier. All apart, that is, from him glimpsing Jo with Richard as he left the palace.

The clock struck eleven in the palace hallway. Thomas and Abberline sat waiting for the king.

Thomas placed his hands on his lap. His fingers locked and unlocked. He wanted to walk along the beach in the fresh air, not sit here in the stuffy, airless building.

Abberline said, 'You're not happy.'

Thomas looked sharply at the man. For a moment, he thought he'd been speaking his worries aloud.

He sighed. 'I'm sorry. I have things on my mind.'

'Oh.'

Thomas intended to keep quiet about what troubled him. The next second the words came tumbling out. 'It's about Jo. Josephine. I think she's fond of me.'

'I see.'

'I like the woman. It's pleasant to spend time with her.'

'There's no doubting her charisma.'

'And her charms, her intelligence, her talent to make people laugh. She's extraordinary.'

'Do you wish she was not extraordinary?'

'I do, because I'm ...' Thomas clenched his fists. The words that came next were awful to say. 'I'm really having doubts about Emma.'

'You're engaged to Emma Bright.'

'Yes, but she won't come back from Ceylon and marry me.'

'Emma is helping her father with important work. Cultivating tea plants that are resistant to disease, isn't that the case?'

'Yes. It's vital work. Nevertheless, it's important that we have a life together. Will I be an old man before she comes back?'

'You told me it might be in the next year or so.'

'Unless she finds another reason to stay in Ceylon.' Thomas dug his fingernails into the palm of his own hand. 'Should I keep waiting for a wedding that will never come? Or should I seize the chance of happiness now?'

'With Jo? Isn't she a close friend of the king's son?'

Before Thomas had a chance to answer, the butler glided from the shadows. 'His royal highness will see you now, gentlemen.'

Inspector Abberline didn't hesitate. The time had come to act decisively. When he spoke to King Ludwig in his office, it was with urgency and absolute seriousness.

'Sir,' Abberline said. 'I cannot guarantee the safety of your people on the island. Not if they remain in their homes. The cottages are isolated and they all can't be guarded at the same time. I believe the killer struck again last night when he cut off the fingers of Mr Kolbaire.'

'Then the killer is losing his nerve.' Ludwig sat at his desk, gazing out of the window. 'The man daren't commit another murder.'

Abberline's fist crashed down on the desk so loudly Ludwig jumped in shock.

'More people will die.' Abberline wasn't intimidated by the king. 'The killer is creating stunts that will draw the attention of the newspapers. He, or she, wants their crimes to be known throughout Britain.'

'You believe he will kill again?'

'Yes, I do.'

Thomas added, 'The killer is clearly resourceful and intelligent. They built an electric battery that was powerful enough to render the boy unconscious when he touched the gate.'

'He must be in league with the very devil.' Ludwig clenched his fists in anger. 'So, Abberline, you told me that my people are not safe. What shall we do to protect them?'

'Bring them into the palace.'

'Everyone?'

'Either that, or evacuate them to the mainland.'

'But it's the time of year when I evaluate the work of academy members. They must remain here in order to submit their papers. This is crucial to the conduct of the academy.'

'Then send out an order, telling everyone to come here at once.'

'But dash it all, Abberline, the place will be full to the rafters! And what about the fishermen and their families?'

'Everyone must be housed here. The palace will become a fortress.'

'Sir, you wish to turn my home into an armed camp?' Ludwig shook his head as the reality of the situation sank in. 'How long will the islanders remain here? Six hours, six days, six months?'

'For as long as it takes to catch the killer.'

Ludwig's eyes darted in Abberline's direction. 'Ha. You're

forgetting something. If the killer is here on the island, and if everyone is brought to the palace, then surely the killer will be in this very building. He will move among us. He can strike while we sleep.'

'If the killer does come to the palace, they will, as likely as not, quickly give themselves away. We'll discover their identity and they will be arrested.'

'I must ask this question, Abberline, even though it's painful to put it into words: do you suspect a member of my academy?'

'There are intense rivalries. We know that academy members have fought duels in the past.'

Ludwig rolled his eyes in despair. 'No one was ever killed.'

'Not until now,' Thomas pointed out.

'The academy must not be brought into disrepute.' Ludwig scowled angrily. 'I have invested a fortune in this venture. All my adult life has been devoted to enabling gifted men and women, whom would otherwise be overlooked, the opportunity to conduct important research and create great works of art.' The man's eyes glittered. Clearly, his academy meant an enormous amount to him. It was as if its strands were interwoven with the fabric of his life and very soul. 'The academy must not fail. It must not.' He pounded his fist on the desk. 'I will hang the rogue myself.' Ludwig slammed his fist down on the desk again.

This time a terrific bang echoed through the house. Windows rattled. A picture fell from the wall with a crash. Ludwig stared at his fist in surprise as if it had caused the tremendous noise.

Another loud *bang* thundered across the island.

Thomas ran to the window. 'That sounds like cannon.'

'Someone's firing cannon at the palace?' Ludwig appeared dazed with shock. 'How could they bring artillery onto the island without it being seen?'

Abberline pointed. 'Over there ... smoke above the trees.'

Thomas stared in shock. 'There's an –'

The third blast of sound came like thunder, drowning what he'd said.

'Someone is detonating explosive.' Abberline hurried to the door. 'Ludwig, send out your male servants in pairs with orders to bring all the islanders here – at once, sir! At once!'

'Of course. Yes ... yes ...' Ludwig had lost his regal composure. He groped on the desk for paper and a pen, knocking over a tea cup as he did so. The man's hands trembled.

Abberline called out, 'Thomas, Ludwig will dictate the order. You write it down.' He briefly paused as he opened the door. 'Whatever happens, don't let anyone go out onto the island alone. Everyone must travel in groups of at least two, and I mean *everyone*.'

Thomas nodded. He drew a chair up to the desk.

Abberline called back over his shoulder as he went, 'And make sure that everyone who can safely handle a gun has one. This is war.'

Thomas Lloyd wrote down the order that King Ludwig dictated to him. Ludwig's hand shook so much he couldn't even grasp a pen let alone write a single word. Eventually, Ludwig did manage to add his rather shaky signature at the foot of the order then Thomas handed it to the butler with instructions that he tell his staff to go out onto the island and gather all its residents and bring them to the palace. Meanwhile, the king's eldest son enthusiastically handed out pistols and rifles, saying in excited tones, 'If you see the killer, aim between the eyes! Shoot the swine dead!'

Thomas felt like pointing out that nobody knew what the killer looked like, whether they were male or female, or if they operated individually or part of a gang. He hoped that the assortment of footmen, gardeners and office staff, now armed with guns, wouldn't fire off shots at the first person they saw approaching the palace. What's more, Thomas realized the killer might be one of those men who now brandished a weapon. Richard could have armed the murderer, and nobody would be any the wiser.

Thomas tried to set aside these troubling thoughts as he headed out of the door. He found Abberline in the courtyard, talking to the three constables who had been sent a few days ago from the local police headquarters in Hull. Just then, another explosion shattered the silence. Birds flew squawking from trees nearby. Everyone looked this way and that for the source of the noise. Presently a large cloud of black smoke rose above the forest. Despite the explosions, male servants ran from the palace. They were in pairs and they hurried to the paths that led to the cottages dotted across the island. Their mission, to bring everyone to the safety … well, conceded Thomas, the *relative* safety of the palace.

Abberline took a pistol from his pocket and handed it to one of the constables. Thomas stared in surprise. He didn't know that Abberline had even brought a weapon with him. Abberline said something else to the men; they saluted before hurrying towards the stables.

Abberline beckoned Thomas.

'Thomas, I've told the constables to bring the fishermen and their families to the palace.'

'The king won't be pleased to house them.'

'He has no choice. This is an emergency.'

'We should start barricading the windows and doors.'

'Professor Giddings is an ex-military man. He'll know what needs to be done.'

'After he drugged Kolbaire? You trust him?'

'Sneaking the drug into the wine was spiteful. But I think what he did was an aberration brought on by his wife's death. I'm sure he'll act properly now and help protect his neighbours.'

Yet another thunderous roar bellowed out across the island. More smoke billowed above the trees.

'Thomas, try and get a fix on the direction of that smoke. Come on.'

Abberline reached into his coat pocket again. When he withdrew his hand he gripped a revolver. Thomas's heart pounded against his ribs. Right now, it seemed a possibility – a decidedly lethal possibility – that soon they would come face to face with the killer that terrorized this island in the River Humber.

Thomas walked through the forest with Abberline. Their intended destination was the site of the latest explosion. Paths criss-crossed the island through the trees. Those paths had plenty of bends so it wasn't possible to see ahead more than fifty paces at any one time. They came upon cottages where Ludwig's male servants passed on the orders that everyone must go to the palace immediately.

They observed academy members leaving their homes. One man carried a trombone, another a crate of books, a woman strode boldly out with a telescope over her shoulder. She told the servant in piercing tones, 'The comet becomes visible in Scorpio in three days. I must have my telescope. Careful with those star charts, man, they are priceless!'

Thomas shook his head. 'The king's orders stipulated that people bring the essentials for a few days away from home. I think these people's idea of what's essential is different from anyone else's.'

William Feasby struggled out of the cottage with Sir Terror in his arms. The wolf with the wings of an eagle looked heavy. A servant helped him.

Feasby sang out in his high voice, 'I will not leave Sir Terror behind. He has been taken once. I won't risk him being stolen again.'

Thomas caught Abberline's eye. 'Would it be flippant of me to compare this island to a madhouse?'

Abberline sighed. 'The word "eccentric" isn't strong enough to describe the behaviour of some of the islanders, is it?'

They continued walking. Thomas constantly glanced through the trees, expecting to see a man appear with a gun. The murderer could easily conceal themselves in the dense woodland. A rustle of bushes made Thomas glance back. Two men in the uniforms of footmen blundered out.

'I told you that Lookout Cottage is back near the old barn,' one of the men grumbled. 'Now look at the mud on my shoes.'

The other scowled. 'I said we should have used the main path. But oh no, you, Sir Know-it-all, said you knew a shortcut.'

The men bickered as they headed back into the forest. Thomas and Abberline pushed onwards along the path. A moment later Abberline held up his hand.

'This is it,' he said.

Thomas saw that one of the trees had about two feet of bark stripped off at head-height. The branches above the bare wood didn't have a single leaf on them. All around the tree were shredded leaves and twigs. Some of them were scorched. Thomas picked up a strong odour of burning and gunpowder.

Abberline sniffed. 'We've found the site of one explosion anyway.'

He examined the tree trunk with part of its bark missing.

Thomas picked up the remains of a metal can that once, according to what was printed on the outside, contained boiled meat in gravy.

Thomas held up the mutilated can. 'This probably held the gunpowder. There's a hole drilled in the top, which could have been where a fuse had been inserted.'

'So, if this bomb had been made by the killer then they know how to construct explosive devices as well as electrical batteries.'

Thomas gazed at the devastation caused by the bomb. Pieces of the metal can were embedded in the tree.

'They failed to hurt anyone this time, thank heaven.'

'They didn't fail, Thomas. These explosions are reminders that the killer is dangerous and they are capable of catching us off guard. The killer is saying to us: "Don't ignore me. I can strike whenever and wherever I want."'

Another loud boom rolled through the trees.

Abberline's expression was a grim one. 'Thomas, it's time we returned to our new fortress and pulled up the drawbridge.' He shot Thomas a direct look. 'All right, we might not have an actual drawbridge, but it's time to barricade the palace doors and see what the devil does next.'

'From past experience, it's bound to be what we least expect.'

Abberline nodded. If anything, his expression grew even more serious as he headed back in the direction of the palace.

That afternoon events moved quickly. The academy members arrived first. They were allocated rooms in the palace. The fishing village lay at the other end of the island so, accordingly, the villagers were the last to arrive. Their living quarters were more humble. Families were put in the refectory where meals were normally eaten. Servants brought blankets and straw-filled mattresses. The fisher-folk had to make themselves comfortable with what they were given. Children ran around the tables and climbed on the king's throne at the top table. The butler clapped his hands and scolded them. Abberline found Ludwig and told him that small gunpowder bombs had been left in the forest, and that each bomb had been detonated by a slow fuse that could have been left smouldering for an hour or more. This gave the person responsible plenty of time to melt back into some remote corner of the island, or – more disturbingly – reassume the guise of a law-abiding academy member, or employee of the king.

Richard, meanwhile, had mounted a huge duck-hunting gun on a windowsill. This weapon had a six-foot-long barrel. He aimed it across the courtyard. Many academy members continued with their work. Already, Kolbaire attempted to play the violin with his hand swathed in bandages. Another man sat in a corner with sheets of paper on his knee. He made notes in pencil, oblivious to what happened around him. Professor Giddings endeavoured to make amends for his reckless behaviour earlier when he'd slipped a drug into Kolbaire's wine. Giddings, helped by a pair of gardeners and Bertie, the ten-year-old, built barricades at vulnerable windows and doors, using wooden boards and furniture.

Tristan, King Ludwig's youngest son, played cheerful melodies on a piano in the ballroom. The fishermen's children immediately hurried there to dance around. The young man smiled and nodded as the little ones cavorted and sang nonsense words to the music. Tristan improvised a game that involved the children dancing when he played – and when he stopped they had to stand as still as statues.

A little while later, Abberline introduced two men of around thirty years of age to Thomas.

'These are my colleagues from Scotland Yard,' Abberline told him. 'The ferry managed to make a crossing to the island, but it won't be able to make the return journey yet. The current is far too strong.'

Thomas shook the men's hands. Both were clean-shaven. One wore spectacles with gold wire frames. The other man was short but very powerfully built. His handshake was crushing. These two detectives wouldn't have looked out of place in a lawyer's office. They were sleek, well groomed, and the way they spoke suggested a good education. Their names were Lionel Metcalfe and Harry Scott. The men answered Abberline's questions fully and were clearly respectful toward their superior. Thomas didn't always get on well with Abberline's colleagues. The other policemen were often suspicious, perhaps believing he would portray them in a poor light in his newspaper stories. Not that there was any evidence to support this. Thomas always wrote about Abberline's colleagues fairly, and portrayed them as conscientious men who strove to protect the public from criminals.

The short man, Harry Scott, smiled. 'This is quite a scene, Thomas – if I may call you Thomas?'

'By all means.'

'Like a scene from a picture book about castles under siege from barbarians.' He grinned. 'Is that lady carrying a bow and arrow?'

Thomas saw Jo with her longbow. She smiled and waved at Thomas before vanishing through a doorway.

Thomas said, 'A lot of the islanders are very keen on archery.'

'Bless my soul.' Lionel raised his eyebrows in amazement. 'An island full of bowmen.'

'And bowgirls,' corrected Harry.

'It seems a long, long way from London.' Lionel shook his head, clearly astonished. 'By the by, Thomas. Do you play chess?'

'I enjoy a game now and then.'

'Would you play later this evening?'

Thomas smiled. 'Yes, I'd be delighted.'

Abberline was clearly pleased that his fellow detectives were on friendly terms with Thomas. 'Have your game of chess, gentlemen, but we will need to take it in turns to stand guard tonight. We don't want that scoundrel throwing a bomb through a window.'

'By Jove, sir!' exclaimed Harry. 'You're right, that wouldn't do at all.'

'I will see that you are armed with revolvers. There is quite an armoury here.'

The palace was a hive of activity. Giddings continued work on the improvised fortifications. Scents of freshly baked bread flowed from the kitchen as the cooks worked to feed the new arrivals. Abberline spoke to the king again. The two detectives, Harry and Lionel, chatted to Thomas and he told them all that had happened. Outside, the shadows grew longer as the sun set on another extraordinary day.

Thomas realized that an extraordinary evening might follow when Jo whispered to him, 'I must see you later. Meet me in the music room at seven. Make sure you're alone.'

At ten minutes to seven Thomas made his way to the music room. This was at the back of the palace, overlooking the lawn. The hallways and corridors were crowded with people. Most talked in excited voices. Even though the palace had been turned into a makeshift fort, and essentially they were under siege from an unknown assassin, the academy members and the fisher-folk talked in loud voices: they clearly anticipated dramatic events tonight.

Thomas encountered the harassed-looking butler. The man told children not to touch the paintings on the walls, and paused to stare in horror at muddy footprints on the rugs.

He said to Thomas, 'I've never seen anything like this. All is disordered. Will Inspector Abberline apprehend the criminal soon, sir?'

Thomas told him that Abberline was doing his best and hopefully there would be an arrest in the near future. Thomas had to admit to himself that what he'd told the butler was shamelessly optimistic. In truth, they were no closer to identifying the murderer than when they first stepped onto the island several days ago. The butler darted away to scold children who slid down the banister of the main staircase.

Thomas wove his way through the crowds. He was eager to reach the music room. Jo had something important to tell him. He wondered what the striking woman wished to confide.

Kolbaire loomed from a doorway to seize Thomas's arm. He brandished his bandaged hand. Part of the wrappings had been cut away to reveal two of his fingers (the other two from that particular hand floated in a glass jar full of gin at Samarkand Cottage).

With a quivery note of triumph, Kolbaire declared, 'See, Mr Lloyd. I've freed two of my fingers from the bandages. I can play the violin again. The injury to my hand will not cheat the world of my music.'

'Are you in pain, Mr Kolbaire?'

'There is laudanum here. I have consumed half a bottle and I feel wonderful.' The man smiled, looking as if he wanted to dance through the hallway crowds. 'I can hear the music *shimmering* in these walls. I divine melody in the hearts of everyone here.' He swayed unsteadily. 'I shall compose such an opera. I will call it *Night at the Enchanted Castle* – it will tell the story of what happens tonight. You shall be in it, sir: the chivalrous knight that moves through this world, haloed by golden light. Protector of everyone here.'

Thomas thanked him before trying to side-step the inebriated man.

Kolbaire wouldn't let go of his arm. 'Mr Lloyd, I will take the opera to Milan, Paris, Vienna.'

At that moment, William Feasby managed to thread his way through the crowded hallway.

'Mr Kolbaire,' Feasby said. 'You promised to remain lying down on the sofa. You must rest, you know? You have lost blood – lots of it.'

'And two fingers.' Kolbaire slurred the words. 'The devil cut off my fingers. What have I done to any man to make him so angry with me?'

'There, there, my good chap. Mr Lloyd is a busy man. He personally assists the great Inspector Abberline of Scotland Yard. Come along now. Let's get you settled under that warm blanket again.'

Thomas nodded his thanks to William Feasby as he led the tottering figure of Kolbaire away. The hands of the grandfather clock now stood at six minutes to seven. He'd agreed to meet Jo at seven. Time to quicken the pace. He once more made his way through clusters of men and women who chatted excitedly to one another.

At one point, he had to stand aside as the butler led a procession of servants, carrying steaming tureens.

The butler called back to his staff, 'Rabbit stew. It's all that Cook was able to muster at short notice. At least there's plenty of bread. This way. Take it through to the refectory. Don't let those children trip you. They are demons!'

Thomas had barely taken five paces again when he saw the king's youngest son, Tristan, who had been playing the piano for the children. As the young man stepped aside, to avoid a servant carrying a basket piled high with loaves, he dropped a wad of paper he was carrying. Sheets spilled over the floor. The man crouched down to pick them up. Thomas hurried forward to help before the paper was spoilt by the muddy boots of fishermen who followed the procession of food. Thomas saw that the paper was covered with musical notation.

'Your compositions?' he asked Tristan.

'Yes, I rather hoped to show them to my father at some point. However, he's frightfully busy.'

'This is like a Covent Garden street on market day,' said Thomas.

'We've never had so many people in the house.'

Thomas stood up and handed the last of the dropped pages to Tristan. The young man smiled.

'Thank you, Mr Lloyd.'

Richard energetically pushed through the mass of people. In each hand he carried a shotgun. 'Mind aside ... mind aside, there.' The powerful man strode up the staircase.

Tristan gave a shy, nervous smile. 'I think my brother rather enjoys all this commotion. Then he does like noise and firing guns.'

'I take it you don't share his passion for firearms?'

'Goodness, no. My melodies have always been enough for me.' He brushed dirt from the sheet music in his hand. 'These musical notes never age. Whenever someone plays them they are fresh and new again. Music – its time signature and its notes – a precisely ordered spectrum of sound that exquisitely transforms disorder into order. Music reflects an instinctive desire we all feel to convert our chaotic lives into ones of serenity.' The young man smiled fondly and somewhat dreamily at the sheets of music. 'If I should be so egotistical as to claim that I have a mission in life it is this: music, beautiful music.' He blushed. 'I do beg your pardon, Mr Lloyd. I am lecturing you, aren't I? Thank you for rescuing my manuscript.'

The grandfather clock struck seven. *Jo! I should be there by now!* Thomas rushed towards the doorway that led to the music room. At last – he'd find out what that remarkable lady had to say to him.

It wasn't what he expected. What's more, there was no mention of the kiss earlier when they sat together on the beach.

Jo stood by the fireplace. The tall, regal woman wore white muslin that shone in the lamplight. The room's shutters had been closed and locked – all part of the makeshift fortification of the building. They were alone in the room full of musical instruments. A bust of Beethoven in white plaster stood on the grand piano.

When Thomas breathlessly entered the room in a rush she turned to him and said, 'I will find the murderer myself. The king has granted me permission to examine everyone in the palace. I would like you to ask Inspector Abberline to watch me at work.'

Thomas Lloyd stared at her in surprise. No. He hadn't expected that this would be the subject of their conversation at all.

'Abberline is discussing important matters with his colleagues from Scotland Yard.'

'What I will undertake tonight is important, too. Vitally important. I can find the man who killed Benedict Feasby and Mrs Giddings and her sister.' Her voice was unusually loud and her manner had become pompous. 'Notes will be taken. I have brought my measuring equipment.'

'You mean to say,' Thomas began in a bewildered, off-kilter kind of way, 'that you intend to use phrenology to identify the murderer?'

'Of course.'

'But, Jo, this –'

Brusquely, she interrupted. 'Don't you see, Thomas? This is the perfect opportunity to test my research. For years I have studied the form and shape of human skulls. I can use what I've learnt to find the killer. And I'll do so tonight.'

'Tonight? But these are difficult circumstances. We are, to all intents and purposes, under siege here. For all we know the person who set those explosions this morning might throw bombs at the palace windows.'

She walked towards him, smiling happily. 'Don't you see? As soon as I discover who the murderer is everyone will be safe again. You and I will have a picnic. There is a lovely little hill with perfect views across the river.'

'Phrenology isn't recognized as a legitimate science. How can the shape of a person's head reveal that they have done something wrong?'

'Soon, phrenology will be the police officer's most important tool when it comes to identifying criminals.'

'Inspector Abberline would disagree. He told me that this business of feeling the bumps and curves of someone's head to reveal their character is ridiculous.'

'Do you think my life's work is ridiculous?'

'I agree with Abberline.'

'Oh, you do?' Her eyes blazed with anger. 'Then you agree with everything the man says. Does he pull your strings? Do you dance like a puppet whenever he wishes?'

'Your theories, Jo, are worse than ridiculous. They are dangerous. Phrenology will condemn innocent men and women as criminals even though they've done nothing wrong.'

'You are Abberline's puppet! I thought you were enlightened. But you are as blind to the truth as the rest.'

She stormed out, slamming the door behind her. Thomas sat down on the piano stool and shook his head in despair. He'd liked Jo so much. Now their friendship had been smashed to pieces in seconds.

Abberline walked along an otherwise deserted corridor on the upper floor. The man was deep in thought. Clearly, he was troubled. When Thomas reached the top of the stairs and saw his friend he realized that the man despaired of finding the individual who had attacked the islanders.

Despite his worries, Abberline smiled, pleased to see Thomas. 'You will have an amazing story to write for your newspaper.'

'If only I could bring it to a satisfactory conclusion. We have no clues. There isn't a suspect that we can put a name to.'

'You're right. This case is a puzzle that I can't unravel.'

They walked together along the corridor. The sound of voices came from far away in the building. Most of its occupants would be in the refectory now, consuming the rabbit stew supper.

Thomas said, 'Do you see any possible motive for the attacks?'

'None.'

'There is intense rivalry among the members of the academy.'

'But why connect a battery to a gate in order to hurt the boy who cleans people's shoes?'

'Perhaps the electric shock was intended for someone else?'

'At that hour of the night?'

'The killer attacked at random then. Does that suggest the person we're searching for is a lunatic?'

Abberline could only shrug. 'I don't know. In fact, this case has less clues than the hunt for Jack the Ripper. '

'The devil has killed with an arrow, with poison, and Kolbaire's fingers were cut off.'

'And don't forget the shots fired at Professor Giddings' cottage.' Abberline shook his head again. The man appeared close to absolute despair.

They continued along the corridor in silence. Where the corridor intersected with another they found Professor Giddings at an open window. A shotgun leant against the wall beside him. The man gazed out, keeping watch, no doubt hoping to spy a shadowy figure amongst the trees. Professor Giddings turned as they approached.

'Good evening, gentlemen.'

'Good evening, Professor,' said Abberline. 'All quiet?'

'As a grave.'

Thomas said, 'There is a distinct possibility that the person we're looking for is already inside the building.'

'Ha.' Giddings gave a grim smile. 'Then I should pray to be transformed into the god, Janus. I would have a face with eyes looking forward, and a face in the back of my head, looking behind me.'

Abberline said, 'You should get something to eat. Food is being served in the refectory.'

'I am denying myself food, Inspector. This is my penance. I will keep watch all night. Every time I set eyes on Kolbaire's bandaged hand I am mortified.'

Abberline nodded. 'But I must submit a report about what you did, putting the drug in Kolbaire's drink. I will say that you acted out of character on account of your wife's death. You may still be charged, though, and then you will face a court of law.'

'So be it, gentlemen. I did wrong. I deserve to face the consequences.' Giddings continued to gaze out as the moon rose above the trees. 'Though I hope to continue my work, for I believe that the countries of our empire should be democratically represented in parliament.'

Thomas said, 'You have submitted your research to King Ludwig for his approval?'

'He has a manuscript of my book.' Giddings nodded thoughtfully. 'If it wasn't for Ludwig, the book wouldn't have been written. I have no money, gentlemen. Without the king's hospitality I would have been forced to take paid employment elsewhere and wouldn't have had the time to write.'

Abberline digested the information. 'That must be the story of most members of the academy. They can only conduct their research or compose their music because Ludwig provides them with a cottage and meals.'

'Ha, indeed, Inspector. You know, we academy members call Ludwig "The Just King", because he is so fair and equitable. He strives to give us time to work in peace here and to prove ourselves.'

'Then I can see why you honour him with the title "The Just King".'

Professor Giddings turned to Thomas and Abberline. His gaze seemed so wise and so serious. 'King Ludwig has such good intentions. No, the *best* of intentions. But you know what they say about good intentions, gentlemen? They pave the way to hell.'

There were at least fifty people in the refectory. Some sat at tables, dunking bread in bowls of rabbit stew. A woman nursed a crying baby. Children played with a ball in the far corner. It was noisy – very noisy.

Thomas saw Jo. She stood in an alcove. The ten-year-old boy by the name of Bertie Trask sat on a high stool. The woman ran her fingers over the boy's head. She wore an expression of stern concentration. Every so often, she made a note on a sheet of paper that lay on a table beside her. When she saw Thomas across the crowded room, she gestured for him to approach. He felt surprise. He was convinced she'd never speak to him again after he'd claimed her work was nonsense. Thomas made his way towards her. He had to dodge a group of boys wrestling on the floor. These were the children of the fisher-folk. They were rumbustious to say the least.

'Thomas.' Jo rested her palm on the top of the boy's head. 'This is Bertie Trask.'

Bertie had a pleasantly rounded face, set with brown eyes that twinkled with good humour. This down-to-earth ten-year-old, who already had a full-time job assisting the gardeners, looked as if he enjoyed nothing more than laughing and having fun in the company of his friends.

'Hello, Bertie,' he said pleasantly. 'We have met. You were trying to scare Wilf by pretending to be the Grim Reaper.'

Bertie grinned. 'I did, sir. I scared the rascal out of his skin.'

'Hush, Bertie. Thomas, will you pass me that, please?' Jo pointed to the paper on which there was an outline of a human head. She'd drawn arrows to parts of the head then added notes.

Thomas did as she asked.

She smiled at him with warmth and affection. 'Despite our little tiff, dear Thomas, I do intend to show you that phrenology is scientifically valid.'

'Most experts would disagree.'

'I will demonstrate that not only is phrenology a *bona fide* scientific discipline, I will also prove it's vital in preserving civilization.'

'That's an extraordinary claim.'

'It is essential that we can identify people in society who will become a threat to property and innocent lives.'

'Psychologists study the workings of the human mind. That is the way forward, surely.'

'Phrenology is more accurate, and much more useful. Run your fingers over Bertie's skull.'

Thomas stared at her. 'I'd prefer not to.'

Jo smiled, tolerating his refusal with good humour. She touched the boy's forehead. 'This bulge in the bone above the eyebrow reveals that he has a highly developed ability to befriend people. He will be a good companion later in life.'

Bertie grinned.

Jo continued: 'The outward curve at the top of his head indicates good numerical skills.'

'I had two bowls of stew,' Bertie declared.

'And the dip here, in front of his right ear, states quite categorically that young Bertie has a big appetite and does relish his meals.'

'And cake,' added Bertie with a delighted smile. 'Three slices, I ate.'

'You can make all these observations from bumps in his skull?'

Thomas shook his head doubtfully.

'Yes.'

'What you can read by touching his skull can't possibly predict the man he will become.'

'Oh, but it does, Thomas.'

'Really?'

'Look at Bertie.' She put her fingers under the boy's chin and lifted his head. 'See how angelic his face is. The big eyes. The sensitive features.'

'He looks a perfectly normal boy.'

'Now, if I run my fingers across the back of his head, like so, I can feel the skull dip inward, almost as if there's a pronounced depression.'

'Just a random formation of the skull, surely?'

'No, Thomas, the phrenology chart identifies this inward depression of the skull as an indicator of violent criminality in the future. According to my chart, Bertie Trask will commit savage crimes one day, perhaps even murder.'

'My God.' Thomas actually felt sick. 'This is a child you are talking about. Why on earth are you telling him that one day he will be a murderer?'

Bertie's eyes watered. He looked scared as he sat there on the stool with his head gripped in Jo's strong hands.

Jo spoke firmly: 'Just as a thermometer tells us if a person is suffering from a fever, a phrenology chart will show us who will become a violent criminal later in life.'

'That's not only ridiculous, it's monstrous.'

'It is the scientific truth.'

'Jo, there is no proof that this boy will become a criminal. He's an innocent child.'

Bertie pushed Jo's hands away. 'She's right! I am bad, sir. I'm very bad! I put salt in Mrs Price's tea. I hid Wilf's shoes. I spied on him taking away that big dog! I shouted rude words at the milkmaid!'

'Bertie.' Thomas tried to soothe the child. 'It's all right. The lady didn't –'

Bertie wriggled down from the stool before running away into the crowded room.

Thomas turned on Jo in absolute fury, but she'd already walked away, carrying her charts and notes. He couldn't stop the thought that sped through his head: *That woman is evil!*

Somewhere in the building a clock sounded the chimes of midnight. Thomas Lloyd gazed out of the window. Moonlight streamed down onto the forest. It seemed so peaceful out there. Yet the forest might conceal the murderous individual that Abberline and his men were searching for. Then again, the murderer might be in the palace, concocting another scheme to cause injury or death.

Thomas felt confused about Jo. Yes, she was beautiful. But what about the mind that lay behind that beautiful face? Her work was nothing less than evil. Because a boy's skull was shaped in a certain way she had condemned him as a criminal of the future. A criminal of the vilest, most brutal kind. Did she believe that Bertie Trask should be locked away in prison now? Or even hanged? Thomas was appalled. His sense of fairness was outraged. The boy was innocent. He'd done nothing wrong other than play the kind of pranks that any other child would play.

Thomas retired to bed in the room that had been allocated to him. He'd been so angry with Jo he thought he would be unable to sleep. Yet within seconds he'd slipped into deep slumber.

His sleep was only interrupted when the door was flung open. Daylight streamed in to reveal Abberline standing there, his face stark with worry.

'It's Bertie!' he panted. 'He's vanished!'

Chapter 11

THE SEARCH FOR the boy had to be one of the most chaotic that Thomas Lloyd had ever seen. From the palace cellars to the attic, people were calling out, 'Bertie? Bertie? Are you there? Hello! Bertie!' A man yelled Bertie's name into the coal cellar. One of the fisherman's children was seized by Virgil Kolbaire, who then dragged the shrieking boy to Abberline. Kolbaire loudly insisted that he'd found Bertie Trask and that the mischievous boy was merely pretending to be someone else.

'After all,' Kolbaire declared in a pompous manner, 'has not the lady applied phrenology to prove that the wretched Trask child is a born liar and rogue?'

Abberline freed the boy (who looked nothing like Bertie) and muttered under his breath, 'Phrenology. That damn nonsense will kill people.'

The only individuals who weren't hopelessly disorganized were Abberline and his two detective colleagues. They quickly assessed that all the doors and windows remained locked. The men who had stood guard at key locations in the palace last night confirmed that no one at all had left the building. These were siege conditions. The detectives were satisfied that no one had entered the building, either.

The palace resembled an ants' nest that had been poked with a stick. People swarmed everywhere in their ineffectual search. The children became excited. They soon made a game of it, running up and down the corridors yelling, 'Bertie! Bertie!' One hooted ghostly sounds before announcing, 'Bertie's gone to hell! You're all next!' Some of the younger children ran screaming, though they were laughing at the same time.

The butler hurried past. 'What a headache I've got. My head's splitting in two!'

Thomas and Inspector Abberline went to the refectory where most of the people from the fishing village had slept last night. Many of the older children were convinced that ten-year-old Bertie had told them he intended to sleep in there last night, as he had plenty of friends amongst the fishermen's children. However, when Wilf appeared he revealed an entirely different state of affairs to Abberline.

Wilf said, 'Bertie told me that he'd got himself a nice warm corner in the kitchen. He was going to bed down there last night.'

After Wilf had gone, Thomas said, 'He sounded confident that Bertie would sleep in the kitchen.'

'And Wilf's testimony seems the most reliable yet.'

Thomas had to ask the most obvious question of all. 'Do you think the killer took Bertie?'

Abberline looked worried. 'I can't rule it out.'

'In that case, Bertie might already be dead.'

'I pray with all my heart that isn't the case, Thomas.'

Cries of 'Bertie, where are you?' came from all directions. Thomas knew it had become increasingly unlikely that Bertie would emerge from some room or other with a mischievous grin on his face, saying, 'I gave you all a scare, didn't I? You thought I'd been kidnapped away.' No, that eventuality became frighteningly remote. Thomas tried to keep mental images at bay of a small figure lying out there in the forest.

At that moment, the two detectives walked briskly up to Abberline. Both had their notebooks open and pencils at the ready.

'Sir,' began Lionel, 'we went our separate ways so we could interview as many people as possible.'

'Seeing as time is of the essence in finding the lad,' added Harry.

Abberline nodded his approval. 'Have you been able to find out when the boy was seen last?'

Harry sighed. 'Unfortunately, the witnesses tend to muddle one child with another.'

'And a good many are vague about the actual time they saw Trask last.'

'We do have some timings, sir.' Lionel referred to his notebook. 'The last sighting I have that convinces me most of its accuracy comes from the boy who cleans the boots, Wilfred Emsall. He'd been sitting opposite the grandfather clock in the hallway, polishing shoes, when Bertie Trask arrived with a piece of apple pie for Emsall. Emsall is certain that this happened at eight o'clock last night, because Bertie Trask performed a comical dance as the chimes rang out.' He turned to his colleague. 'Do you have a later time, Harry?'

'My witness is much more vague and doesn't have a precise time. However, the cook states she saw Bertie dragging a mattress across the kitchen floor. He said he'd sleep next to the pantry. Of course, this isn't usual for staff to sleep in the kitchen but there are so many people in the palace that every corner is being used. That would have been after nine o'clock, she insists, because she only returned to the kitchen between nine and ten in order to check that the kitchen maids had cleaned the pots.'

Abberline had been listening carefully. 'Did the cook see Bertie bed down for the night?'

'No.'

'Did she notice if Bertie left the kitchen?'

'She says that she was busy checking if the pans had been cleaned properly. When she turned back the boy had gone. She assumed he'd gone back upstairs.'

Thomas asked, 'Was there any sign that the mattress had been slept on?' Immediately he regretted asking the question. Abberline's fellow police officers could be touchy, to say the least, when he asked them questions like this.

However, Harry didn't seem to mind at all. 'No. A blanket was left neatly folded on the mattress. And in my experience young boys don't neatly fold blankets. He must have been given the blanket from a laundry room and taken it and the mattress into the kitchen.'

Abberline mulled this over. 'Then it appears that Bertie vanished between nine and ten o'clock last night. Until we have information to the contrary, this is now a case of kidnap.'

Abberline and the two detectives organized a thorough and this time coherent search of the palace. Rather than having everyone in the building look for Bertie, small groups led by either a detective, or one of the three constables on loan from Hull, conducted the search. Normally, Thomas would be at Inspector Abberline's side but not this time. Abberline asked Thomas to question the cook again, just in case she remembered anything else about Bertie's visit to the kitchen last night that might prove useful. Thomas felt a stab of disappointment.

It seemed as if the policemen preferred to work together. Thomas had to admit to himself that he felt left out. He knew the feeling was a childish one. However, he no longer seemed part of the investigation team that he and Abberline had created.

Thomas chatted to the cook as she ran the kitchen, just as a captain runs a consummately well-ordered ship. She efficiently gave orders to her staff as they kneaded mounds of white dough. Consumption of bread had become formidable now that so many people were staying in the palace. Thomas couldn't help but picture the deserted cottages and the fisherman's silent village now that the entire population of the island had been moved to the palace.

The cook tried to be helpful. In truth, however, she simply did not recall anything else relevant to the case. Bertie had brought the mattress and blanket into the kitchen. That had been the last anyone had clapped eyes on the lad – unless one of the people interviewed wasn't telling the truth.

Inspector Abberline came down to the kitchen to look at where Bertie Trask had been seen for the final time. He examined the floor. He even searched the pantry.

'If a boy wants to hide himself,' he explained, 'it's astonishing the places they can tuck themselves away. Up chimneys, in cupboards. I even found one in the bottom drawer of a desk: he'd decided he didn't want to go to school.'

The search of the kitchen revealed nothing new. Thomas and Abberline returned to the refectory where coffee was being served, and it was there that Abberline's conversation centred on what the boy had been doing yesterday. Thomas told him about Jo's examination of the boy's skull and what amounted to her diagnosis that the boy had been born bad.

Abberline's face turned crimson. 'What a blasted crock of nonsense! Phrenology has been chucked out by the scientific world. Why the woman persists with such cock-and-bull beliefs is beyond me.'

'She upset Bertie when he heard her say that he would grow up to be a criminal.'

'The woman should be arrested.' Abberline turned to glare at Jo, who sat at the far side of the room with Mr Feasby. 'The trouble is she hasn't actually broken any law that I can think of. Blast her.'

'Bertie certainly made off quickly after he'd heard what she had to say.' Thomas paused. 'He was extremely distressed. I wonder if he decided to run away. So maybe he hasn't been taken after all?'

'He can't run far. This is an island. The ferry won't be sailing until later today at the earliest. One of the fishermen said that the full moon is producing unusually high tides.'

'The poor little chap. I hope we can find him soon.'

Abberline withdrew into his thoughts for a moment. At last, he said, 'Thomas, before the boy left you and Jo last night, how was he? His manner? His mood?'

'As I said, he was upset to hear Jo accuse him of being ... well, to put it bluntly, naturally evil. He had tears in his eyes.'

'Did he say anything in response to the accusation?'

'Yes, he started shouting that she was right. I don't know if he thought he should agree with what an adult told him, even if it was unpleasant.'

'Please tell me his exact words. This could be important.'

Thomas closed his eyes for a moment. He brought to mind the memory of the boy sitting on the high stool. He'd plenty of experience as a journalist in recalling the exact words of people who he interviewed. He did this now. He pictured the boy's frightened face and the words that had poured from his lips. Thomas opened his eyes again. 'He said: "She's right. I am bad, sir. I'm very bad. I put salt in Mrs Rice's tea ..." No, that should be: "Mrs Price's tea. I hid Wilf's shoes. I spied on him taking away that big dog. I shouted rude words at the milkmaid." That's all he said before he ran out of the refectory.'

'I see.'

'Probably every boy in this room could make a similar confession. Bertie can get up to mischief. To say he's evil, however, is evil in its own right.'

'Agreed.' Abberline rubbed his forehead as he thought about what he'd heard. 'Those words of Bertie's are interesting.'

'They were just the outburst of a little boy. Surely they aren't relevant to the case?'

'I disagree. They could be extremely relevant.'

'I don't see how.'

Abberline held up three fingers. 'In three instances Bertie identifies the three people he played tricks on – Mrs Price, Wilf and the milkmaid.'

'But he didn't say who he spied on.' Thomas felt a tingle run down his backbone; he sensed that this conversation was about to become extremely interesting.

'Exactly. Now ... why didn't he name that person or identify them in some way?'

Thomas felt baffled. 'He simply didn't choose to, that's all.'

'Imagine I told you a story about four people. Three of the people aren't in the room with us so, naturally, I'd name them. However, if the fourth person in the story was actually there with us then I might ...' He allowed his voice to trail off, leaving Thomas to complete the train of thought.

'Then you might find it unnecessary to name the person because they're in the room with you. You'd simply say "he did such-and-such a thing", and I'd know who you referred to.'

'Examine the words Bertie used. He said, "I spied on him taking away that big dog."'

'I took it that Bertie had watched someone take away a dog. Though it's hard to see such an incident would be important.'

'Break it down, Thomas. Look at particular words in detail. Bertie admits to "spying" on "him". That means he secretly watches a man or a boy. Why is he "spying"?'

'He doesn't want to be seen.'

'Why?'

'He might get into trouble if he's found spying on someone.'

'Why?' Abberline used the word 'why' like a hammer to crack open the hard shell of the mystery.

'Perhaps he realized that someone should *not* have been *taking* the dog, so he watched in secret.'

'Why? Which dog was taken?'

'A big dog.'

'No, he used the words "that big dog". The big dog was special in some way.'

'Ah ...' Thomas understood at last. 'It wasn't a big dog at all. It was Sir Terror. The wolf with the eagle's wings.'

Abberline leaned forward to whisper the next words so nobody else in the refectory could possibly hear. 'To be a detective is to be infuriatingly pedantic. We must not just look at the surface of things, we must bury deep and examine every word of a statement, every inflection in a voice.' For the first time in days the man wore an expression of relief as if he, at long last, had begun to make progress in a mystery that had steadfastly refused to reveal useful clues. 'Those nine words the boy spoke have just given me vital evidence.'

Thomas repeated that potentially key part of Bertie's statement: 'I spied on him taking away that big dog.'

'That's the most important sentence I've heard uttered on this island. Do you see why?'

Thomas felt an exciting flash of revelation. 'Bertie admitted to seeing a man or boy take the stuffed wolf from the Feasby cottage. The same wolf that was hidden in the tree in order to draw Benedict Feasby out along a branch and into the open so the bowman could kill him with the arrow.'

'What's more, when Bertie Trask made that admission to you last night, he didn't have to name the man or boy who took the wolf, because he could see that person was here in this room.' Abberline turned to look at the men and women in the refectory: they were all busily talking amongst themselves. Abberline nodded as he let the implications of what he discovered sink in. 'In fact, the boy was probably looking at the murderer at that very moment he spoke.'

Abberline moved quickly. He now suspected that the killer had been in the refectory last night. Thomas had not been able to identify many people who'd been there. After all, there had been at least fifty or so. Some had been eating supper. Children had been scampering about. The butler had been scolding them. Thomas had been engaged in the heated conversation with Jo as she declared that Bertie Trask had a skull formation that suggested an inborn malevolence. So, at that moment, he hadn't been looking back at the crowded room. He couldn't even begin to guess who Bertie had been looking at when he said: 'I spied on him taking away that big dog.' This, Abberline maintained, was the boy confessing to secretly watching another boy, or a man, making off with the stuffed wolf creature known as Sir Terror.

Abberline walked briskly into the hallway. For a moment, he gazed at the front door, which was guarded by Richard. The young man peered out through a small window at the forest.

Abberline spoke to Thomas. 'It would be a waste of time examining the door. It was guarded last night. It's unlikely Bertie, and whoever abducted him, would use that route.'

'There are plenty of windows at the back of the building.'

'A corridor runs alongside them. They were all visible to the sentries there.'

'All the other doors were locked and guarded too. Professor Giddings has done an excellent job of turning this place into a fortress.'

'So how would the kidnapper remove a child from the palace?'

'An upper window?'

'Much too exposed. And wouldn't we have found a rope or a ladder?'

They passed a room where the two detectives, Lionel and Harry, sat at a table. They both used fountain pens as they worked.

Abberline said, 'I've asked them to write up the case notes while the details are still fresh in their minds.'

'They're good men. I don't think I've seen such dedicated policemen. Apart from yourself,' Thomas added quickly.

'Thank you, my friend. Yes, they have plenty of energy as well as dedication. I think I'll soon be testing them to their limits.'

In the next room, King Ludwig stood watching a man of about forty turn the silver wheels of some apparatus that rested on four metal legs.

Abberline murmured to Thomas, 'I see the academy work goes on.'

'The annual assessment. The king and the academy members take it very seriously.'

'More seriously than a missing boy.'

'It would seem so.'

Abberline stopped abruptly. 'Let me think. Bertie was last seen at ten o'clock last night at the latest. It was only at seven this morning that staff realized he was missing.'

'Which means the kidnapper could have removed him at any time during the night.'

'So they had ample time to carry the boy to the other end of the island, if need be, and still return here before he was missed.'

'Do you think that the person who took Bertie overheard him telling Jo and myself that he'd seen someone steal the wolf?'

'I'd say it's most likely. They realized they must make Bertie vanish before he revealed anything that would lead us to identifying the killer.'

'They're going to do away with Bertie, too, aren't they?'

'Yes, they will, if they haven't already.' Abberline's expression was grimly determined. 'Which means that while there's a chance we might find the boy alive we have to devote every moment to searching for him.'

'We must organize a search party.'

'You're absolutely right. Just wait here, won't you? I'll be right back.' Abberline hurried to the room where the detectives sat writing at the table. Abberline soon returned. 'I've told them to gather the able-bodied men. We'll begin searching the island twenty minutes from now.'

Jo swept along the corridor towards them. She was conventionally dressed in long skirts and a white blouse. 'I've heard about Bertie.' Her manner was brisk, almost cold. 'Have you any idea where he is?'

Thomas glared at her. 'Why? Do you intend to arrest him for possessing the wrong shaped head?'

'I want to help,' she told him.

Abberline's expression was an unhappy one. 'I regret to say that I haven't even been able to discover how the kidnapper took the boy from here.'

Thomas added, 'All the doors and windows have been in sight of the guards all night.'

'Even the entrances to the basement?' Without waiting for a reply, she strode towards a doorway. 'Follow me.'

At the top of a staircase she used a match to light a candle. After that, she hurried down the stairs. Thomas and Abberline followed her into the shadows.

'The place is used mainly to store firewood and coal,' she explained. 'I sometimes use it as a darkroom when I develop photographs.'

She led them past mounds of coal. A rat scuttled within inches of her feet. Even though she saw the creature, she didn't react.

Abberline said, 'I expect that nearly everyone on the island will know about these cellars?'

'Yes. Some of the fishermen are hired to carry sacks of coal up from the ferry to the palace. It's tipped down a chute. And there –' She raised the candle to illuminate another set of steps, leading upwards '– is a door that wasn't guarded last night.'

Abberline climbed the steps to the door. 'There is no lock,' he said. 'It's merely secured from the inside by bolts.'

'There you have the kidnapper's exit, gentlemen.' Triumph flashed in her eyes. 'He took the boy through that door, left it unlocked, and returned later to close the bolts. And nobody in this building was any the wiser.'

Abberline looked her straight in the eye. 'How do you know this?'

'I have an imagination, too. Though I believe I have imagined the sequence of events accurately, don't you?'

Abberline gave a sharp nod. 'There's no time to lose. We have to search the island. Find the boy before it's too late.'

Abberline descended the steps before moving quickly away across the basement. He was desperate to send the men out in the hope of locating the child.

Jo walked alongside Thomas, holding the candle high so it illuminated the way for all three. She lightly touched Thomas's arm.

'Thomas. I'm going to look for Bertie, too.'

'You feel remorse for what you said about him?'

'What I said about his innate criminal tendencies is true.' She shot him a meaningful glance. 'I must also make another statement that is true: We're playing into the killer's hands. He wants us out there in the open. Just as he lured Benedict Feasby into the open with that monstrous wolf, so he's luring us out into the forest.'

Jo went to change into her outdoor clothes. Perhaps she was keen to make amends after all? But was she really going to admit that her belief in the quack 'science' of discovering personality by feeling the curves of a human skull was pure nonsense? Thomas doubted it. There were so many qualities in the woman that he admired, however. If only she didn't devote her life to the mean-spirited doctrine of phrenology. The phrase 'fly in the ointment' came to mind. The meaning of that homely phrase attained a new clarity as he pictured a jar of fragrant balm spoilt because a small yet ugly insect floated there. Jo's radiant personality was marred by her vile dogma. Thomas clenched his fists. He realized that thinking about Jo had become a habit. No, thinking about the woman had gone beyond habit – it was an obsession.

Thomas followed Abberline to the refectory. Around two dozen people sat at the tables. A little child stood at the piano, hitting keys at random and smiling as the plinking notes echoed around the room. The butler sat with his collar undone and feet splayed out. The man was exhausted from having to cater for so many people.

Abberline pointed to the alcove. 'That is where Jo examined Bertie Trask last night?'

'Yes.'

'That is the stool he sat upon?'

'Yes, it's the same one.'

Abberline's gaze took in the room. The man was thinking hard, no doubt turning possibilities over in his mind. When he spoke it was in a whisper. He didn't want anyone else in the room to overhear what he said. 'Thomas, please put the stool where it was last night.'

Thomas positioned the stool in the centre of the alcove.

Abberline nodded. 'Will you sit on it just as Bertie did when he said those words?'

Thomas did so. Abberline, meanwhile, took hold of a long wooden pole with a hook on the end that was used to open and close the windows that were too high to be reached with arms alone. He held the end of the pole so the hook part was in his two hands.

'Thomas,' he whispered. 'Visualize the little boy as he sat there last night. Try to remember *exactly* where he was looking when he spoke the sentence about the dog. As you do so, look in the direction Bertie looked.'

Thomas pictured Jo standing there with her hand resting on the boy's head. He took a deep breath and tried as hard as he could to remember every detail. When he spoke he kept his voice as low as possible so that no one, other than Inspector Abberline, would hear: 'The room was crowded, very noisy. Bertie looked over in that direction as he said: "I spied on him taking away that big dog."'

Thomas stared in the same direction as Bertie had last night.

Abberline raised the five-foot-long pole and held it level with Thomas's gaze just in front of his face.

'Don't move,' Abberline told him. 'Keep looking in the same direction as he did. Now imagine you're looking along the barrel of a rifle. What do you see?'

The pole directed his gaze to a small area of the room.

Thomas said, 'I see a table. Beyond that is open floor. And beyond that …' His voice trailed away as shivers ran through him. The child now stood on the piano stool, hitting the keys at random, producing discordant notes. '*The piano.*'

Abberline lowered the pole. 'So, Bertie's eye-line was directed at either the table just there, or at the piano.'

'I don't remember exactly who sat at the table. The fishermen's families, I think.'

'And the piano? Who sat at the piano?'

Thomas found himself holding his breath with astonishment. His heart pounded. 'The king's youngest son. He played music for the children as they danced.'

Abberline gave a sharp nod. 'Tristan. He's now become our main suspect.'

'We should tell the king.'

'No, Thomas. We'll tell no one. If Tristan doesn't know that we suspect him then we retain the element of surprise.'

'We should at least find Tristan's whereabouts. He might have hidden the boy somewhere in this building.'

'That's what we must do, and as quickly as possible. Remember, Bertie can identify Tristan as the man who stole the wolf.' Abberline's expression revealed what he was thinking. 'Tristan, if he is the killer, will want to get rid of witnesses. Even if that witness is a little child.'

Finding Tristan, the twenty-two-year-old prince of Faxfleet, wasn't easy. The two detectives and three constables had already led the search teams away from the palace and into the forest in order to begin combing the island. Inspector Abberline asked the men guarding the main door for the names of the people that comprised the search parties. Once again, Thomas saw that witnesses could be far less than perfect. The men listed the individuals who had left the palace in order to look for the boy. However, the men couldn't remember all the names. One footman insisted that the head gardener had left with the first party. However, a moment, later the head gardener emerged from a room that led off from the hallway.

The gardener blinked in surprise when Abberline asked if they'd had any luck with the search. 'No, sir,' said the man. 'I haven't been out of the palace this morning.'

Abberline patiently continued to question the guards. In a seemingly careless way he mentioned a few names of people who might have headed out with the search parties this morning. Casually, he dropped the name of Tristan into the list. A guard said he was sure that Tristan had been with one of the groups. Another declared he was certain that Tristan wasn't, and thought he'd heard him playing the chapel organ just a few minutes ago.

With a tight smile, Abberline thanked the men for their help. He motioned for Thomas to follow him.

When they were some distance from the guards, Abberline said, 'If our luck's in, we can catch our man in the chapel.'

Abberline broke into a run as he made his way along the corridor. The chapel doors were in sight. Thomas followed. His heart pounded and he wondered what they'd find there. Organ music suddenly filled the corridor. The booming notes grew louder and louder. Abberline threw open the chapel doors. The music immediately stopped dead.

They approached the man in black as he sat at the organ. He turned on the stool to face them.

'Ah, good morning, gentlemen.' Virgil Kolbaire lifted his bandaged hand. 'I am delighted to tell you that I can play this instrument with just one hand.' Turning back to the keys, he began to play a doom-laden melody. 'See, gentlemen! Anything is possible if one tries hard enough!'

Abberline snarled with frustration. When they were back in the corridor again, Abberline checked that nobody was close enough to hear.

'Thomas. Tell no one that we're looking for Tristan, otherwise someone is bound to inform him. We must catch him by surprise. If we don't, he'll kill Bertie to make sure the child is silenced forever.'

'What now?'

'We'll have to search the palace for Tristan by ourselves. If anyone asks, pretend we're looking for the boy again.'

They hurried back into the main part of the building. Thomas had seen Tristan's name on a door on the upper floor. That was clearly Tristan's room and their obvious destination. Abberline agreed. However, when they entered the room they found it deserted. Abberline's expression became increasingly grim and more desperate. He knew time was running out for the kidnapped boy. In fact, it might already be too late.

'Inspector,' Thomas said, 'I have a feeling that we won't find our man in the palace.'

'My instincts are saying the same. It's time we headed outdoors.' Abberline reached into his jacket and pulled out a revolver. After checking the gun was loaded, he pushed it back into his pocket again. 'We're entering the stage of high stakes. This will be life or death. Are you ready?'

'I'm ready.'

'You've become a good friend. I wouldn't trust another man with my life. I trust you, though.'

'Thank you, Inspector.'

Abberline nodded then led the way downstairs to the main entrance.

Abberline called out to one of the footmen, guarding the door. 'Give Mr Lloyd your shotgun, and the bag of ammunition.'

The footman obeyed. As Thomas took the weapon, Jo breezed along the corridor. She wore the leather kilt and pantaloons again, together with boots, a riding jacket and a red scarf. Thomas noted that she carried the longbow. A quiver full of arrows was slung across her back. She cut an astonishing figure, one that blazed with energy and determination.

'Gentlemen,' she called out in a powerful voice. 'You will inform me that I am a mere woman. You will insist that it isn't safe for me out there. You will tell me, dear Thomas, that I should stay here.' Her eyes shone like those of a huntress from legend. 'Let me tell you, gentlemen. I will not remain within these walls. I am coming with you.'

Thomas realized that they made a strange sight as they left the palace. Two men in suits and hats – one in his thirties, the other in his fifties – and the young lady carrying the archer's longbow. What would have been sure to turn heads (if there were any heads to turn nearby) was the short leather kilt she wore over the pantaloons. She looked like a female Cossack – a fierce horsewoman from the Russian wilderness.

There was nobody else in sight outdoors. Thomas glanced back. Several people gazed at them from the palace windows. Thomas recognized Mr William Feasby, who waved. Thomas waved back. *Will we catch the killer of that man's brother today? Could it really be that Tristan is the murderer? If so, what is his motive? Benedict Feasby was a harmless eccentric with a love of all God's creatures. And what could Mrs Giddings have done to Tristan that was so awful that he felt compelled to poison her?* Thomas would have liked to discuss Tristan at that moment, especially as so many ideas were coming to the boil inside his head, but Jo was there. Abberline had insisted that they keep their suspicions about Tristan between themselves for the moment. Abberline believed that this would, when the time was right, give him the advantage.

They walked along a woodland path. A strong breeze tugged at the branches, making the leaves hiss and the trees creak.

Jo asked, 'Where do we look first for the boy? The cottages?'

Abberline shook his head. 'We should join one of the other search parties.'

'If we can find them in all this.' Jo waved an arm at the forest.

'There will be five groups of men in all,' Thomas told her. 'We should come across one of them before long.'

They pressed on through the forest. The sound of a body crashing through the bushes behind them caused them to spin round. In one fluid moment, Jo had plucked an arrow from the quiver and placed it on the bow, with the string in the arrow's notch ready to fire. A stag broke through the greenery. It bounded across the path and vanished again.

'The animal seemed frightened,' Thomas pointed out.

'Is there any wonder,' Jo said. 'There are dozens of men with guns tramping through the woods.'

Abberline eased the revolver from his pocket. 'And possibly a man who commits murder, acts of mutilation, and kidnap.'

'A man?' Jo's eyes were sharp. 'So, you have a suspect?'

'I beg your pardon, miss.' Abberline continued walking. 'I shouldn't make slipshod statements. The killer could be a man or a woman.'

'Do you suspect me?'

'Is there any reason I should?'

She shot a loaded glance at Thomas. Her expression was of someone who had been cruelly misunderstood. 'No doubt Thomas has revealed what we have discussed together. He'll have told you that I had been examining the skulls of the islanders.'

'Ah, phrenologists. I'm sure if they went to dinner with members of the Flat Earth Society they would become the best of friends.'

'That is a hurtful comment, Inspector.'

Just then, a gunshot came from some way off. They froze on the path, listening.

Thomas said, 'It sounded more like a shotgun, rather than a pistol or a rifle.'

Jo's eyes scanned the trees. 'The gun must have been fired by one of the men in the search party.'

Abberline cocked his pistol. 'Or fired by whoever kidnapped the boy.'

Thomas peered into the shadows beneath the trees. 'This is hopeless. The forest is as thick as a jungle. There aren't enough people on the island to make a proper search.'

'Nevertheless, for now, we're on our own,' Abberline told them.

Thomas shook his head. 'Then perhaps the island should be evacuated before anyone else is hurt or abducted.'

Jo gave a regretful sigh. 'The ferry's unable to make the crossing to the mainland because the tides are unusually high. There's so much water coming in from the sea that the currents speed up to the point that boats can't make any headway.'

Abberline led the way along a narrow, twisting path. 'All of which means nobody can leave, we can't bring in reinforcements. And there is no way of sending a message to the outside world.'

Thomas felt a growing sense of being trapped here on this little patch of land in the river. 'Ludwig should have a telegraph wire run across the riverbed. It's time he brought modern ways to this place. Surely it would be simple enough to –'

A savage blow struck both of Thomas's ears at the same time. For a moment, he thought an attacker had landed punches on him. That is, until he saw white smoke billow in front of his face. He smelt burnt gunpowder, and realized he hadn't actually been struck with fists. No, there had been a tremendous explosion that had half deafened him.

'Inspector?' he called.

Jo crouched down over a dark mound on the earth. That's when Thomas saw what that mound really was.

'Inspector!' He lunged forward, his ears still ringing from the thunderous bang.

Inspector Abberline lay on the ground. His face was twisted in pain.

Jo shouted, 'He's been shot!'

Thomas saw blood seeping wetly through the fabric of the man's trousers, just above his right ankle. 'He's been hit in the leg. Do you have anything we can use as a dressing?'

Jo pulled squares of lace from her jacket pocket. 'I have clean handkerchiefs.'

Thomas called out, 'Inspector. Can you hear me?'

He unlaced the injured man's boot.

Abberline sat up, pushing Thomas's hand away. 'No! Keep your wits about you! Look around. Can you see the gunman?'

Thomas quickly got to his feet, raising the shotgun to his shoulder as he did so. Jo drew an arrow back on the bow, ready to fire the second she saw the attacker.

Smoke from the gunshot drifted away into the trees – a white ghost of a shape.

'I can't see anyone,' Thomas hissed, 'can you?'

She shook her head. 'But the weapon was fired close by. It went off just a yard from the inspector.'

Thomas searched the ground. Masses of dry leaves lay across the path. Frowning, he kicked them aside.

'Look.' He pointed at a long strip of iron that had been partially exposed when he kicked away the leaves. 'It's one of the old spring-guns that gamekeepers used against poachers.'

Jo eased off Abberline's boot. He grunted with pain.

'An automatic gun?' Her expression was one of horror. 'Anyone could have been killed by it. A child. Anyone.'

Thomas pulled the device from the undergrowth. Essentially, it was a long iron strip attached to a short gun barrel.

Thomas glared at the device in fury. 'See? If anyone stands on the metal strip when it's hidden under leaves or grass, it releases a spring that causes the gun to fire.'

He glanced at a tree trunk at the other side of the path. Metal beads peppered the bark.

Jo beckoned Thomas. 'Hold his leg steady so I can press the handkerchiefs against the wound. I have to stop the bleeding.'

Thomas ran his fingers over the metal shot embedded in the tree. 'Fortunately, most of them missed.'

'Thomas, help me. It's important.'

He crouched beside her. He supported Abberline's leg beneath the calf and the heel as Jo pressed the squares of lace against a puncture wound just above the man's ankle. The blood was a rich red. It glistened wetly.

Thomas looked at Abberline's face. He was very pale but conscious.

'Do you know what happened to you?' asked Thomas.

'I stepped on a spring-gun.'

'Spring-guns have been illegal for years.'

'They have.' Abberline flinched as Jo exerted pressure on the handkerchiefs to stem the flow of blood. 'But someone has been setting them as mantraps again. The gunshot we heard earlier might have been another one of the damn things going off.'

'So the killer might have set mantraps for the search parties?'

Jo said, 'That won't deter us from looking for Bertie.'

'No.' Abberline grimaced as the pain bit deep. 'But they have a sense of the dramatic. They know that the use of mantraps will result in ... in plenty of ... agh ... newspaper stories and ... and public interest. The killer wants their activities to become famous. Agh, my leg stings like fury.'

Jo said, 'It looks as if the pellet gashed your leg rather than becoming embedded in the flesh.'

Thomas felt a great deal of relief that the wound wasn't a very serious one. 'Don't worry, Inspector. I'll get you back to the palace. We can treat the wound properly there.'

'He won't be able to walk,' Jo said. 'Moving his leg will open the wound up again.'

Thomas spoke firmly. 'I can carry him.'

'My friend.' Abberline managed a smile. 'It's too far. You'll need a cart for these old bones.'

Thomas stood up. 'I'll go back to the palace and bring help.'

Jo shook her head. 'I'll go.'

'I can run there.'

'I would bet an entire pot of gold that I can run faster than you, Thomas. Besides, I know shortcuts. You'll take twenty minutes to reach the palace. I can be back there in ten.'

Thomas gave her a direct look to show he was concerned for her. 'Are you sure?'

'Absolutely. Here, keep pressure on the wound. Don't let this policeman move one inch, otherwise his leg will start bleeding again.'

Thomas knelt down beside where Abberline lay on the ground. He pressed his fingers down onto the delicate lace handkerchiefs that were now sodden with blood.

Jo picked up her bow. 'Keep applying firm pressure, Thomas. I'll be back as soon as I can.'

She darted away into the forest. Her red scarf fluttered, and her long legs were a blur. It was almost like watching a deer flitting amongst the trees.

Thomas knelt beside Abberline as he lay on the path. There was nobody else in sight. No sounds, either, that even hinted people might be nearby. Abberline's face had become pale. Every moment or so he grimaced in pain. The shot from the automatic gun had left a deep gash above the man's ankle. Thomas hoped the metal pellets hadn't shattered the bone.

Abberline took a deep breath. 'Don't look so worried, Thomas.'

'You've bled a good deal.'

'Blood renews itself in the veins, doesn't it?' He smiled. 'I'm sure I'll be back on my feet in no time.'

Thomas pulled out his pocket watch. 'Jo has been gone nearly thirty minutes.'

'It'll take time to bring a handcart through the forest.'

'The devil.' Thomas felt the heat of his anger surge through him. 'It was Tristan who did this, wasn't it? He hid that damn spring-gun so it would injure the first person who walked along this path.' Thomas glanced at his shotgun leaning against a tree. 'If he comes this way, I'll blast him to kingdom come.'

'It's justice we want, Thomas, not revenge.'

'The man's clearly trying to make his attacks famous – murder by bow and arrow, using exotic poisons, electric shocks, mutilating a composer's hand – now this: mantraps. Those will be the kind of stories that will capture the public's attention. Tristan must be afflicted with some kind of egomania or narcissistic condition.'

'We don't know that it is Tristan who carried out the attacks. He's a suspect, that's true. But we can't assume that he's the perpetrator. Ack … Thomas. My leg isn't Tristan's throat.'

'I'm pressing too hard? I'm sorry.' Thomas released pressure on the handkerchief that he'd been forcing against the wound. Gently, he lifted the pad of lace. 'The bleeding has stopped.' He glanced back along the path. 'I thought Jo would have brought help by now.'

'No doubt she will be here soon.' Abberline patted Thomas on the arm, a gesture of affection. 'When she does, we won't be able to discuss matters openly. Don't mention that we suspect Tristan is the killer.'

'But he should be found.'

'We must retain the element of surprise.'

'He might be holding Bertie prisoner. Considering what Tristan has done in the past then he'll be planning to kill the lad in … let's say a spectacularly newsworthy way.'

'Thomas, your expression suggests that we should tell everyone that Tristan is our suspect. But imagine the king's reaction. If I tell him that his son might be the murderer he simply won't believe me. He might even have me locked up in the palace cellar because he thinks I've lost my mind; then I will be of no use whatsoever.'

'I see.'

'So you understand that keeping our suspicions about Tristan a secret might determine whether Bertie Trask lives or dies?'

The sound of voices came along the path.

'This sounds like our rescue party.' Abberline tried to be cheerful although he grunted with pain.

To Thomas's surprise the group wasn't brought here by Jo. In fact, a constable in uniform led half a dozen fishermen. One man carried another man on his back. A single glance told Thomas that the man being carried had suffered an injury to his leg.

The constable rushed forward with the words: 'Good Lord. Another one of those damn guns has gone off. Inspector, are you hurt bad?'

'Just a cut,' Abberline said.

Thomas said, 'The bleeding's stopped.'

One of the fishermen stepped forward. 'I'll carry the gent on my back.'

'I'm not light,' Abberline warned him.

'Don't worry, sir. I can manage you.'

The fisherman had white hair and bright blue eyes. The broad shoulders suggested that the man possessed a massive physical strength. A lifetime hauling nets had given him plenty of muscle. A couple of other men helped Abberline onto the fisherman's back, so he'd be carried piggy-back style like the other wounded fellow. Soon, the strange procession continued on its way through the forest.

Thomas, meanwhile, began to feel increasingly uneasy. 'Jo should be here by now. What's happened to her?'

Fifteen minutes later, the group made it back to the palace grounds. The fishermen had taken it in turns to carry Abberline and their injured friend. Both men were conscious, and both were in pain. As they approached the palace Thomas broke away from the group to run the last hundred yards to the front doors. The doors opened to reveal one of the footmen he'd seen earlier.

'Where is Miss Hamilton-West?' he asked, using Jo's surname.

The footman appeared taken aback. 'The lady left with you.'

'She came back here about an hour ago.'

'I haven't seen her, sir.'

'You've been here all the time?'

'Yes, sir. I watched you leave with the lady and the Scotland Yard gentleman. Nobody has been through these doors since then.'

Thomas felt the skin all over his body become cold. He wanted to find Jo as quickly as possible, yet there was another important matter to be dealt with first. He said, 'There are two injured men on their way. Is there anyone here with medical knowledge?'

'Yes, Mr Manvers was a doctor before he became an artist.'

'Good. Make sure he's called to the entrance hall. The injured men will be here in no more than two minutes.'

Thomas raced back to the half a dozen men accompanied by the police constable. 'There'll be help waiting for you when you reach the palace.' He turned to Abberline. 'Inspector, I must speak with you.'

Abberline asked the fisherman to set him down. He put his arm around Thomas's shoulders in order to support himself.

Abberline spoke to the constable. 'Get everyone indoors. I'll join you in a moment.'

The constable nodded and led his search party towards the palace.

Thomas waited until he was sure they wouldn't be overheard. He whispered. 'Jo didn't return to the palace.'

Abberline gave a single, sharp nod. 'Then it's likely that she's been taken, too.'

'But where on earth could she be?'

'Even though this is a small island, there are still plenty of places to hide prisoners. Empty cottages, huts; the forest is as dense as a jungle in places.'

'I'm going to look for her.'

'Don't forget that Tristan is still out there.'

Thomas raised the shotgun. 'I've got this.'

'Very well, but take care.'

Thomas reassured Abberline that he would.

Abberline said, 'When I see Metcalfe and Scott I'll tell them that Tristan is the murder suspect. I can trust my own men not to give the game away until Tristan is caught. As I said earlier, I don't want to be in a position where I have to persuade Ludwig that his own son might be the killer. If he doesn't believe me, I'll lose what authority I have here. Now ... leave me. Go find Jo and Bertie.'

'You can't walk.'

'Don't worry about me. One of the footmen will help. Go, Thomas. Every minute counts. If you see any of the other search parties tell them that I gave you permission to take charge of the search.'

'Thank you.'

'Oh, and keep out of the forest as much as you can. There'll be more of those infernal spring-guns in there.'

Thomas made sure that Abberline could stand by himself. That done, he gripped the shotgun tightly in one hand, and raced back along the path.

This part of the forest didn't have another human being in it as far as Thomas could see. He smelt the damp earth beneath the trees. Rabbits hopped across the path in front of him. Birds sang in the branches overhead. More than once he thought he saw a crouching figure. He'd whip the shotgun up to his shoulder only to realize that what he took to be an assassin was an old tree stump.

His imagination showed him in vivid detail what may have happened earlier, when Jo had headed back in the direction of the palace. Perhaps Tristan had been watching them all along. Might the automatic gun he'd hidden be as much to warn him that people were moving around the island, rather than a means to wound or to kill? The man was intelligent. He manipulated his victims' behaviour before he attacked. The sound of the gun, which had hurt Abberline, might also have drawn Tristan to them. When Tristan saw Jo leave, he followed her. Moments later he must have pounced. Where was she now? Was she even alive?

Thomas ran faster through the forest, searching at random, hoping to come across a clue. A mound of leaves covered the path in front of him. He skidded to a stop. Picking up a fallen branch from the ground, he brushed aside the leaves and stood quickly back. It was another of the old spring-guns that had been used as mantraps many years ago before they'd been outlawed. Landowners used these potentially lethal devices to injure trespassers and poachers. Long strips of metal were connected to a spring trigger fixed to the gun barrel. The automatic weapon would be loaded with gunpowder and metal pellets.

Thomas moved to a point where the open mouth of the gun's muzzle pointed away from him. He swung the branch down onto the long strip of iron. A click! The spring had been activated, which operated the trigger. There was a terrifically loud bang, a jet of smoke, and the pellets struck a nearby tree, stripping away bark. If he'd stepped on the thing, before noticing it, it's likely the skin of his leg would have been violently torn away just like the bark of that tree.

Thomas concealed himself behind some bushes. Would the sound of the gun firing bring Tristan again? Would the man want to see the result of his pernicious handiwork?

Five minutes passed. Rabbits returned to hop around the glade. They seemed content to nibble the dandelion leaves that grew there, suggesting that they hadn't heard another human approaching. Thomas waited another two minutes. No. It seemed that Tristan wouldn't be drawn into the open again. He'd realized, no doubt, that others would have guessed that the spring-guns were also a device that warned him people were in the forest.

Thomas continued along the path to the river. The tide had rolled out, exposing areas of sand and mud. He decided it would be safer to move along the shore. There, nobody could spring out from a tree behind him. Also, there wouldn't be any of those vicious automatic guns hidden on the beach.

Of course, he didn't know where to search. So, once again, he found himself walking in the simple hope of seeing Tristan, or some indication that he was nearby. It wasn't long before he noticed marks in the sand. He knelt down in order to examine them more closely. Two sets of footprints. One set seemed to be made by a man's shoes. The other set was smaller, with pointed toes. He recalled Jo's boots that tapered towards the toes.

Could these be Jo and Tristan's footprints? But why would she come to the beach with Tristan? After all, she was returning to the palace to bring help after Abberline had been wounded. These thoughts sped through Thomas's mind as he studied the footprints amid a scattering of white seashells. Of course, she had no reason to be suspicious of Tristan. Only Thomas and Abberline believed that the king's youngest son might have a connection to the killings and the abduction of Bertie Trask. Tristan could have invented a story to deceive Jo. *Come quickly,* he might have said. *I've found the child. He's badly hurt. I need you to help him.* It was quite reasonable in those circumstances that Bertie should be helped first. Especially if she believed that his life was in danger.

'So ...' Thomas murmured to himself. 'Jo goes with Tristan. She doesn't know she's alone with a murderer.'

Thomas gazed at the line of footprints. They told him the direction the two people had walked. However, after no more than a dozen paces they turned towards a broad line of pebbles where they disappeared. Thomas tried to pick up the footprints again. The land above the high-tide mark consisted of hard-packed soil, covered with grass. He could see no prints whatsoever. Jo and Tristan might have headed into the forest, or even backtracked across firm ground that wouldn't show any prints. Or they might have continued heading along the strip of grassland between the beach and the trees.

All Thomas could do, in the circumstance, was hope for a lucky break. He checked again that the shotgun was loaded. A moment later, he began walking quickly, following the line of the beach, scanning the area ahead as he went.

Thomas Lloyd continued walking. He kept his shotgun at the ready. Flocks of birds had settled onto the beach to feed. At the water's edge, a seal watched him walk past, its dark eyes glistening in the sunlight. Way off, in the centre of the river, big steamships lay at anchor, waiting for the turn of the tide before they could safely make for the open sea, which lay several miles to the east.

Thomas passed the old windmill at the water's edge. Twenty years ago this would have been on dry land. But now this derelict structure straddled the beach. The river had been steadily eroding the Isle of Faxfleet for the last decade or so. No doubt in a few more years the mill and its outbuildings would tumble into the river and be gone for good. The tall mill tower that once bore the sails of the windmill was nearest the water. Even from here Thomas could see huge cracks in its brick walls. The tides must already be eating away at the tower's foundations.

Thomas pushed on, walking briskly. He decided to check a cluster of vacant cottages in the forest that he'd noticed when he'd first arrived on the island. One of those could have been used to imprison Bertie and Jo. He turned inland. Almost straightaway he heard it – something like a clatter of falling stones.

Thomas looked back at the old windmill. Immediately, he saw the flash of red from the biggest outbuilding. This was a substantial two-storey structure. The flicker of red came again from a window.

Thomas stared in shock. 'That's Jo's scarf,' he breathed. 'I've found her.'

He ran back down the beach towards the derelict building. Jo must have seen him. Was she held captive there? And where was Tristan? The man was dangerous. Thomas realized that only too clearly. He tightened his grip on the shotgun, simultaneously curling a finger around the trigger. Perhaps it would have been safer to find the constables and Abberline's colleagues. However, if Tristan decided to kill Jo it would only take a moment. Finding the policemen might take hours, considering that the men were searching elsewhere on the island.

No, he told himself, *I must act now. This is the only way.*

He raced towards the two-storey building. The red scarf fluttered in the breeze. Jo remained out of sight. Perhaps she couldn't come to the window? She might have only just been able to extend her hand, holding the scarf, as far as the opening.

Thomas reached a door that hung askew from its hinges. He stepped into the building, alert to the slightest movement, his head turning as he listened for a noise that would suggest that Tristan was about to spring out at him. He heard nothing. Quickly, he found the room where he'd seen the scarf. And there it was, tied to the rotten frame of the window, fluttering and snapping sharply as the breeze caught it.

Is Jo still here? he wondered with a growing sense of fear for the woman's safety. *Or is she already dead?*

Thomas couldn't continue this furtive search of the mill. He threw caution to the wind and loudly called her name.

'Jo? Jo! Are you there? It's me, Thomas!'

Instantly, voices echoed from somewhere in the building. A woman and a child.

Thomas's heart surged. That must be Jo and Bertie. *They're alive!* He rushed along the corridor that stank of rot and damp.

'Jo? Tell me where you are?'

The voices that answered seemed to shimmer from far away. They were almost like the voices of spirits from another world.

'Jo! Keep shouting! I'll find you!'

The cries of the child and woman continued. They were full of terror, as well as a clamouring kind of hope, yet he couldn't make out any actual words amid the chaos of echo upon echo.

Then he realized why the voices sounded so ghostly. A doorway yawned to reveal steps descending into the earth.

With triumph soaring inside of him, he shouted: 'They're in the basement!'

Thomas clattered down the steps to find himself in a vault lit by candles. The smell of damp filled his nostrils. There was a strong odour of seaweed, too. At the bottom of the staircase, vaults ran to the left and to the right. He saw a scattering of debris on the floor that included pieces of furniture – stools, chairs, cabinets – along with bottles, jars and food cans – these must have been stored down here when this had been a working mill. His feet squelched in wet dirt when he entered the vault.

'Jo!'

'Thomas, here. Quick!'

An extraordinary sight met his eyes – so extraordinary it stole the air from his lungs and left him gasping in shock. For there, in the candlelight, were six iron cages. They must have measured five feet by five feet. In fact, the ironwork formed a cube that had been sealed at the top. The cages were old, red with rust: they must have been used to contain animals, perhaps just prior to slaughter, because huge iron hooks protruded from the ceiling where the carcasses of sheep and pigs might have once been hung.

Most extraordinary of all – two of the cages were occupied. In one, Bertie. In the second, Jo.

She threw herself at the cage bars, seizing one in each hand. 'Thomas! Don't stay down here! Fetch help!'

Even as she finished shouting those words, a tremendous thud echoed through the basement.

Thomas knew that was a door being slammed shut. Bolts rattled as they were shot home. He raced back to the steps but knew what he'd find. The basement door would be locked. They'd be trapped down here.

*

Candles set in holders fixed to the wall illuminated the scene. The brick-lined vault was as cold as a tomb. Strewn across the floor were pieces of wood, chairs, broken tables. All were rotting. Damp oozed from the walls in glistening beads.

Thomas had checked the door to the basement. This was made from heavy slabs of timber. The thing was soundly bolted from the other side. He tried to pull it open. The door didn't budge. He returned to where Bertie and Jo stood in the iron cages. The gates to the cages were padlocked shut. Those were formidable padlocks. Even though he knew he'd try his hardest to jemmy them open he doubted if he'd be successful with the bits of rusty metal lying here and there in the wet dirt. Maybe he could shoot off the locks with the gun? That could be possible, but it would also put the child and Jo in danger. They might be hit by deflected shotgun pellets. He stood before the cage that held Jo. The woman stared out at him.

'Tristan?' That was all he asked.

She nodded. 'I met him in the woods. He told me he'd found Bertie in the windmill and needed help freeing him. So I went with him. When we reached here he pulled out a pistol and made me come down into the cellar.'

'Did he hurt you?'

'No. In fact, he was remarkably courteous.'

'He killed Benedict Feasby and the two women.'

'Yes, at that point I realized that he had. That's why I didn't argue when he told me to step into this cage.'

Thomas looked through the cage bars at Bertie. The little boy shivered with cold and, no doubt, sheer fright. His eyes were large and his face bore the marks of tears. 'Bertie? Are you all right? He didn't hurt you?'

'I'm hungry.'

Jo said, 'Bertie told me that he hadn't been harmed.'

'I'm very hungry.'

'I'm sorry,' Thomas said, 'I don't have anything to eat. You're cold, though, so take this.' He slipped off his coat and fed it between the thick iron bars of the cage. 'Put it on.'

Bertie did as he was told. The huge overcoat seemed to engulf the lad. Its sleeves dangled down almost to the floor.

Thomas said, 'Jo, have you seen Tristan recently?'

'The last time was when he locked me in the cage. That's when he took my scarf.'

'He used it to lure me to the mill. I found it tied to a window frame.' He tugged at the gate, hoping that the hinges might give way. No such luck. They were strongly made. 'Did Tristan say anything to you?'

'Nothing, other than pretending he needed my help. That and telling me to go into this thing.' She slapped an iron bar with frustration. 'I can't believe I was so gullible.'

'Don't worry, I'll get you out.' He turned to Bertie. 'Did Tristan put you in the cage, too?'

'No!' Bertie pulled back the long sleeve so he could point. 'She did!'

'I did not,' Jo protested. 'Why on earth did you say that, Bertie?'

'You poked away at my head, you said I'd been born bad, and I was going to grow up to do nasty things to people. I heard you say that people like me should be locked up in jail before we did anything wrong. That's why I've been put in a cage. You're a nasty lady.'

'Bertie,' she began, trying to soothe the boy. 'Bertie –'

'Have you had that thing done to you?' Tears filled the boy's eyes. 'Have you had your head looked at to reckon if you were born bad, like me?'

Jo couldn't speak. She looked stunned.

Thomas said, 'I'm sure the lady would never do anything to hurt you, Bertie.'

'You can hurt people with words, can't you?' Bertie trembled with anger as much as distress. 'Things can be said that go into your heart and make you sad. That's what she did to me.'

Jo's own eyes glinted with tears. 'I'm so sorry, Bertie.'

The boy turned his back to her.

Thomas asked gently, 'Who brought you here?'

Bertie said nothing.

'Bertie, it wasn't Jo, was it?'

The boy shook his head.

'Who was it?'

'The king's lad.'

'Tristan?'

Bertie nodded.

'What's important now,' Thomas said, 'is to get both of you out of those cages.'

Jo pointed out an obvious fact. 'Even if you do that, how do we get out of the basement?'

'The search parties will find us before long.'

The woman shuddered. 'There's a very real danger that Tristan will come back here before anyone else. We can identify him as the man that abducted Bertie and myself. Tristan will want to make sure that we never speak to anyone.'

'Don't worry. I've still got this.' Thomas held up the shotgun. 'I can deal with him before he can deal with us.' He chose the words carefully to avoid scaring Bertie.

There was silence. Bertie stared into the corner of the basement. He seemed deep in thought.

At last, he turned to Thomas and said in a clear voice, 'Mr Lloyd. There's water. It's coming into the cellar.'

One look at what was happening in the corner of the vault was a revelation. Not a pleasant revelation at that. In fact, Thomas Lloyd experienced a sickening jolt of pure shock. But he realized now why the pieces of furniture lay all higgledy-piggledy on the floor. He knew only too clearly what had left the layer of wet mud under his feet. The mill stood on the beach, and the basement was a good twelve feet below ground level.

'The tide's coming in,' he said. 'The river will flood the basement. That's why the furniture is strewn about. Every time the water comes in it washes all this junk about and leaves mud on the floor.'

'Remember what I said when we first met on the beach?' Jo spoke in a tense way. 'When the tide comes in, it rises fast.'

Thomas did remember, and here he was, facing the incoming tide again. This time the water streamed through the vault's brickwork. He wondered if he could block its entrance somehow. However, he quickly realized that the river didn't flow into this subterranean room at any single point. It came through hundreds of little gaps in the brickwork. The water even oozed up through the floor beneath his feet. When he walked back to the cages his feet now splashed through two inches of water. And still it kept on coming.

'I don't want to drown,' Bertie said. 'My cousin drowned last year. He fell into the dock. They didn't find him for a week and his face had gone all green.'

'Don't worry,' Jo told him. 'The water won't come in very much.

All we'll get is wet feet.' She tried to make a joke of it. 'Once we've dried your shoes out by a fire they'll be right as rain.'

Thomas agreed, 'You're safe. The water won't get very deep.'

Even as he said the words his eyes were drawn to white speckles clinging to the iron bars at the top of the cage. Barnacles. He touched them. Yes, definitely barnacles. The presence of the tiny shellfish sent him to check the walls. Soon he found what he was looking for.

Jo watched him anxiously from her cage. 'What have you seen?'

He returned to her and put his face close to the bars.

'There's a high watermark,' he whispered so Bertie wouldn't hear. He didn't want to scare the boy if he could help it. 'It's six feet above the floor.'

Her eyes snapped open wide as she heard his words. Then she looked up at the iron bars that formed the top of the cage. They were barely five feet above the floor. The tall woman had to stoop in the space that confined her.

'We have to get out of here,' she whispered back at Thomas. 'The water will rise higher than the top of the cages.'

Bertie sensed there was something wrong, even though he couldn't possibly hear what they were whispering. 'What's going to happen?'

Thomas made sure he was smiling when he said, 'Don't worry. I'm going to open the cages and get you out.'

'How?' Bertie looked down at the water. It had reached his knees. 'You aren't strong enough to break the padlocks. We're going to drown, aren't we?'

By now, water poured through the cracks in the walls with a rushing sound. Chairs began to float out of the shadows. Thomas picked up a burning candle and quickly searched the entire basement. There was a second entrance. This was a wooden trapdoor set in the ceiling. Like the door to the basement, it was made of massively thick timbers, reinforced with strips of iron. He couldn't lift it at all – not even by a fraction of an inch, and by the time he returned to the cages the water was waist deep.

That's when he stopped and stared at the glistening cascade that gushed through the wall. Because it didn't seem so much as if water entered the vault – it was as if Death itself had stepped into this place. It had grown colder. Much, much colder. When Jo and Bertie breathed out, their breath came in big white clouds. It looked as if every time they exhaled, part of their spirit escaped from their bodies.

Thomas knew that he had no more than twenty minutes to free the woman and child from the cages. Twenty minutes from now the river water, which flowed down through the earth and into the basement, would reach the top of the cages. That's when the pair would drown.

Thomas surged through the water. He tugged at both of the cages' gates in turn. They were fixed lethally tight by huge padlocks. Quickly, he checked the height of the padlocks. They were now a couple of inches above the water's surface.

'It's now or never.' He took a firm grip on the shotgun. 'Bertie, go to that corner of the cage. Turn away from me. Cover your ears. You too, Jo.'

The boy did so immediately. Thomas aimed the gun at the padlock in such a way that the blast would be directed away from Jo and Bertie.

He fired. In the confined space the noise of the gunshot slammed back so fiercely that Thomas grimaced in pain. The pellets struck the padlock, causing lots of little dents in its metal casing. He tried to tug the padlock hasp open. No, it wouldn't budge.

'I'm going to try again.'

The flood now reached the padlock. If he didn't blast it free soon, the water would cover it and no amount of shooting would smash it apart. The water would effectively shield the device. He aimed.

'No!' Jo yelled. 'Lift the stock of the gun up so you're firing down onto the top of the padlock. That way it'll be like a hammer blow.'

Thomas glanced at Bertie. The child stood facing away from the gate, his hands over his ears. The water now reached his chest.

Thomas fired in the way that Jo had suggested. The pellets hit the lock, others splashed the water. Quickly, he tugged at the padlock. A terrific yell of relief burst from his lips as the padlock hasp slipped out of the lock. He worked the hasp free of the iron loops, swung the gate open and pulled Bertie clear. The water now threatened to float the little child away. Not wanting to delay for another moment, he lifted the boy onto the top of the cage. At least there he would be safely clear of the flood.

He turned round to attack the padlock on Jo's cage. To his dismay he saw it was submerged.

'Jo. Turn round and cover your ears.' He reloaded the gun.

'It's too late,' she said. 'The water will slow the shot down. It won't hit the lock hard enough.'

'I'm still going to try.' He fired at the lock as it became blurry under water. He fired again. He checked the bolt. 'It's still holding tight.'

'It's no good!' she cried. 'We'll have to think of something else.'

Even so, he reloaded and fired again. By this time the padlock was a foot deep. The water was up to his chest. He knew it was hopeless. He laid the shotgun across the top of the cage along with the satchel of ammunition, and he cursed himself for not shooting both locks off earlier. In truth, however, he had been afraid to try in case he'd hurt Jo and Bertie.

Thomas searched the basement, looking for a heavy iron bar that he could use to jemmy the gate. Some of the candles that were lower down on the walls were going out as the water drowned the flames. The higher ones should be all right for now. For the first time it occurred to him that Tristan must have left the candles there. Had he planned to capture more people and bring them here? Perhaps he intended to hold islanders to ransom? By now, Thomas could no longer stand up. The flow of the water carried him along with the swirling furniture and empty jars. He had to swim. That was the moment he heard screams. As quickly as he could, he swam back to the cages.

Bertie was safe. He stood on top of the cage that had once held him. However, he yelled as he pointed at the cage which imprisoned Jo. The water was just inches from its topmost bars. She had to stand with her face pressed upward against the iron slats in order to breathe. Two minutes from now the water would cover her little prison and she'd drown.

Thomas scrambled up onto Jo's cage. She looked up at him with such an expression of desperation he could have wept. She held her hand up through the bars. He seized hold, gripping tight.

'Keep holding my hand, Thomas dear,' she said in a soft voice. 'Don't let go until it's over.'

'I won't let you die,' he said.

'I know,' she said in those gentle tones. 'I know.'

But he could tell she had accepted her fate now, because she could not escape. Death waited just a few heartbeats away. She gazed up at him. Here in the gloom, her eyes seemed enormous. Her expression had become serene. She was at peace now. The water covered her entire body as far as her upturned face. Her nose and mouth were no more than a single inch above the water. Her short hair floated around her head. The woman was just on the other side of those bars. He could hold her warm, living hand yet there was nothing he could do to save her.

Jo continued to gaze up at him as the water crept higher.

That's when a volcano of rage erupted inside Thomas.

'I'm not letting you die!' he shouted.

'It's all right, Thomas. This is how it's supposed to be.'

'No.'

'Will you put your hand through the bars so I can kiss it?'

He rose to his feet.

'No ... No!'

'Please, Thomas.'

'No! Hold your breath and put your head underwater. Keep well down below the bars.'

She did as he asked. Thomas immediately stood up. He stamped down on one of the top bars with all his strength. A tremendous crash rang out through the flooded basement. He stamped again, and again, and again ... and then ... yes, he felt it move. He bent down and grabbed the iron bar as bubbles escaped from Jo's mouth. The iron had become weakened – the salt water that flooded the cellar twice a day had rotted the metal.

Thomas forced the bar aside, reached down into the water, grabbed hold of Jo and drew her up through the gap he'd created. The air that greeted her as she emerged was icily cold and smelt of brine. But it was good, clean air. She could breathe. The woman inhaled deeply. Her eyes were open but she seemed dazed for a moment. Thomas sat her down on top of the cage.

Bertie clapped his hands together. 'You did it, sir. You did it! You saved the lady!'

Jo's eyes cleared. Sucking in the air, she smiled and put her arms around Thomas's neck.

'Thank you,' she panted. 'You kept your word.'

'Now it's time to get out of here. Stay where you are – both of you. The water won't rise much higher.'

He grabbed the shotgun and bag of ammunition. After that, he lowered himself into the shockingly cold water. He managed to swim, holding the gun and bag above his head in one hand. He reached the steps that led up to the door. As silently as he could, he climbed the staircase. But not all the way to the top. He had a hunch now. What if Tristan intended to return to see the results of his handiwork? The man would surely believe that Jo and Bertie had drowned, but he'd know that Thomas must have survived. After all, the tide wouldn't fill the basement as far as its roof. No doubt the king's son had another means of execution planned for Thomas.

Thomas lay forward against the steps, his eyes level with the floor that led to the doorway. He saw a gap of perhaps half an inch between the bottom of the door and the floor. Something moved beyond it.

Yes ... he'd been right. Tristan lurked out there. He was sure of it. Thomas examined the bottom of the door. At the side nearest the hinge was a gap of perhaps three inches wide and two high. No doubt a persistent rat had gnawed an opening at the bottom of the door so it could pass to and fro. Thomas positioned himself so he could see through the rat's entranceway. Now he could hear the scrape of feet as they moved slowly back and forth. That had to be Tristan, surely. After all, if it had been a member of a search party they wouldn't be so furtive. Either the searcher would open the door to check the cellar, or they'd have moved away by now, believing that nobody was in the mill. Thomas didn't make a noise. He didn't want Tristan to know he was there, on the other side of the door. Carefully, silently, he eased the shotgun out onto the floor in front of him until the muzzle almost reached the hole made by the rat.

Thomas knew what he must do. The notion that this would be violent and cruel did cross his mind. But then he recalled Mr Benedict Feasby's death. That man loved animals and birds so much he devoted his life to protecting them. Of course, the Feasby twins had made those quirky creatures from the body parts of other animals, but those animals had died of natural causes. Then there were the gruesome deaths of Mrs Giddings and her sister. One poisoned, the other gassed.

Tristan had killed without even considering the pain he would cause his victims or the grief of their loved ones. Callously, he'd left a woman and a boy to drown in cages. Did the man deserve to be spared pain?When the brown shoe appeared directly beyond the hole at the bottom of the door, Thomas did not hesitate. He fired the shotgun through the opening and into the man's foot, which was no more than ten inches from the weapon's muzzle.

As the explosive bang of the gun died away, Thomas realized he could hear screaming. Blood seeped under the door. A different kind of tide this time – warm and red.

Thomas couldn't see much through that small hole. However, he saw legs, flat against the floor. A torn shoe. A bloody foot. Prince Tristan of Faxfleet wouldn't feel much like hurting anyone else for a while.

Thomas had an idea. He reloaded the double-barrelled shotgun and went back down the steps to their halfway point. From there, he leant forward with the gun aimed at the wooden hatch-door set in the ceiling. He fired into the wood at almost point-blank range. Splinters of wood cascaded down. The shot had scooped out an inch of wood. He fired again. This time the smoke from the shotgun was immediately sucked upwards and out of the basement. He reached up and pushed his hand through the opening he'd made. The hole was only a small one. There'd be no way of using that route to escape. It did, however, present an opportunity. He retrieved a couple of burning candles from the shelves. He placed them in glass jars so they wouldn't be blown out by the breeze then he pushed them up through the hole and left them standing outside on the trapdoor.

Thomas could see it was dark by this time. In such a remote place as this, the light of even just two candles burning in the blackness would be like a beacon.

Then Thomas returned to the cages where Bertie and Jo sat. He climbed back on top of the one where Jo sat shivering in the cold. He beckoned the child to join him and Jo.

Smiling, Thomas told them that everything would be all right; that they were safe. He put one arm around Jo's shoulders and the other arm around the little boy, and drew them both close to him. They sat like that for a while until there came the sound of bolts being drawn back, and suddenly the light of lanterns flooded the basement along with the voices of the men who had come to set them free.

Chapter 12

KING LUDWIG OF Faxfleet stared out of the window in utter despair. Thomas Lloyd sat in a corner of the bedroom, balancing sheets of paper on his lap, as he made notes with a pencil. Inspector Abberline sat in a wheelchair close to the bed, the bottom half of his leg and his entire foot swathed in white bandages. Abberline fixed his eyes on the king's youngest son, who lay on the bed. One of his feet was bandaged too. Tristan gazed dreamily at the ceiling. Thomas wasn't at all surprised by Tristan's faraway expression. He'd drunk a large tot of laudanum. Several glasses of brandy had followed that heady potion of opiates blended with wine.

Ludwig turned to Abberline, flung out his arms, and thundered, 'You will not arrest Tristan. I forbid it!'

'Sir, you must accept my authority as a senior police officer.' Abberline spoke firmly. He did not shout, yet his personality dominated the room. He was in charge. 'Your son has admitted to killing Benedict Feasby with the bow and arrow. He has described how he stirred poison into the rice that Mrs Giddings ate.'

'No, damn it.' Ludwig glared at Abberline. 'I am king of this island. I am the law. I will not permit you to arrest my son. You shall not take him to the mainland.'

'Tristan has admitted assault, kidnap and murder.'

'English law has no power on Faxfleet. You, sir, have no authority here.'

Abberline said, 'So, you will try your son for those crimes? Who will be the judge? You?'

'There will be no trial. Lloyd fired the shotgun at my son's foot. Tristan has lost three toes. He will limp for the rest of his life. I want you to arrest Thomas Lloyd, not my boy.'

'Mr Lloyd saved the lives of a woman and a child. He prevented a killer from striking again. He shouldn't be arrested; he should be awarded a medal.'

'Nonsense.' Ludwig looked as if he wanted to attack Thomas. 'Now, I demand that you leave Faxfleet.'

Abberline nodded. 'And Tristan shall go with us. He'll be taken to the jail in Hull where he will await trial.'

'No, he will not.'

Ludwig stormed forward to grab the arms of the wheelchair that Abberline sat upon. The king turned the chair away from the bed as if he couldn't abide Abberline looking at his injured son.

Tristan gave an inebriated chuckle. 'I shot little Feasby from the tree like he was a pigeon. As for Mrs Giddings and her sister? Well ... two birds with one stone I killed. One poisoned. One overcome by gas emanating from Giddings' belly.'

Abberline didn't look back at Tristan. He merely asked, 'Why?'

'Because ...' Tristan gave a long sigh. 'My blessed father's academy must be done away with. He invites ... to this island ... a vile assortment of eccentrics, lunatics, charlatans, and men with less artistic talent than a pig in its sty. He houses them for free, he feeds them, he gives them salaries ... and his wretched, wretched academy uses up all his money.'

Ludwig patted his son on the shoulder. 'There, Tristan. All is well now. There is no need to talk.'

Abberline spoke quickly. 'But your father needs to know your motive for murder, doesn't he?'

'Yes, he does, Inspector. He does indeed.' Tristan smiled at the ceiling as the drugs and alcohol swirled through his brain. 'This island shrinks day by day. When Faxfleet vanishes into the river it will take the kingship with it. The royal line will end. Our family will no longer be able to sell royal titles to wealthy men ... our income will then vanish and we shall become destitute.'

'So,' Abberline said, 'you wanted to embarrass your father so much by killing academy members in such a spectacular and newsworthy way that he'd be forced to dissolve the academy?'

'Yes.'

'If that happened, and the academy was no more, what should he do with the income that he earns every year?'

'It is searingly obvious.' Tristan rolled his head sideways on the pillow in order to look at where Thomas sat making notes. 'Mr Lloyd, the island is shrinking as the river shaves it away inch by inch. What would you do?'

Thomas realized that the man was so steeped in opiates and alcohol that he seemed to bear Thomas no ill-will for blowing part of his foot off. Thomas said, 'There must be an engineering solution to the island being eroded. Perhaps walls could be built along the beaches to prevent the island from being gradually destroyed.'

'Exactly!' Tristan sat up straight on the bed. 'Exactly! Father, old blunderbuss Lloyd here knows what should be done. But you, Father, waste your money. You have given away a fortune to absurd people who believe the earth is flat, or the shape of a skull determines whether the individual is good or evil ... you shower men with gold coins so they can daub hideously incompetent portraits or compose music that sounds like a chorus of demented cats. You, Father, are like Nero who happily played his fiddle while he watched Rome burn to the ground. Damn you, sir. You are a fool!'

'Tristan,' began Ludwig with tears in his eyes. His son's tirade clearly crushed him. 'Don't say these things. I care about you deeply. I have always –'

'Always done what? Done the *wrong* thing! Don't you realize that it will cost millions to fortify the island against it being washed away? You should dissolve that joke of an academy today and save every penny of your income for the next ten years ... only then will you have enough to reinforce this mound of boulder clay and dirt with granite. Then the island will last for a thousand years and so will our family's wealth.'

The young man had come close to raving. Ludwig sat on the bed with his head in his hands.

Abberline said, 'The ferry is sailing to the mainland today. My colleagues and I will be on it. Tristan shall, too. He is to be taken to Hull where he'll await trial.'

Ludwig shook his head. 'No ... no. English law has no jurisdiction here.'

'Faxfleet lies in the heart of England. If the public hear that a man will literally get away with murder in this country, there will be uproar. Neither the British royal family nor the government will protect you.'

'What am I to do, Abberline?'

'Surrender Tristan to me. He must face justice.'

'If I refuse?'

'There will be consequences. You must know that?'

Thomas spoke up, addressing Ludwig. 'Sir, Tristan was prepared to kill in order to protect the royal line and its wealth. Forgive me for stating this so plainly, sir: I believe that you, yourself, would eventually fall victim to him. Tristan is ruthless.'

Tristan lay on the bed and giggled.

Abberline spoke firmly: 'I agree. If you had stood in the way of his schemes then he would have found a way to dispose of you without drawing attention to himself.'

King Ludwig stared at his son, lying there, grinning, chuckling.

Tristan's head moved in an exaggerated theatrical nod. 'Father ... those gentlemen are much wiser than you.'

King Ludwig looked a broken man. At last he sighed. 'Very well. I surrender Tristan to your care, Inspector.'

Abberline asked Thomas to fetch one of the constables. The time had come to prepare for departure. However, Abberline told Thomas there was one other matter to settle.

As Thomas wheeled Abberline along the corridor, Abberline said, 'Would you please take me to the conservatory? Then ask Lionel Metcalfe to join me there.'

'Of course.' Thomas's mood had lightened. The dangerous and troubling times on the island were behind them. 'Would you like me to find Harry, too?'

'No, thank you. However, when I am alone with Metcalfe I would like you to hide outside the conservatory in the bushes and eavesdrop on our conversation.'

'Really?' Thomas was so surprised by this request that he stopped wheeling Abberline. 'Why on earth do you want me to do that?'

'It will become clear in the next few minutes. But it's vital you hear every word. Please make notes, too.'

Thomas did as he was asked. After wheeling Abberline into the conservatory, he went and found the detective by the name of Metcalfe and asked him to join Abberline. After that, Thomas made his way outside, where he settled down behind a bush close to an open conservatory window – there he could hear everything without being seen by Metcalfe.

Lionel Metcalfe arrived at the conservatory. Thomas couldn't see the two men. He heard every word, however, with absolute clarity.

Abberline spoke first. 'Please sit down, Metcalfe.'

'Thank you, sir.'

'I've been reading the witness statements you took yesterday.'

Metcalfe sounded concerned when he spoke. 'Is there something unsatisfactory about them?'

'I found them completely satisfactory.'

'Thank you, sir.'

'You wrote them in your own hand?'

'Yes.'

'As you know, as your commanding officer, I have to sign each one in order to verify that I've read them. Ah ... may I borrow your pen? I forgot mine.'

Thomas frowned. *Abberline never forgets anything.*

'Thank you.'

Thomas couldn't risk lifting his head above the bush to see what was happening. Metcalfe would notice him. However, Thomas guessed that Metcalfe had handed Abberline the pen so he could add his signature to the written statements.

What Abberline said next made Thomas's heart lurch with shock.

Abberline spoke quite calmly. 'Metcalfe, recently you forged a number of letters, supposedly from the Whitechapel Ripper, and sent them to me. Why?'

A pause. A long one, then Lionel Metcalfe exclaimed, 'Inspector? In God's name, why do you accuse me of such a thing?'

'The forgeries are excellent. Although when I see your handwriting here, on these statements, there are faint yet telling similarities to the letters I received that are signed "Jack the Ripper".'

'I deny it.'

'I have also studied earlier documents, which you've written using this pen you've just handed to me. I have compared the writing under a microscope with the latest Ripper letters.'

'Sir, you are mistaken.'

'I don't think so, Metcalfe.' Abberline spoke with complete confidence. 'The nib of your pen is slightly damaged. The downward stroke of a letter "l", for example, is split into two downward strokes running parallel to one another. The left-hand stroke is slightly, but measurably, wider than the right-hand stroke. Look, see for yourself. This is one of the Ripper letters. See how the downward strokes are formed by two lines, not one.'

'Why would I send hoax letters to you?'

'For some reason you wish to discredit me.'

'I'm sorry that you've drawn these bizarre and inaccurate deductions.'

'I shall tell you what I have concluded,' Abberline told him. 'You forged the Ripper letters, knowing that these would draw the newspapers' attention to me, the detective who failed to catch Jack the Ripper two years ago.'

'Sir, I would not –'

'Please let me finish. You forged the letters. Somehow, you discovered the body of Mrs Ruth Verity in a river in another part of London. You cleaned the body, dried the clothes, dressed her again, then smuggled the body into Whitechapel where you left it in a derelict house after mutilating it, so the poor woman resembled the original victims of the Ripper.'

'Why would I do that?'

'You wanted to publicly humiliate me so that I'd be forced to resign. Because I never would find Mrs Verity's killer, would I? The woman drowned in another part of the city. I daresay you want rid of me because you don't like my approach to policing. I am sure you are not acting alone, Metcalfe. I believe you, together with a number of your colleagues, want to build your own little kingdoms in London that you will rule. You will grow rich on the bribes you receive from criminals. You and your crooked friends might even resort to crime as well. After all, how did Mrs Verity die?'

'I freely admit that Mrs Verity took her own life. After I discovered her body in a river in Wembley I went to her house and found a suicide note, which I destroyed.'

'You will make an official confession.'

'Ha, never, Abberline. But I did want to see your face when I told you that I'd outwitted you.'

'I have evidence, Metcalfe. See this pen with the ever so slightly splayed nib? I can scientifically prove that this pen of yours wrote the Ripper letters that you sent to me recently.'

'Yes, of course you can prove that exact pen was used by the forger. I will make a statement saying that I found the pen on the floor at Scotland Yard just before I came to Faxfleet. If you insist the pen was used to forge the letters then, in effect, you are accusing every police officer based at Scotland Yard. After all, who is to say which man wrote the letters? Your accusation will outrage every constable and detective. They will despise you.'

'So, that's your plan, is it? You have engineered hoax letters and a false murder in order to publicly humiliate me.'

'Yes.'

'You know that would mean I'd have to resign from the police force? Without a salary I can't pay the rent on my home. My wife and I will be penniless.'

'That, Abberline, would be a deliciously satisfactory state of affairs. You, and your high-minded kind, have denied the ordinary policeman the right to earn a little extra on the side.'

'The "ordinary" policeman? The correct phrase is "corrupt policeman".'

'Well, seeing as we're done here, Abberline, I'll go and pack my things. We're returning to London today, aren't we? Oh, cat got your tongue? I wonder what kind of stories the newspapers will publish when they tire of your incompetence at finding Jack the Ripper – even though he's returned to Whitechapel under your very nose. Tell Mrs Abberline to pawn her wedding ring. You will need that money very soon. I'll join you on the ferry, sir. Cheerio.'

Thomas waited for the man to leave. A moment later, he heard Abberline say: 'He's gone, Thomas. Please come in.'

Thomas all but stormed into the conservatory. Lionel Metcalfe's vile words had made him furious.

'You heard, Thomas?'

'I'll say. Every poisonous syllable that man uttered.'

'Good. I'm pleased the matter of the letters has been cleared up and that devil they call Jack the Ripper hasn't returned to Whitechapel after all.'

'Pleased? Metcalfe is an absolute scoundrel. You will arrest him?'

'You heard what he said, Thomas. If I accuse him of writing the letters, he'll claim he found the pen at Scotland Yard. He's right. I'd be making every single person who works at Scotland Yard a suspect. They would hate me for making such a wide-ranging accusation.'

'So, what will you do now?'

'With regard to the hoax letters and the body left in Whitechapel? Nothing, Thomas. Absolutely nothing. My hands are tied.' Abberline looked up. 'Don't worry, my friend. We've succeeded here on Faxfleet.

Or, rather, you have. You will be able to write some very exciting articles for your newspaper.'

'But it's not finished, though. Not properly. Metcalfe must be brought to justice.'

'We can't win every battle, Thomas. Sometimes we must admit defeat. Now, will you wheel your grateful friend down to the jetty? The ferry leaves in twenty minutes.'

The sun shone down on the River Humber's wide waters. Many of the islanders came to the jetty to watch Prince Tristan being carried onto the ferry-boat. The young man's foot was heavily bandaged. Thomas saw spots of red on the bandages that covered the toes, or what was left of the toes. When Thomas fired the shotgun at the man's foot in the mill it had torn away the end of his foot. Thomas had expected to feel remorse at inflicting such mutilation; he realized he felt nothing of the sort. Tristan had killed innocent people and intended to kill more. In the end, the killings became a sort of game for him. He chose his victims on a whim, for his real motive was simply to draw public attention to his father's academy in the hope that there'd be widespread ridicule of the academy members and their bizarre work.

Thomas watched the constables lift Tristan aboard the ferry. The man was still inebriated and he waved to people on the jetty. Abberline's colleagues from Scotland Yard took their seats on the boat. Harry Scott chatted to Abberline, who sat beside him. It seemed that Scott had no idea that his friend and colleague, Lionel Metcalfe, had hatched a plot to discredit Abberline. Of course, Abberline could say nothing. He'd have to keep that loathsome conspiracy a secret. Thomas had to force himself not to glare angrily at Metcalfe.

As for Metcalfe, he sat opposite Abberline. He gave Abberline knowing smiles that were nothing less than gloating. He'd got the better of his superior officer and he knew it.

'Mr Lloyd, Mr Lloyd!' Bertie ran along the jetty to throw his arms around Thomas's waist. 'Sir, why don't you stay on the island? You have become a good friend to us.' Bertie turned back as he said the words. He looked directly at Jo, who walked towards them.

'I'm sorry, Bertie,' Thomas said. 'My home is in London. My place of work, too.'

'You're a newspaperman, aren't you, sir? Will you put all that happened to us in the paper? Will I see my name written there?'

'You will, Bertie. I shall write about you specially.'

'Thank you, sir.'

Jo approached. Her smile was as friendly as ever. 'So, it's farewell, my dear Thomas.'

He nodded. 'Tristan will be taken to the jail in Hull. Then I'll head back to London with Inspector Abberline and his colleague.'

'We shall see each other again, Thomas. I know we will.' She held out her hand.

When he took hold to shake it, she pulled him forward and kissed him on the cheek.

'It's been remarkable knowing you.' The woman held his gaze as she spoke. 'I found you somehow ... what's the correct word? Luminous ... yes, I found your presence here illuminated something inside of me.'

The ferryman called out, 'Going in two shakes, sir. Please come aboard.'

'Right you are,' Thomas replied. He turned to Bertie. 'Listen. You are a fine boy and you will grow up to be an honest man with a good life ahead of you.' He stared Jo in the eye, daring her to disagree with what he'd just said.

'Bertie,' she began pleasantly, 'remember Mr Lloyd. If you grow up to be like him then you shall accomplish all that your heart desires.'

Thomas nodded his farewells to both then took his place on the boat. He felt the tug of the current that would carry them away. Already, the river itself seemed eager to remove them from this unusual little kingdom.

Thomas sat beside Metcalfe, but only so he could face Abberline.

'King Ludwig didn't come down to watch his son leave,' Thomas said.

Metcalfe nodded. 'The man knows when he is beaten. Ludwig has retreated to his den to lick his wounds, as it were.' He stared at Abberline as he said the words. 'Ludwig will be too ashamed to show his face in public.'

Thomas would have dearly liked to throw the corrupt and mendacious Lionel Metcalfe overboard. All he could do, however, was watch the island dwindle into the distance, and the people, there on the jetty, waving as they shrank away to specks. Soon they had vanished completely.

One week later

Strands of mist ghosted along the street. London was as silent as a graveyard tonight. Thomas Lloyd had been at his desk writing all day and wanted nothing more than to move his limbs and try and work the stiffness from his shoulder; something that he'd acquired from sitting for so long with a pen in his hand.

From the mist came the sound of horses' hooves. Thomas watched a carriage approach, drawn by a pair of horses. He recognized the vehicle straightaway. The driver stopped the carriage alongside Thomas and touched the brim of his hat by way of a respectful greeting.

'Mr Lloyd, sir, would you kindly step into the coach?'

Thomas didn't hesitate. He opened the coach door, climbed in, and took his place in front of the man he'd spoken to before his trip to Faxfleet. The gentleman, aged seventy or so, didn't have a single hair on his head. Once again, Thomas looked into a pair of grey, intelligent eyes that regarded him with an air of calm authority.

'Mr Lloyd, you are quite well, I trust?'

'Very well, thank you.' Thomas didn't linger on niceties and said firmly, 'This is a remarkable coincidence, you passing by as I walked along this street, or did someone tell you where I'd be at this precise time?'

'I wished to speak with you.'

'So someone is spying on me?'

'Nothing so melodramatic, I assure you.' The stranger picked up a newspaper that lay on the richly upholstered seat beside him. 'My colleagues and I have been reading your account of the murder investigation on the Isle of Faxfleet. We are all agreed that it is wonderfully written and portrays Inspector Abberline as the kind of modern policeman that we admire so much. What's more, the story is an exciting one. The public at large will find it satisfying to read how you brought the young man, Tristan, down to earth, literally, with that well-aimed shot through the bottom of the cellar door. A most exciting narrative.'

'Thank you.'

'One can imagine families gathering together in their homes to read about those dramatic events that your pen captured so well.' His thin lips formed a smile. 'We hope you will continue to accompany

Inspector Abberline on many more investigations.'

'The case isn't finished yet. I'll be in the courtroom when Tristan is tried for murder, assault and kidnap.'

'There will be no court case, Mr Lloyd.'

'Why?'

'Young Mr Tristan has been diagnosed with lunacy. Therefore, he will not be tried for any crimes.'

Thomas couldn't believe his ears. 'He is not insane. He deliberately, coldly and rationally committed those murders. His motive was to preserve the family's income.'

'Nevertheless, the authorities have now classified Tristan as a lunatic.'

'Are you saying that a self-confessed murderer will go free?'

'Tristan has been sent to a private hospital in Switzerland. He will not be released until he reaches the age of forty.'

'That means he will be kept under lock and key for less than twenty years.' Tristan escaping responsibility for the murders so lightly enraged him. What's more, he pictured that hospital in Switzerland – there would be flowers in vases, walls painted in pleasant pastel colours, lawns where patients could sit out in the sun or play croquet. 'What is to prevent me from writing a news story about how a privileged young man escapes the hangman's noose?'

'That would not serve the interests of the nation.'

Thomas glared at the man. 'What will serve the interests of the nation, then?'

'Mr Lloyd, King Ludwig will be the last of the royal line. In return for the British justice system declaring Tristan unfit to stand trial due to insanity, King Ludwig has agreed that the Faxfleet monarchy will cease to exist upon his death. What's more, his sons are, as from today, no longer princes. They are commoners. Just like the two of us.'

'When we first met you told me you had such great plans to create a true civilization in Britain, yet I've seen you pervert justice for your own ends. Tristan should be tried in a court of law.'

'More powerful individuals than my friends and I wanted the Faxfleet monarchy to be abolished. I had nothing to do with stifling justice.'

Thomas turned his lapel over to reveal the gold pin with the pearl. 'Inspector Abberline found one of these on the island. Do you have colleagues there?'

'Yes.'

'Who?'

'I am not at liberty to say. Our society is a discreet one. We do not publicly reveal who our members are.'

'Mr Feasby? Miss Josephine Hamilton-West? King Ludwig?'

'Thank you for your time, Mr Lloyd. I'll bid you good evening, and please continue to write your excellent news reports about Inspector Abberline. You are helping build a better future for all.'

Thomas remained sitting in the carriage. He refused to leave without revealing what constantly preyed on his mind. 'You were right about Inspector Abberline having enemies.'

'Ah, you have something to tell me in that regard?'

'Yes, recently an attempt has been made to discredit the inspector and force him to resign.' Thomas told the man about the hoax Jack the Ripper letters, the discovery of the mutilated body in Whitechapel, and about what he'd overheard when Abberline had confronted Lionel Metcalfe in the conservatory. Thomas decided to test his place in this society represented by a gold pin – yet he did so without any firm belief he'd be taken seriously. He said, 'Detective Constable Metcalfe is clearly trying to damage Abberline's reputation; therefore, he should be sacked.'

The man nodded. 'I agree. Metcalfe will be dismissed.'

'Aren't you going to persuade me that he should remain a detective until you make enquires?'

'You are a fellow member of our society, Mr Lloyd. I have absolute trust in you. Tonight I'll write a letter. Who to doesn't concern you. However, by noon tomorrow Detective Constable Metcalfe will no longer work for Scotland Yard. Naturally, he won't be accused of planting the body or forging letters. He must not know the real reason. Simply, witnesses will say that Metcalfe was seen drinking alcohol while on duty. That is sufficient. The man will be dismissed from his post and removed from the premises.'

'You can do that?'

'Yes, I can – or, rather, we can. Of course, Inspector Abberline must never know about this conversation we're having now, or that you are responsible for Metcalfe's employment being terminated.'

'May I ask why?'

'There are reasons why we work in such secretive ways. We have enemies, too.'

A moment later, Thomas stood in the street, watching the carriage vanish back onto the mist.

One month later

The summer of 1890 was turning out to be a warm one. The evening heat had become almost tropical as Thomas Lloyd took his seat in a small theatre in Bloomsbury. When the curtains slid back they revealed a lectern. Behind the lectern stood Miss Josephine Hamilton-West. He found it difficult to think of her as the cheerful, bohemian 'Jo' that he'd encountered on Faxfleet. Tonight the woman was dressed in a black jacket and long, black skirt. The theatre was, perhaps, almost half full. He watched as the woman lectured the audience about the marvels of phrenology.

Jo's voice rang out clearly: 'It is possible to discover a human being's future behaviour by examining the contours of their skull. We can examine the head of a child and know whether that boy or girl will grow up to be a sinner or a saint.'

Jo delivered her lecture with powerful authority. She used a cane to point at a phrenology chart of a skull – the chart, in effect, was a map of the head that indicated areas of character traits upon the skull. When she lifted a cloth from an easel to reveal a photograph of Bertie Trask, Thomas quietly left the theatre.

He walked out through the doors into a street where people strolled under the night sky. Horses trotted by, pulling hansom cabs. The gas in the streetlights burned brightly. So brightly, in fact, that Thomas could easily read the letter in his hand.

Dear Thomas,

I shall be giving one of my lectures at the Coptic Theatre in Bloomsbury, 16th June. Would you attend? It would be lovely to see you there. I will notice you immediately in the soft, warm darkness of the auditorium, because didn't I tell you once that you have such a personality that is, without a shadow of doubt, luminous?

Do be there, Thomas. There is no place for me on Faxfleet anymore. I plan to go to New Zealand and start afresh there. Wouldn't it be enchanting if you were my travelling companion? Wouldn't it be an adventure!

Meet me in the theatre after the lecture. We will talk. We shall make plans.

Yours, with a fierce and heartfelt affection,

Jo

Thomas recalled the effect she'd had on him on the island all those weeks ago. She had been like a spirit creature from a marvellous dream. The woman had cast her spell. He'd been happy in her company. He also recalled her condemnation of the little boy Bertie Trask: *born bad*. Thomas looked up into the night sky above bustling, noisy London. The spell Jo had cast seemed to float away like a soap bubble – a fragile thing in the end. The bubble had burst, and Jo's vile philosophy made him shudder. He screwed the letter into a ball and dropped it through an iron grate in the pavement that led down into one of the sewers.

Thomas had begun to walk away when he heard someone calling his name. He turned to look into the crowds. A familiar face appeared.

'Thomas, just you wait there a moment.'

'Magglyn, what are you doing here?'

The smiling face of the man that lived in the next room to his, under Mrs Cherryhome's hospitable roof, appeared.

'Thomas. Friend, Thomas. I have Mr Abberline in tow.'

Abberline emerged from the crowds. He used a cane still, and had a slight limp. However, the wound caused by the spring-gun was healing well.

Thomas shook both men by the hand, laughing as he did so. 'How the dickens did you know I'd be here?'

Magglyn beamed. 'You told Mrs Cherryhome this evening that you were going to the Coptic Theatre. Mr Abberline dropped by – oh, I should call you Inspector, shouldn't I? – well, the gentleman dropped by ... we got talking. Supper was suggested in quite a roundabout way, and I recommended that we find you and carry you to a restaurant for a dish of something tasty.'

Abberline said, 'I hope you don't mind us hunting you down?'

Thomas laughed. 'Not at all. In fact, I'm rather glad that you did. It's very nice to see friendly faces.'

Magglyn clapped his hands together in sheer delight. 'I shall forge ahead to the House of Spain café over there. I'm sure I've just spied an empty table. If I'm swift, I'll have that table before anyone else.'

'Thank you, Maggs,' Thomas said. 'We'll follow you there.'

Magglyn crossed the busy street to the café.

Abberline paused for a moment. 'My ankle still feels stiff from time to time. But the doctor told me that I'll probably only need the cane for another week or two.'

'Jo gave a lecture at the theatre tonight. Phrenology. She used a photograph of Bertie Trask as if he was a laboratory specimen.'

'Oh?'

'I left early.'

'I see.'

'I've heard from Emma. She should be back in London for Christmas.'

'That's excellent news, Thomas.'

'Yes. I've now realized that it is.'

'We should cherish these pleasant surprises, shouldn't we? I remember how surprised I was to hear that Lionel Metcalfe had been dismissed from the police force. Drinking on duty. Who would have believed it of him?' Abberline linked arms with Thomas. 'You know, there are times when I find myself believing that I have friends in high places. I don't know who they are, or whether they are close to me or far away, but for some reason they wish to protect me. Or, rather, they wish to protect my work as a policeman. Oh ... after you, Thomas. Mr Magglyn has found us the best table in the house.'